WAKING HOURS

A. N. P. Emmanuel

Longlisted for the SI Leeds Literary Prize

To my parents, with gratitude and love, for their enduring faith, love and support.

CONTENTS

CHAPTER ONE

January 2007

As the train murmured through the suburban dusk, gliding unassumingly past back gardens and starving foxes, Aidan McGuinness jolted awake. He was embarrassed to have fallen asleep in public. It made him feel weak and vulnerable. He checked the corners of his mouth for dribble and straightened himself in his seat, hoping no one had noticed.

As he eased himself up, he felt his boot catch something soft on the floor. He peered down and found not the dead rodent he'd feared it to be, but a glove. He reached down to retrieve it.

A middle-aged woman was standing by the doors. The possible owner. Aidan tensed as he considered calling after her, but she was pressing the exit button, so he decided to leave it. He relaxed as he watched her step out into the snowy evening, telling himself it probably wasn't hers anyway.

The train was almost empty, travelling in the opposite direction to the main commuter flow. As it pulled away from the station, Aidan turned to gaze at the warmly lit kitchens and dining rooms that punctuated the darkness outside. He usually found these cubes of domesticity comforting, but this time struggled to see past his moody reflection.

He turned his attention to the glove, which he was holding with both hands. It was red, intricately knitted and had a bow around the wrist – a particularly feminine glove. Probably not very functional, but pretty. He slipped it on.

An elderly man seated on the other side of the aisle, fully in beige, stared listlessly. Aiden nodded at him as he stood in readiness for his stop. He quit the train, his right hand still encased in the red glove.

After the cosy lethargy of the carriage, the frozen air was exhilarating, burning his face. It stirred in him a sense of anticipation.

This was dampened as soon as he turned the corner to his treeless street. He found the sullen terraces wilfully joyless.

His father, Gordon, was coming out of the kitchen when he got home, holding a mug of tea. He smiled when he saw Aidan.

'What happened to the other one?' he asked, nodding at Aidan's right hand.

'Oh, I found this on the train.'

His father came closer to examine the red glove. A sigh of disappointment soon followed. 'Why do you always have to spoil things?' he said, then turned and limped into the living room, tea spilling from his mug.

Aidan remained by the front door, silently seething, wondering what to do. He could go back out, slamming the door behind him. He could confront his father in front of the regional news. Instead, he opted for his usual course of action following such encounters. He sprinted upstairs to his bedroom, locked the door and threw himself onto the bed, surprising the dozing cat. Angry tears fell, as expletives filled his head.

Eventually his tears were spent and his head throbbed. He stood up, slightly giddy, and walked towards his mirror. It was a full-length dressing mirror that had belonged to his mother. He appraised himself. Everything about his appearance, he was fully aware, was a reaction against his father. He had stopped short of wearing lipstick, only because he felt it might reduce his chances of getting a girlfriend.

Skinny jeans - garments he'd once mocked - had become part of his standard daily attire since starting sixth form college. While his friends had looked forward to the freedom of no longer having to wear a school uniform, it had been a pressure Aidan could have done without. He had made a rare foray into a department store the weekend before term started, in an effort to bulk up his wardrobe. Until then it had consisted almost exclusively of faded t-shirts and sweatpants. His father had given him money for the endeavour.

An enthusiastic shop assistant had suggested he try skinny jeans and had herded him into the changing rooms with a range of subtly differing shades of grey. He had let her because she was pretty and it was easier than refusing. He had scowled at his reflection after awkwardly pulling on a pair, hating what he saw. But as he removed them he had thought about how much they would annoy his father. He bought three pairs, using his father's cash plus the birthday money he'd saved to buy a computer game.

This form of rebellion had been in keeping with his temperament. Going off the rails required too much effort. Now he found even this mild defiance wearying.

As he stared at his face, streaked with eyeliner tears, he acknowledged that this was not really him. He was not sure who he was anymore.

Downstairs, Gordon sat in the living room. The news was on, but he wasn't paying attention. He was thinking about his son. Why would he wear a woman's glove?

He had never understood his son. He had held him in awe when he was a young child, amazed that he had been involved in producing this human being. As his son grew, he became even more of a mystery.

The snow that evening had reminded him of his last winter with his wife, a decade earlier. The tiniest details of those days were engraved in his memory. There had been a night of heavy January snowfall. He couldn't help but smile as he remembered Aidan, then eight, eagerly calling him to the window to see their magically transformed garden.

His foreman had called to tell him not to bother coming to work. It was a day's wages lost, but he had been relieved. He had witnessed enough accidents on that site.

Aidan had begged his mother to take him to school. Expecting it to be a fruitless mission, Gordon had watched them from the living room window until they were out of sight. He was still there when ten minutes later they trudged back into view. They looked beautiful, he thought, in their colourful winter coats against the white landscape. The snow had transformed their grim little street into something picturesque and expansive. As they got closer, he could see his son blinking excitedly as snowflakes landed in his eyelashes.

The three of them had gone out to the common with a hastily constructed dustbin lid sledge, then come home for steaming jacket potatoes and board games until the early evening news.

He had reluctantly returned to work the next day. The day after that, the snow had turned to ice. In the afternoon, after another day off school, Aidan had gone out into the street to play with a friend. He had slipped and cried out, so his mother had run to him, just as a car came skidding down the road. She was killed instantly as the vehicle mounted the pavement and smashed into their neighbour's front wall.

Gordon had blamed his son for their loss. There had been no outbursts. Instead, he kept him at arm's length. The anger subsided, but the distance remained as he went through the motions of parenthood. Eventually, even when he wanted to get close to him, he found he didn't know how to.

The snow that evening had reminded him of how badly he'd treated his son. Aidan had witnessed the accident, yet had never spoken to him about it. Gordon felt wretched. He wanted to ask his son for forgiveness, to tell him he loved him, to make amends before he lost him forever. But then he walked in with that stupid glove.

*

The train was busier than usual due to an earlier cancellation. Though it was not heaving, there were no clusters of empty seats left, so Lily Jansen took a spot opposite a sleeping young man. He looked like an art student, she thought, but then noticed he didn't have the large portfolio they all seemed to carry. Perhaps a drama student then.

The train was more than adequately heated, so Lily removed her gloves and laid them on her lap. She unfolded her free newspaper and flicked to the Sudoku. The young man was gently snoring, which she found soothing.

It had been a tiring day, as they all seemed to be lately. Grief had that effect. In the weeks after her husband left her, she had spent most of her hours sleeping. She was determined not to fall into that void again.

Her manager had been particularly belligerent that day, setting her an unreasonable deadline and drawing attention to trivial typing errors in front of her colleagues. This had particularly upset Lily - she took pride in her attention to detail. It had been in the rush to meet the deadline that she had not had time to properly check her work.

Lily sometimes worried that her temperament made people think she was a pushover. Perhaps she was. The thought made her bristle. She would start looking for another job that weekend.

She peered out at the dusky gloom and tried to think positive thoughts as she glimpsed her anxious reflection. Perhaps she should try a new career. For some time she had harboured the idea of opening a cafe. She could look into that. She brightened as the train approached her station.

The young man was still asleep, his brow furrowed. Lily considered waking him in case he missed his stop, and leaned forward, but then changed her mind.

She had been holding her gloves loosely and as she stood, one fell. She didn't notice.

After alighting, Lily pulled on her left glove, then anxiously searched her handbag and pockets for the other one. By the time she turned around to check the carriage, its doors were resolutely shut. As the train lurched away, she could see the young man through the window, now awake, holding her glove. She felt inexplicably sad as she walked away. It was just a glove, after all.

As Lily made her way home, the snow started falling faster, which made her feel strangely light. Her pace quickened. As she thought of her daughter waiting for her, her heart swelled with love. She would tell her about the cafe idea and perhaps they could bake something together that evening. Perhaps that cardamom and coffee cake recipe she wanted to try.

The front door opened before she could find her keys, as it almost always did, her daughter listening for the click of the gate.

'Are you late because of the snow?'

'Am I late, darling?'

'Where are your gloves? It's cold, you should wear them.'

That's why she had been so upset. The gloves

had been a Christmas present from her daughter, how could she have forgotten?

'I'm so sorry, darling, I've been careless. I lost one.'

'You're always losing things now,' her daughter said quietly and ran upstairs.

Lily remained by the door, the other glove in her pocket.

*

Iris had not actually lied to her mother. The original plan had been to go Christmas shopping with her best friend Amma and her older sister, but Amma had been sick that week and asked to postpone. This was not an option for Iris. She urgently needed to buy all her presents before she and her mother left to go to her aunt Veena's for the Christmas holidays.

Iris had decided the night before that she would make the trip by herself, but felt it would be unhelpful to tell her mother of this change of plan. She had reasoned that as she was almost nine, she was both old enough and sensible enough, even though she had never travelled alone on public transport before. She was also desperate to get out of the house, having been confined to it for much of the past month. Planning the shopping expedition had helped take her mind off her loss, though she had to try hard not to dwell on the significant gap in her Christmas list.

To her delight, a bus appeared within a minute of her arrival at the bus stop, but it was already crammed with flustered Saturday shoppers. Iris squeezed on, positioning herself by the exit, where she determinedly remained for the duration of the journey. She ignored the pointed looks and muttering directed towards her.

She was the first to alight when they reached the shopping precinct. As she walked hastily towards the central mall, she almost fell over as her foot slid on something. She looked down, to find a foot-long smear of fresh dog muck that ended at her left foot. As she despondently scraped her trainer against the kerb, her fellow passengers rushed past her. She searched for a puddle to wash her shoe in. There were none. It had been an exceptionally dry autumn.

Iris continued walking, conscious of the smell drifting up from her foot. She wanted to go home, but knew she would feel more depressed if she returned empty-handed. The trip would be curtailed, but she would leave with at least some of the presents. She had already decided what she was getting her mother: a cookery book and gloves.

A pair on the hands of a shop window mannequin soon caught her eye. They were red, with some crochet work. Probably not the warmest, but pretty and reasonably priced. She had expected to spend at least a couple of hours traipsing around shops, weighing up prices and other factors, but felt confident about this choice. Iris wondered if the ease of finding them was to make up for her shaky start.

She stepped inside the shop, aiming for a quick transaction, as the odour wafted from her shoe. She located the accessories section and strode purposefully towards it. Then suddenly stopped. A group of girls from her school were looking at scarves, just opposite the gloves. Iris had suffered at the taunts of one of them in particular, Sky Lacey - Psycho Lacey as she called her - and had no desire to be seen by them.

She started rifling through a railing of mini-skirts. As people walked by she noticed them wrinkling their noses in disgust and confusion. She caught the eye of one of them and did the same in an attempt to distance herself from the smell. She glanced back at the gloves. The mean girls were still there.

Perhaps she should come back later, she thought. Get the book first. Or at least go and sort out her footwear situation. She began to head towards the exit, then stopped again. This was ridiculous. She would just walk towards the gloves, pick up a pair, then stroll to the check-out. They were too absorbed in themselves to notice her and as long as she kept her back to them she could carry out her assignment undisturbed.

Iris pulled up the hood of her duffel coat and walked towards the gloves. As she got nearer, a small child wandered in front of her, slowing her approach.

She kept her back to the group as she slid off a pair of gloves from the railing. As she did so, it came loose, depositing all its wares onto the floor. She stepped over them.

'Are you gonna pick those up?'

Iris froze at the familiar sound of Sky's snarky voice.

'You're rude. You should pick them up,' another joined in.

Iris felt someone shove her in the shoulder.

'You can't go into a shop and throw things around. Other people have to buy this stuff, you know.'

'Eh, what's that smell?'

'Yeah, I was wondering that.'

'Is it you?'

Iris still had her back to the group but was unable to move.

'You're disgusting,' Sky said contemptuously before yelling loudly at a passing shop assistant. 'Excuse me! Can someone come over here please! You're gonna have to wash these gloves. You may want to bring some air freshener as well.'

This prompted Iris to move briskly to the cash register, tears soaking her eyes.

The cashier dealt with the transaction without looking at her, for which Iris was grateful. As she hurried towards the exit, she could still hear the girls complaining about how out of order it was that people behaved like that.

In her haste to leave the store, she bumped into someone coming in. Iris braced herself for a scolding but instead felt someone lightly touch her arm as they apologised. She turned to look. Heading inside was an older boy, in skinny jeans.

CHAPTER TWO

November 2003 – May 2004

Professor Carl Jansen blamed the radiator, jammed on the highest setting, for his inability to concentrate. He had stopped seeing words on his computer screen half an hour earlier and was allowing his thoughts to meander as they pleased.

A hesitant knock at the door interrupted his reverie. His voice was unintentionally gruff when he answered.

It was his research assistant, Nadia Behnam. At 27, she was exactly half his age as they shared the same birthday, something he had noted from her CV. She had featured prominently in his day-dreaming.

Nadia looked at Carl gravely, which made him instinctively stand up. She then walked towards him and handed him an envelope.

'It's a letter of resignation,' she said, fixing her

eyes on the desk.

Carl sat down, as if her words had literally deflated him. He looked at the envelope. She remained standing, waiting for a response.

'Have you found another post?' he asked eventually.

'No,' Nadia answered quietly, glancing up briefly before settling her gaze on his stationery pot.

'What will you do?'

'I've nothing concrete planned...I still enjoy my work here at the university, but feel I can no longer continue in this position.' She answered carefully. Carl kept his eyes trained on her as she spoke. 'I have some annual leave, which means I have two weeks left in the office.'

Carl stood again, pressing his hands against the table to steady himself. Nadia nodded a goodbye, then left. He remained standing, staring at the door for a while, then turned towards the window. Soon he saw her walking briskly across the car park. He moved closer to the glass, watching until she was out of sight. The radiator burned his legs. He didn't move, feeling it was a just punishment.

He eventually sat down and opened the envelope. He was disappointed to find the letter contained only the bare minimum required for notice. No reason was given. No reason was needed. He knew.

He despondently turned off the computer,

stuffed papers into his battered leather case and left the office, struggling to lock the door. He was in no mood to play the cheery host at his daughter's birthday party. He felt an overwhelming sense of disappointment, tinged with guilt, which remained with him throughout his drive home.

After parking his sensible estate next to his wife's practical hatchback on their neatly sandbricked driveway, Carl turned to survey the well-lit *cul-de-sac*. He found the blandness of its 1960s architecture particularly offensive that evening.

An abundance of small coats, piled up on the banister, greeted him as he entered the house. Dainty shoes were lined up against a wall, almost neatly. It was unexpectedly quiet. On reaching the living room, he discovered this was due to it being a key moment in a game of musical statues. His daughter, Iris, who was turning six, was balancing precariously on one foot, grinning widely. She had inherited his height and was a good two inches taller than most of the other little girls in the room. Her normally tidy fringe was askew from all the dancing. As soon as she saw Carl hovering by the door, she ran to him, instantly disqualifying herself from the game. He held her tightly.

Carl often wondered how someone like him could contain so much love for another and, more remarkably, how they could love him back. His wife Lily, controlling the music, looked over at them and smiled.

His melancholy lifted as the party continued. He took immense delight in seeing Iris happy and giggling with her friends. Later, as he lay in bed, he wondered why he had felt guilty about Nadia. He had done nothing wrong. Her resignation, though regretful, prevented the possibility of any future indiscretions. He would, of course, write her a glowing reference.

He turned onto his side and found Lily looking at him. She whispered, 'Thank you', and the earlier feeling rose up in him again, clouding his chest. He felt resentful that she was still present, while Nadia would soon be gone. He realised how unreasonable that was.

*

'I've got an early meeting,' Carl lied, before gulping down the coffee Lily had made for him. The cooked breakfast beside it remained untouched as he rushed to the door.

He had been unable to look at his wife directly that morning and left for work aware he had hurt her with his brusqueness. She was an intelligent woman, he thought, why did she have to be so fawning?

Nadia was already at her desk when he arrived. Carl had recently acknowledged to himself that he was attracted to her, but it was only now that he felt an urgent sense of longing. He wondered if she could sense this in his two word greeting.

After sitting at his desk for seven minutes, staring at a pile of books, Carl stood up and walked into the neighbouring office, where Nadia sat with her back to the door. None of the other staff had arrived yet. He coughed, which startled her. She swivelled her chair round to face him.

'I just wanted to say that you'll be missed...by everyone in the department. And I wondered if you might reconsider your decision,' Carl said as affably as possible.

'I've been thinking about this for a while.'

'Just think about it a little more. You don't have to make a decision right this minute.' Carl smiled, attempting to feign how relaxed he was about the whole situation. Nadia nodded and turned back to her computer.

'Perhaps we could go for lunch later?' he said as nonchalantly as he could manage.

'To go through the Morley bid?' Nadia asked, looking over her shoulder.

Carl nodded, then quickly left the room.

He had a particularly productive morning, having forced his normally stubborn window open to bring in the November chill. He did not allow himself to think about anything other than what he was working on - an article for the alumni magazine. Neither his wife or daughter, nor the impending lunchtime appointment with Nadia. When he visited the bathroom, he deliberately avoided his reflection. He did not want to be reminded of his grey hair or the dark circles around his eyes.

At one o'clock Carl braced himself for the knock on the door. At five past, he was still waiting. It would be inappropriate for him to go next door and prompt her, he thought. At eight minutes past one, the knock finally came. He pretended to be reading when Nadia entered the room. She did not apologise for the delay. He made her wait a minute before standing up and retrieving his coat from its antique stand.

Nadia was carrying a ring binder of documents. 'You can leave that here; we won't be needing it today,' he said.

*

Carl wished he had given more thought to the lunch. The anecdotes that used to flow so easily with Nadia were absent. Instead, they both studied the pub menu intently, making occasional comments about its contents, then smiled thinly at each other once they'd ordered.

'I brought you here to bribe you into staying, with gastro pie and mash,' Carl said eventually. 'But I think I've failed miserably.'

He was relieved to see her smile. The admission seemed to act as a reset button and the lunch continued in a more relaxed vein. But Carl was acutely aware that he had not yet accomplished everything he wanted to.

It was in the car that he kissed her. Awkwardly, mechanically, more a statement of intention than anything else, but she had not objected. He had not kissed Lily like that in years and the feeling both thrilled and terrified him.

*

Carl picked up a bouquet of carnations for Lily on his way home from work. He nearly backed out of giving them to her in case they were an obvious signpost to his guilt. As he sheepishly handed them to her in the kitchen, a few of the heads fell off.

'I'm sorry for being so aloof lately. We've just been very busy and I've not been coping very well.' Carl found the effort of lying made his throat ache.

Lily was speechless with gratitude. He wanted to flee when he saw tears welling up, but instead stood rigidly as she embraced him. He awkwardly patted her shoulder, as she lay her head against his chest.

For the next month, Carl overcompensated at home, even taking Lily out for a meal on their anniversary, something he had stopped doing two years into their marriage. He had wondered if his mother-in-law had suspected something as she bade them farewell at the front door. She had looked at him quizzically. He had responded by staring at his unpolished shoes. He had almost suggested calling in another babysitter to avoid such an encounter.

He then reverted to his usual polite indifference, and Lily continued with her uncertain attentiveness. For some time, Carl had found Lily's unrelenting cheerfulness and confidence in him wearying. Now he found even her innocuous questions about work irritating, as it forced him to lie to her. His answers became monosyllabic and gruff. She would then apologise for troubling him when he was tired, which annoyed him even more.

He began comparing her looks unfavourably with Nadia's. Her skin was not as supple. Her straight mid-length hair was boring compared to Nadia's curls, her slim figure not as enticing as Nadia's curves. Her dark eyes, he relented, were kind. Too kind. Quite similar to Nadia's.

Carl's relationship with Iris also suffered. He felt unclean and did not want to tarnish her by association. He noticed her behaviour around him changed. She used to climb into his lap after dinner as he read the paper, asking him about the headlines and photographs. Now she would sit beside him, quietly reading a book, careful not to disturb him. He found the guilt unbearable at times, but continued to see Nadia.

*

Keeping their affair secret from colleagues required no special effort from Carl or Nadia as neither was given to public displays of affection. Their relationship went unnoticed for several weeks until a department administrator witnessed a 'flirty exchange of looks' one Wednesday morning in a corridor.

The following Friday evening in the pub, emboldened by a couple of large glasses of house white, she had asked Nadia about it. Unused to lying, Nadia had stuttered an unconvincing denial and by the end of the next week, most of the history department knew of their liaison.

Cocooned in his office behind the carnage of books and yellowing papers, Carl was oblivious to most of the gossip and ignored the smirks of fellow professors.

*

Carl stared at the email, his hands reflexively clasping his knees. His eyes were fixed on the line: *'An official invitation will be posted to your home address in the next few days.'* When he first read it, he had physically recoiled.

It was an invitation to a formal dinner for staff and their spouses in celebration of the university's 150th anniversary. Carl had never considered the possibility of Nadia and Lily meeting and the prospect horrified him. He sat up straight in his chair and rubbed his throat, which often felt tender these days.

He had generally avoided thinking about the wider implications of the affair, as whenever he did so he became agitated. The email was an unwelcome reminder of the complexities of the situation.

Carl took a deep breath and tried to process the matter rationally. The invitation would be addressed to both him and Lily. She would see it first, as she arrived home before he did, but she would wait for him before she opened it. She would be excited at the possibility of a rare evening out. He would agree to go, but on the day itself feign illness, thus averting the danger.

Carl shut down the computer, relieved at his plan, but unsettled at how easily unsettled he was lately.

*

The invitation arrived two days later and things played out as Carl had predicted. Lily had waited for him before opening it. She was excited, as he'd expected, but he hadn't anticipated being moved by her enthusiasm.

'This sounds very posh, Carl.'

'It's no big deal. I mean, they say 'black tie' but I doubt anyone will take any notice of that.'

'But I should probably get a proper outfit for it, shouldn't I? I mean it's the 150th anniversary.'

Carl smiled uncomfortably. Lily had never been demanding, just grateful for any small diversion offered to her, which was rarely. He began to doubt his ability to go through with his plan.

'Lily wants to come to the dinner,' he told the back of Nadia's head the next morning.

'I'm sure it will be fine,' she said, and continued typing.

*

Lily descended the staircase and did a twirl for Carl. He smiled, embarrassed.

To him, Lily's newly purchased outfit looked more or less like the rest of her wardrobe: a longish flowing skirt with colour coordinated blouse. Though her face remained smooth, almost girlish, and there were hardly any silver strands in her hair, she had looked middle-aged from the time they'd first met, he thought. She had never been youthful.

'You look very nice,' he said, then coughed.

'Thank you, darling.'

Carl coughed again.

'Are you alright?'

'Yes, I'll be fine.' Carl knew he had left it too late. He had attempted a few coughs in the morning which had gone unnoticed, as Lily had been preoccupied with her own toothache.

'Yes, you'll be fine,' his mother-in-law appeared in the doorway of the living room, her hands resting on Iris's shoulders.

'Mummy you look beautiful!' Iris threw her arms around Lily's slender hips.

'Enjoy yourselves.' It sounded like a command from his mother-in-law. Carl knew he had no choice but to grin and bear the evening. He contemplated getting rolling drunk, but thought better of it. He had to have his wits about him.

The dinner was being held in the university's Whitfield Hall, which a few weeks later would host a seemingly endless roster of graduation ceremonies. Church candles had been placed liberally around the room, their effect somewhat diminished by the competing sunlight that still streamed in through the stained glass windows. Carl wondered how wise it was to place unguarded flames around inebriated academic staff.

He scanned the hall for Nadia and was dismayed to find her by the drinks table, glass in hand. He had never seen her drunk and wondered if she morphed into someone different to the quiet person he thought he knew.

'Hello, Carl. And who's this delight?' William, one of his colleagues, had grabbed Lily's hand and was kissing it.

'This is my wife Lily. Lily, this is Professor William Dunbar.'

'Well, what's he done to deserve you, my dear?'

'Brilliant news on your paper!' Another colleague, Lionel, patted Carl on the back, spitting out half a *vol-au-vent* in his congratulations. 'A few titbits might even make the national press, I hear.'

'Nadia helped quite a bit with that. She's the one who worked on the press release,' Carl replied, to which Lionel grinned knowingly.

'Loved the title. It's the kind of popular history people like: *Misogyny and Mayhem-*'

'*Mischief.*'

'What?'

'It's *Misogyny and Mischief in Early Modern Lancashire.*'

'Yes, that's the one. About the cross-dressing serfs.'

'Well, it's a bit more complex than that.'

'Is that lady over there your wife?'

Carl turned and was surprised to find Lily was no longer beside him.

'Over there,' Lionel indicated with his absent chin.

Carl felt his stomach hollow. Lily was approaching Nadia, who was pouring herself more Prosecco. In the foreground, William turned and raised his eyebrows mischievously at Carl.

Carl started to make his way over to them, but was intercepted by a young PhD student who wanted to congratulate him on his paper, as well as introduce him to his girlfriend, a model. Carl half-listened as she described at speed a recent trip to LA, in which he caught references to Corey Feldman and cat food. Out of the corner of his eye he watched his wife and assistant. In due course, there was a pause in the young woman's narrative as she took a sip of her sparkling water, at which point Carl excused himself and made a beeline for Lily and Nadia.

He felt a hand on his shoulder. 'No use bothering them. Won't do you any good. Nadia's a good girl, she won't let slip,' William said, almost soberly.

Carl had never officially acknowledged the affair so was unsure of how to respond. He was also reluctant to take advice from someone with four failed marriages.

'Get some of this fizzy stuff down you. Not as good as ale, but it's quite fun when it tickles your nose.'

William furnished him with a glass, which Carl obligingly downed. He spent the remaining time before dinner accepting compliments on his paper, with nods and a fixed smile that made his face ache. He had positioned himself so that he could observe the two women. Lily had her back to him. Nadia appeared to be doing most of the talking and was gesticulating in a way he had not noticed in her before. He put it down to nerves.

A printing malfunction meant the seating arrangements for dinner were a free for all. Carl was relieved to be able to exercise some control over the situation and beckoned Lily over to two seats in which they would be surrounded by colleagues from the Natural Sciences department.

'But what about Nadia? Please don't split us

up, darling.'

Carl looked at Nadia who was smiling blankly behind Lily.

'What about over there? There are three seats.'

Lily made her way towards them and placed herself in the middle seat. Nadia and Carl trudged behind. He simultaneously pitied and resented his wife.

Nadia had reached the lethargic stage of drunkenness and was quieter than she had been earlier. It was Lily who did most of the talking, pausing often, always conscious that she might be boring her listeners. It was fairly innocuous at first: documentaries she'd recently watched, articles she'd read, cooking. The trivial things she used to talk to Carl about at the dinner table. Then she mentioned in passing that Iris shared her father's interest in history.

Having his wife take such a liking to his girl-friend was bad enough, but having his daughter's name brought up was more than Carl could bear. He leaned forward. Nadia's discomfort at the situation was obvious from her expression, but Lily was oblivious.

'Darling, can we go after dessert? I have a headache brewing.' Carl never used any terms of affection for Lily and he wondered if, like the flowers, they were an obvious indication of his transgressions.

'Of course, darling,' Lily smiled, appreciating

his use of the word in public, suspecting nothing.

In the taxi home, she linked her arm through Carl's and rested her head on his shoulder.

'I'm so proud of you. Everyone I spoke to was brimming with how brilliant you are.'

'Nadia has been a great help to me.' Carl caught Lily's eye as he said it, but her expression remained unchanged.

'She seems like a lovely, bright girl. So sad about her sister.'

Carl was surprised that Nadia had confided something so personal to Lily in such a brief period and wondered what else she had shared. His muscles tensed under her grip.

He decided then that he would leave, convincing himself that it was for the sake of Lily and Iris. What good was he to them, he thought. Just another body taking up resources in the household, contributing nothing of worth. He would ensure they were well provided for.

Carl was not an impulsive person. He had contemplated the idea of leaving Lily before, but until recently had never thought he would actually act on it.

He lay awake for most of the night, mentally composing his departure letter. He kept telling himself that life would be better for his family without him there. He did not ponder for too long the possibility that his absence might be devastating for them.

He left for work earlier than usual the next day. Lily had been quiet, sitting at the kitchen table holding her jaw. Iris had been full of questions about the previous evening, while his mother-in-law, who had stayed overnight, regarded him silently as she sipped her tea.

He spent two hours at his desk writing and re-writing the letter, by hand. He was not satisfied with the final draft, but reasoned that one never really could be with such a communication. Nadia was away that morning, so he had not been able to inform her of his plans.

At 11am, he returned home and hurriedly packed his belongings, reluctantly leaving his books for a later time.

He stood in the doorway of Iris's bedroom, the walls still in the pastel green and yellow they'd chosen for her as a baby. She was already a freakishly neat child, having taken after her mother. As he looked at her tidy room - her toys displayed in an orderly manner, her small shoes, her piggy bank - he began to sob. He allowed himself to do so. He longed to step inside, but felt he would sully the air.

A dull headache was developing as he drove back to the university. The crying had drained him. He felt fragile.

Nadia was at her desk, eating a sandwich and flicking through a newspaper, when he arrived.

'Could I have a quick word, please? In my office,' he said with as much restraint as he could manage.

Nadia got up immediately and followed him, sandwich still in hand.

'I've left Lily,' he announced before she could shut the door.

The words made Carl want to vomit. He started crying again. Nadia stood, her eyes glazed, as if his words had hypnotised her.

'I have some errands to do and a tutorial this afternoon. We can talk about this later,' she said eventually, then left Carl alone in his office.

He turned to the window and gazed out. A while later she came into view. He had a strange feeling of déjà vu and recalled the day she handed in her letter of resignation. He opened his desk drawer and found it there, beneath packets of staples and mints. He was too exhausted and numb to muster any feelings of regret, so slowly closed it again.

He picked up his office key and held it tightly until it began to hurt him. He started to entertain the idea of returning to Lily. It was not too late to pretend this had never happened. That would be the right thing to do. He had not considered what Nadia's response would be. He should have spoken to her first, he realised. She had featured very little in his planning.

He stood up purposefully, gathered his belongings and rushed to the car, grateful he had no appointments scheduled for that day.

As he turned out of the university car park he

tried to picture his life with Lily 10 years down the line. She would be 60, Iris 16. Nadia would be 38. He tried to imagine life with her. He found he could not.

As he took the familiar roads home, he began to relax. It was a strange sensation, one that he realised had become alien to him. The life he thought he resented began to seem appealing, desirable. It offered the potential for happiness. He felt hopeful.

He would go home and speedily unpack, then return to the university and speak to Nadia.

He felt a prang of fear as he thought of her. What should he tell her? Should he end it? How would she respond? Would she tell his wife? Would she try and blackmail him? As scenarios flooded his mind he started to panic. He pulled over to the side of the road.

Carl reasoned that Nadia was not that kind of person. If her earlier reaction was anything to go by, she might even be relieved. But if she felt he had betrayed her, there was no guarantee of a discrete response. He realised that he did not know her very well. He had once or twice pondered whether he loved her and had not come to any conclusions. He had used her, he admitted. He had been flattered that a young, intelligent woman held feelings for him. She had tried to behave honourably by tendering her resignation; he had not let her. If she reacted badly, he deserved it, but Lily did not.

Carl gnawed his index finger. He would tell Nadia that he was not yet ready to leave his wife. That would buy him time to apply for a position at another university. There was a recurring offer from Boston that he could look into. Lily would be willing to move if she believed it would benefit his career. Iris was still young. They could start afresh.

He pulled away, grateful for the lack of traffic.

On reaching the house, he bounded upstairs to the bedroom where he'd left the note on Lily's pillow.

It was not there.

He lifted the pillow and pulled back the duvet, then checked under the bed. He became frantic. He knew he had definitely left it there as he had spent some time thinking about where to put it before deciding on its final resting place.

Carl sat on the bed, transfixed by a woodlouse making its way slowly across the carpet. He had no idea of how to fix the situation. He started weeping, realising he had cried more that day than he had in a decade. Eventually he stood and gloomily made his way down the stairs and into his car. He grasped the steering wheel to stop his hands shaking. As he drove away, he kept saying to himself, over and over again, that he was a coward and that whatever bad happened to him now, he deserved.

CHAPTER THREE

May – December 1990

Flora Ratnam stared impatiently at the newsreader. Her daughter was normally home by six - it was now ten past. It had felt like a particularly long day. The rain had kept her indoors and she was not enjoying her library book. She would finish it though, on principle.

At twelve past she heard the click of the gate and rushed to the door. Her daughter, Lily, looked drawn as she walked up the path, but smiled when she saw her mother.

A pot of tea was made, accompanied by homemade *muruku*, and they sipped and munched for the remainder of the news. It transpired that a fault on the preceding train had caused the delay.

After changing out of her work clothes, Lily made dinner. She always made it from scratch, with leftovers kept for their lunches the next day. Rice was on the menu at least twice a week, with the accompaniment determined by whatever Flora had picked up from the market. Lily was always happy to experiment and had mastered a variety of cuisines. At Flora's request, chilli was always added to her portion, whether required or not. After eating at the dinner table, they would move to the living room to watch television, read or knit.

Their weekday evening routine had remained unchanged for fifteen years, since Lily finished her bookkeeping course at the local polytechnic. The only exception was Wednesdays, when she attended a Bible study. Although Flora was keen for her to go, she would watch the minutes until she returned. Even with the television or radio on, the house always seemed quieter at night, especially in winter. As though the darkness, like a blanket, had smothered it.

Flora also attended a Bible study on Wednesdays, but in the morning. She would regularly share her concerns about her daughter's marital status, or lack thereof. Her friends would smile placatingly, squeezing her hand, telling her not to worry. Though she loved her group, she found this indifference frustrating. It was as though they viewed her concern about Lily dying alone as a silly cultural quirk.

Flora thought about this as she tried to read her tedious book and realised that it was probably because many in the group were themselves spinsters. A number of them former missionaries, who had fought off disease and militias in remote tropical villages, with nothing but prayer and fortitude. Annoyed at her own insensitivity Flora slammed shut her book before she had placed the bookmark, compounding her frustration.

She turned her gaze towards Lily, who was engrossed in a wildlife documentary.

She thought about how weary she had looked as she walked up the path, for a moment appearing older than her 36 years.

'I'm sorry that I've been such a bad mother to you!' Flora burst out.

'Why would you say that, mummy? Of course you're not a bad mother.'

'It's my fault you're alone.'

Lily walked over to her mother's armchair and bent down to embrace her. 'Don't be silly.'

They remained silently entwined as dramatic music played over the closing credits of the programme.

'Shall I put the kettle on?' Lily asked.

Flora nodded.

'You deserve better than to be stuck here with your old mother,' Flora said when Lily returned with steaming mugs of cocoa.

'What do you mean? I'm happy here with you.'

'Don't you want to find someone, darling?

Don't you...' Flora was unsure of how to complete her sentence.

Lily stared into the depths of her mug of cocoa. 'It would be nice, but I'm too old now.'

'Don't talk nonsense, Lily. If you're old, then I must be dead.'

'Who would want me, when they can have someone young and beautiful?'

'Any man would be lucky to have you as a wife. I'm sorry that I've neglected my duties. I've been selfish, keeping you to myself.'

'It's not your fault, mummy. I'm a grown woman.'

'But would you be interested in meeting someone?'

Lily shrugged.

*

Flora had a course of action in mind to remedy Lily's situation, but decided to keep it from her until she returned from work the next day, in case it distracted her. She, meanwhile, was restless with the weight of it. When she returned her half-read book to the library she had been unable to concentrate enough to choose another. Nor could she focus on her afternoon quiz programmes, getting up to make herself a cup of tea before the first ad break. When she returned to her seat, she found herself holding the milk bottle, having placed her tea cup in the fridge.

When Lily finally returned home, Flora used

her remaining reserves of self-control to hold back until they had both sat down with their tiffin.

'How would you feel if I called Frieda? To see if she knows of anyone suitable for you?' Flora said casually before taking a sip of tea.

'Really? I thought-'

'Only if you want me to. If you prefer not to then-'

'No, I don't mind you calling her if you think she can...If she knows anyone.'

Flora was surprised at how readily Lily agreed. She had prepared a few encouraging comments, which she had planned to drop into conversation over the next few days in order to persuade her. She again felt guilty about her inertia. 'I'm sorry, darling,' she said.

'Why, mummy?'

'For doing nothing for so long.'

'Most people are able to find their own spouse. I can't even do that.'

'Stop talking like that. Give me the phone, I'll call her now.'

Flora knew her older sister would be surprised to hear from her as it was not one of their regular calling days, which were Thursdays and Sundays. She also realised that she would have to enquire after the family and Frieda's health before she could get to the main issue.

She was disappointed to be greeted by the answer-phone. 'Fred, it's Flo. Where are you? Are you alright? Anyway, call me straightaway. It's urgent.'

When Frieda called back over an hour later, it startled them as it came at a particularly tense moment in *Coronation Street*.

'Flo, what's wrong? I just got back from choir practice and heard your message.'

'Lily's not married and it's my fault,' Flora replied.

'You called to tell me that?'

'Yes.'

'Well, you're right, but don't ever leave me a message like that again, unless it really is life or death. I thought something terrible had happened.'

'This *is* terrible. I need you to...'

'Help? Are you asking me for help?'

'Well –'

'If not for your pride, Lily would have been settled long ago.'

'I know.'

'So many times I kept telling you, then I gave up.'

'I know.'

'The older they are, the harder it is. Most of the good ones have been taken. You're usually left with the weirdoes or used ones.'

'I don't want a weirdo for my Lily. Are you going to help us, Fred?'

Frieda sighed. 'As it happens, there may be someone.'

'A good one?'

'I don't know all the details yet. What is Lily looking for?'

Flora turned to Lily who was watching anxiously, trying to get the gist of the conversation.

'Well, a good fellow,' Flora said.

'Height? Age? Profession?' Flora repeated the questions to Lily, who shrugged, so she decided on her behalf. 'Well, not too short. Average to tall. Lily is 36, so not an old fellow. Someone educated.'

'I'll make enquiries about this boy. If you'd called me a day later it would probably have been too late - someone else would have snapped him up. Do you know how many nice boys have passed by because of your pride?'

'I know. I'm trying to put it right,' Flora answered quietly. She would not normally have accepted such haranguing from her sister, but felt she deserved it on this occasion. Ten years earlier, Frieda had contacted her with a proposal which she had violently rejected, informing her that Lily did not need any help securing a husband and would easily find someone.

'I'll call you back. How's your chest?'

Within ten minutes the phone rang, which again took them by surprise.

Frieda reeled off the information she had acquired, 'Name is Carl Jansen. Age 41, 6'1" tall, slim, fairly quiet, UK born. Parents dead. Father: Johan Jansen, Dutch Burgher from Mount

Lavinia. Mother: Navamani, formerly Miss Pillai, Jaffna Tamil from Wellawatte. He: Dutch Reformed, she: Methodist. Met at Cambridge University – love marriage. Both were teachers.'

Frieda paused as Flora repeated the information to Lily.

'He's a lecturer at the University of the North West of England. Poni doesn't know what subject. Not science, maybe humanities,' Frieda continued to read from her scribbled notes. 'Aunt trying to fix a match, but he doesn't yet know.'

'He doesn't know?'

'Not yet.'

'Oh.'

'Do you want me to pursue this?'

Flora turned to Lily. 'What do you think, darling? Are you interested?'

Lily smiled. 'He sounds nice.'

'Find out more, Fred. Keep me informed.'

*

Within a fortnight, a meeting had been arranged between Lily and the lecturer. Flora restrained herself from offering much advice, for fear of saying the wrong thing. She gave only tentative suggestions on what to wear and recommended applying a little make up, something she had no experience in whatsoever.

'Just be yourself,' she told Lily as she was about to leave for work. 'If he doesn't accept you for who you are then he's not worth it.'

She felt this was sound advice, but could see the uncertainty in her daughter's eyes. She called her at lunchtime to check that it was still going ahead and resisted the urge to call again. In the evening, she calculated Lily's expected time of arrival. If she met him at six for an hour, then took about 45 minutes to get home, she should be back by eight at the latest. She was surprised to hear Lily's key in the door just after 7:20 and rushed to greet her. Lily was smiling shyly.

'Well? He's not a weirdo?'

'He's a lovely man,' Lily replied.

Flora had not wanted to ask Lily too many questions, but couldn't help herself. Was he good looking? Clever? Did it seem like he had common sense? Lily was happy to entertain her enquiries. Yes, he was handsome, tall and intelligent. She was particularly taken with his pale green eyes. And more importantly, he was willing to see her again.

*

Flora stared blankly at the familiar faces on the TV, then glanced at the clock. It was 9:30. Lily was at her Bible study. She was out of the house more often these days since she had started seeing the lecturer two months earlier. As he lived on the other side of the city, as a compromise, they often met in the centre. It meant Lily had to get the bus home alone, which made

Flora anxious, even though the evenings were light. She was annoyed the lecturer had not once offered to drop Lily home, even if it meant a lengthy round trip once in a while.

The phone started ringing. Flora regarded it suspiciously. She was not used to phone calls at this time of night and knew that none of her friends would call at such an uncivil hour. She let it ring and turned up the volume on the television. The phone was persistent so she heaved herself up, suddenly fearing something had happened to Lily.

'Hello?'

'Mrs Ratnam?'

'Yes.'

'This is Carl. Professor Carl Jansen. I've been seeing your daughter Lily?'

'Oh, hello.'

'Are you well?'

'Yes, thank you.'

'Good. I was just calling to let you know that I think it's been going quite well.'

'Oh, good.'

'Yes. So I thought, if you don't mind, I'm happy to take this forward. I just wanted to ask your permission, as it were.'

'Right.'

'I mean there's no point dragging this out. Neither of us is getting any younger.'

'I don't believe anyone is.'

'True! So, are you happy with that?'

'I am, if Lily is.'

'Oh yes, I think she'll be fine about it.'

'Right.'

It was Flora's first direct contact with Carl Jansen. She knew she should be excited at this turn of events, yet she felt flat. She kept telling herself he was a good catch for Lily and would provide for her, but she couldn't help feeling that something was missing. It had all been too easy, too quick. Like a smooth business transaction, lacking any warmth. She reminded herself that she had got too caught up in emotions when she married, and it had gone horribly wrong. This kind of clear-minded practicality was surely better.

*

Flora looked up from her weeding as she heard the front door shut. A moment later, Lily burst into the garden.

'Carl asked me to marry him!'

Flora slowly stood and embraced her daughter.

'I'm so happy for you, darling.'

It was not a lie. She was happy for Lily, but wondered if the speed of the courtship was actually penance for her previous lack of action. She hadn't had time to adjust and before she knew it, Lily would be gone and she would be alone.

*

Lily laid out brochures in front of Flora. She could smell the newness of them.

'Your honeymoon?'

'No, mummy. They're retirement flats. I thought you may just want to have a look. Just to get an idea of what's out there if you ever considered downsizing. These ones are ten minutes from Carl's. It's just to see.'

Flora had kept her concerns about her future to herself, not wanting to tarnish Lily's happiness. She should have known her thoughtful daughter would be thinking about these things too. She flicked through one of the brochures as Lily went to make tea. The rooms were tiny and she would no longer have a garden to herself, but they would be close to her daughter.

As Lily brought the teapot to the table, Flora said, 'They look lovely. When can we go and have a look?'

*

Flora watched Lily plump up the cushions in the living room for the second time in ten minutes. It was a fortnight after the proposal and Carl was coming for dinner. Flora would be meeting him for the first time face to face. She didn't blame Lily for not bringing him home before this, but was a little hurt to have so far been excluded from such an important development in her daughter's life.

Twenty-two minutes after Carl's expected time of arrival the doorbell rang.

Flora had resolved to say very little. She would ask questions that were interested but not intrusive. She would not mention her infirmities.

Carl looked much as she imagined he would. He was tall and trim, and had obviously shaved for the occasion. She suspected he normally favoured stubble. His pale eyes hinted at his father's European ancestry, as did his skin, which was light for a Sri Lankan though not much different to Lily's in tone. He was cleanly presented and not bad to look at, but there was something intrinsically dishevelled about him. His white shirt and navy chinos, which she assumed were his 'good clothes', were slightly crumpled. His gradually greying hair, though straight and fairly short, did not sit politely on his head. She wondered if that was because he was prone to rubbing his hands through it. Her father used to do the same as he sat at his typewriter waiting for inspiration.

As he sat awkwardly on their low sofa, Flora wondered why he had agreed to this arrangement. He seemed too western and worldly to consent to such a match.

When Lily came in with a tray of drinks, Flora was momentarily distracted by how her daughter had bloomed. She hadn't noticed it before. She seemed a brighter, glossier version of herself.

'Doesn't she look pretty, Carl?'

'Yes,' Carl answered, glancing quickly at Lily before focussing on the coaster on which she was about to place his ginger beer.

'She's a good catch, Carl. I hope you realise that.'

'Mummy!'

Flora could hear her tone was uncongenial, which hadn't been her intention.

'Well, you've brought up a lovely young lady, aunty. Her manners are exquisite. She's a very good listener. She has a lovely temperament.'

He makes her sound like a well-trained dog, Flora thought.

'Hasn't the weather been glorious?' Lily said as she took her seat.

Flora wept that night as she lay in bed. Her own loneliness she could deal with, but the thought of Lily stuck in a loveless marriage was more than she could bear. And like everything else that went wrong, she thought, it would be her fault.

*

Four months later, Carl and Lily wed. Flora was relieved that Carl had turned up at all, let alone on time. She watched him closely during the service. While Lily was unable to stop smiling, he looked serious. He livened up at the reception, his hand tightly around Lily's waist, which had partially reassured Flora.

They honeymooned in Sorrento, leaving her to sleep alone in the house for the first time in years.

CHAPTER FOUR

January 1991 – November 1997

As Flora gazed at the pavement through the balcony railings, she thought about her miniature roses. She hoped the new owners of her house were maintaining the garden.

The sale had gone through unexpectedly quickly, leaving her wondering if the house had been undervalued. She had watched helplessly, as a procession of potential buyers traipsed through her home of thirty years without removing their shoes, while suited agents murmured that it 'could do with modernisation, but was extremely good value'. The young couple who had gone on to purchase the house had been complimentary about the garden, Flora recalled, though it was with regard to its potential for sunbathing and barbecues rather than her double-petaled clematis.

It was Lily who had suggested putting the house on the market soon after the engagement, so the funds could be used to purchase the retirement flat. They had been told they were in luck - a 'much sought after' first floor apartment with balcony, in a popular sheltered complex had just become available. And if they didn't move quickly they would miss out.

Flora wrapped the blanket around herself more tightly. Events had moved so fast that she sometimes felt breathless with the effort of keeping up with them. Sleep, which had been a great comfort to her throughout her life, now evaded her. She had started rising early, before dawn, and would sit on her lauded balcony in the dark. There she would drink in the frozen air, think about the past, worry about the future, until her eyelids became heavy.

*

Flora glanced up from her porridge and looked disapprovingly at the phone. She was not used to receiving calls so early in the day. She took a moment to clear her throat before answering.

'Hello?'

'Mummy, it's me.'

'Lily?'

'I've got some news.'

'Good news, I hope.'

'I'm pregnant.'

Flora went out soon after breakfast and pur-
chased new wool, choosing a pale yellow. She
couldn't understand people who dressed their
infants in bright colours, overwhelming the
poor mites. She already had patterns that she'd
used for Frieda's grandchildren, which she'd
carefully stored in the hope that one day she
would use them for her own. But as she started
to knit a tiny cardigan, the needles began to feel
heavy, and she felt strangely sorrowful. She un-
ravelled her work and put the patterns and wool
to the back of a drawer, unwilling to contemplate what it might mean.

*

Four months had passed since Flora's move;
two since Lily announced her pregnancy. In
that time, Flora had discovered the communal
garden in the central courtyard and taken two
plots. The flowerbeds, raised a metre above the
ground to cater for the residents' arthritic limitations, were some consolation for the loss of
her garden. As the days grew gradually longer
and warmer she spent much of her time outside - weeding, sowing, tending, or reading on
one of the nearby benches. She would exchange
nods and pleasantries with other restless residents who also sought respite from their lonely
confines.

Flora had registered at the local library a day after moving, and reluctantly conceded to Lily that it had a bigger crime fiction section than her former place. She still commuted to her church on the other side of the city, her friends having drawn up a rota for lifts. Though none had expressed resentment, Flora felt uncomfortable being so dependent and had once attempted the journey by bus. Having taken a wrong connection, she arrived an hour late for service and had to endure the gentle chiding of her friends for being so silly.

Lily had invited her to join her local church, but Flora wanted to hold on to at least one thing that was familiar, that connected her to her former life.

What she missed most from that life was her daughter. She had been able to cope with the solitary days after her retirement, knowing that she had Lily's company to look forward to in the evening. Now there was nothing to break up the monotony of her loneliness. Though she spoke to Lily daily, it was no compensation. Though she visited regularly, it always seemed so brief and her departure left Flora feeling more melancholy. She knew she had to accept that things would never be the same again.

Flora put down her Father Brown mystery and checked her watch. Lily would be at work, but Flora sometimes called the house while having her mid-morning tea, to hear her daughter's voice on the answer-phone. She made her way back to her flat, which always seemed so gloomy after the brightness of the garden. After settling down with a half-filled mug, she picked up the receiver, only to find no dial tone.

'Hello?'

'Mummy?'

'Lily?'

'You picked up straightaway.'

'I was about to call you. Why aren't you at work?'

Flora could hear a quiver in her daughter's voice. She stood up and pulled the phone towards the door where her coat was hanging.

'Tell me, darling. What's happened?' Flora slipped her arm into the jacket sleeve.

'I've lost the baby.'

'Oh, Lily. I'll be there soon.'

*

Flora sat on the edge of the bed and stroked Lily's hair as she slept. There were a few grey strands, which she had not noticed before. Carl was away at a conference.

Three more miscarriages were to follow in as many years. Lily announced the last to Flora as they sat in the kitchen one Thursday evening. In the background, Carl noisily opened and closed cupboards in search of coffee. 'Where is the stupid thing?'

'Where it always is,' Lily said, staring impassively at the washing machine.

*

'They're for Mrs Everley,' Flora said in a slightly raised voice as she handed the prescription over to the pharmacist.

She was glad to make herself useful running errands for her less mobile neighbours, but found some of their medical requirements embarrassing and was keen to distance herself from them.

She had been living in the flat for five years, but referred to it as 'the new place.' Though she still found the rooms poky, she had to admit they kept the heat in better than her draughty house and were easier to maintain. She had made a few friends, with whom she played cards in winter and visited garden centres in spring. Sleep was still elusive.

After a year of commuting to her old church she had reluctantly started attending Lily's. It was much livelier than what she was used to, with a drum kit and clapping, but after some initial reservations she had grown to enjoy it. She had joined the Women's Fellowship, which had a much wider age range than her former place, and had put herself on various rotas. It had invigorated her. It also gave her valuable time with Lily.

They had established a routine, spending Sunday afternoons and Thursday evenings together, with occasional visits in between. Flora knew it was as much as she could ask for and had come to accept it. She had not anticipated further change, so was caught by surprise when one Sunday Lily casually revealed a potential disruption to their arrangements.

'We're thinking of going to Boston, mummy. For Carl's sabbatical. It's not definite yet though.'

'Boston, America?'

'It's a wonderful opportunity for him. And I think the change will do us both good.'

'What about your job?'

'They're open to letting me take unpaid leave. I'm sure I'll find things to do over there. Maybe a distance learning course, or something at Carl's university.'

'Sounds like you've got everything planned.'

'It'll only be for a year, mummy. Less than a year, in fact. We'll be back before you know it.'

Flora had excused Lily's flippant comment, but was hurt that the news had come out of the blue, with no warning at all. Then, within just a week of her daughter announcing the move as a possibility, it was confirmed as a certainty.

As Flora walked from the chemist to Mrs Everley's, she tried to focus on the potential benefits of the move on her daughter's marriage. She spent relatively little time with her son-in-law, but felt her initial instincts about him were correct. She sometimes sensed a hint of resentment at her regular presence on Sunday afternoons: a quickly fading smile, a note of frustration in his voice. She was unconcerned at this and accepted it as part of the normal relationship between mother-in-law and son-in-law. It was his attitude towards her daughter that was troubling. Flora had noted the lack of social engagements, his disregard for their church ('too hippy') and matters of faith, and the fact that he made no attempt to assist Lily around the house. Flora only ever heard him compliment Lily on her cooking, and that when prompted. He seemed to get easily irritated by her.

Lily never complained and was defensive if Flora ever raised these issues, so she had stopped for fear of raising discontent where there was none. But lately she had noticed Lily's lacklustre tone when she spoke of Carl. Flora was certain the words 'will do us both good' were significant.

When they left, Flora did not see them off at the airport, fearing the solitary taxi ride home. She waved them off from their house and prayed they would return safe and happy.

*

The months immediately after Carl and Lily's departure were especially difficult for Flora as they coincided with her enforced winter break from the garden and a spike in the mortality rate at the complex. January had been especially harsh, claiming Mrs Everley and two friends from her card group. It had also taken a young woman from the church whom she had befriended; killed on an icy road by a sliding car.

After the young woman's funeral, when the snow and ice had completely withdrawn, Flora made her way to the bereaved household, taking a chicken casserole. She had met the husband only once or twice before and had thought him aggressive-looking, but found him crumpled by grief. She watched helplessly as he sobbed, uncertain of what she should do. His son looked so small, small even for his eight years, sitting alone in an armchair, silent. He clutched a red scarf that Flora recognised as having belonged to his mother. She hugged the boy before she left and was heartbroken at how tightly he held on to her. Though she tried to arrange another visit, she did not see either of them again.

As the year progressed and the days became milder, Flora came to terms with her revised routine, which included twice weekly phone calls with Lily. She was relieved to hear a change in her tone. She sounded more relaxed, at ease with herself. Even Carl sounded conciliatory.

*

'We're expecting.'
'Expecting what, darling?'
'A baby, mummy! A baby girl!'
'A baby?'
'I'm in my third trimester. We didn't want to

say anything too early, you know, just in case, but the doctors seem positive.'

'That's wonderful, Lily!'

'We're going to stay here for the birth. We don't want to risk anything with the flight.'

'Of course. You do what you have to, darling.'

'I wondered if you might consider coming out here, mummy? I would love to have you here with me.'

Within a month, Flora was on a plane, crammed between a slumberous flatulent man and an indefatigable yoga teacher. After attempting some stretches that had been insistently suggested for her aching legs, Flora feigned sleep. The experience reminded her why she had not boarded a plane in a decade.

It was almost forgotten when two months later she held her granddaughter Iris. Flora had never been fond of newborns, finding them squashed and uninteresting. To her, Iris was an exception, her face already expressive and intelligent. She had inherited her father's green eyes and according to others, Flora's chin, though she thought it too early to tell. When they joked that Iris would be eligible to stand for president, Flora replied solemnly that though it was a possibility, it would probably be beneath her capabilities.

CHAPTER FIVE

*September – Novem-
ber 2003*

N adia made herself a cup of tea and sat down at the kitchen table. She sprung up immediately to rinse the teaspoon, then sat down again and began gnawing at the side of her right index finger in a vain attempt to stop grinning.

Carl Jansen had taken her first lecture at the University of the North West of England. He had a dry sense of humour that occasionally aired itself in lectures and tutorials. Because of its sporadic nature and subtle delivery it was lost on most students, who duly noted down his asides only to be later confused when revising. Nothing had been lost on Nadia, and she had allowed herself to fall into what she regarded as an innocent infatuation.

It had been five years since she left the university, after completing her masters. She'd had less contact with Carl in her final years and her feelings had gradually faded, so she was surprised at how excited she had been to be called for an interview for a research assistant post. It had prompted her to dig out photographs and mix tapes from her student days to wallow in bittersweet nostalgia.

She had braced herself to be disappointed with Carl at the interview, but instead found him disarmingly relaxed and charming. As they shook hands at the end he had said he was glad his lectures hadn't put her off the subject. She had been flattered that he remembered her, then later realised he had merely gleaned this from her application form.

A letter offering her the position had arrived that morning, two days after the interview. She had emailed her acceptance immediately.

As she cradled her teacup in both hands, Nadia's eyes came to rest on a photograph on the windowsill, in which her older sister Sasha had her arm protectively around her. It had been taken on a day trip to the seaside when they were seven and four respectively. While Sasha smiled eagerly at the camera, Nadia was preoccupied with a pebble in her hand. As she gazed at the familiar image, she wondered if this upturn in her life was to compensate for the dreadful past year, which had begun with her sister's death.

Nadia had feared that Sasha would die young. For as long as she could remember, she had regarded her as both charmed and tragic. She was impulsive, desperate for affection, and full of uncertainty.

One night, when Nadia was 17, Sasha had run into her bedroom panicking, having swallowed a packet of paracetamol. Nadia had forced her to regurgitate, angry and scared at her sister's behaviour. She gave in to her pleas not to call an ambulance nor tell a soul, insisting she went to the doctors the next morning if she felt ill. She'd kept vigil overnight, comforting her sister, stroking her hair.

In the end, Sasha had died in dramatic mundane circumstances. On the way home from the supermarket she had collapsed and died of an undiagnosed aneurysm. Nadia sobbed as she thought of her lovely sister alone on the pavement, groceries scattered around her.

Soon after Sasha's death, Nadia had started her first serious relationship, with a colleague from the journal where she worked, *The New Socialist Historian*. Grief and gratitude had initially blinded her to certain character flaws that became more apparent as the months progressed. He was controlling and resented the progress she was making in her career. When she suggested that perhaps they weren't suited to each other, he had responded by telling their editor that

Nadia had been plagiarising other people's work for her articles. No one had believed him, but by then she found his presence unbearable and was desperate to move on.

And that was how she found herself back in her old university city, house-sitting for a globe-trotting friend. Though she had instructed friends not to inform her ex of her whereabouts, letters from him were being re-directed from her old flat. They were whining bitter missives that she was largely able to disregard, but some parts moved her. He said he was lonely and missed her, that he was sorry for what he'd done and would put it right.

As Nadia got up to wash her cup, she decided that if another letter came from him, she would bin it without reading. Emboldened by this re-solve, she started to prepare dinner.

*

Nadia frowned at the clothes scattered on her bed. There had been no dress code at her pre-vious workplace - her editor had come to work in a pyjama top on more than one occasion – so she had very few items of formal clothing. After much deliberation she settled on a knitted dress that was uncharacteristically figure hug-ging. She convinced herself that she was defin-itely not dressing to impress Carl Jansen, and had to remind herself of this when she discovered he was away at a conference. She tried not to be disappointed at the note he had left her apologising for being absent on her first day. It was attached to a batch of papers that he suggested she familiarise herself with.

The following day Nadia looked into Carl's office on the way to her desk. She found him staring out of the window. Before she could interrupt, he turned to his computer and typed a handful of words. This was followed by a shorter pause and more typing. She coughed to attract his attention, causing him to visibly tense. He smiled when he realised it was her.

As she walked into the room, he stood and stepped forward to shake her hand, which he clasped in both of his. 'I'm so glad to have you working with us, Nadia. I just have to finish something off, I'll be with you shortly.'

'I'm looking forward to it.' As Nadia walked to her desk she wondered if that had sounded too forward, flirtatious even, then scolded herself for being over-analytical.

She was unable to concentrate on her reading as she waited for Carl to arrive. Her back was to the door and she did not want to appear startled. After attempting to read a paragraph for the fourth time she felt her morning coffee reach her bladder. She was hesitant to leave in case Carl turned up while she was away, worried he would think her slack if he found her desk unoccupied. She again dismissed these thoughts and left to do the needful.

As she left the room she immediately ran into Carl, narrowly avoiding a head on collision. She stifled a guffaw and felt the pressure on her bladder increase.

'I'm sorry to have kept you waiting for so long, Nadia. I always struggle to close addresses. Never know whether to end with a joke or something poignant.'

'It's fine. Could I just...'

'And, I'm really sorry, I'd forgotten that I have a departmental meeting. I'm actually already running late for it. Why don't you join me? It'll be good for them to meet you.' He looked expectantly at Nadia.

'OK. I just have to...' Nadia sighed, grabbed her bag from under the desk and followed Carl.

The meeting was in the office of one of the department lecturers. Very little distinguished it from Carl's. A chewing gum-pocked blue rug obscured much of the parquet flooring. Precarious piles of books and dusty batches of papers obscured much of the rug, as well as most other surfaces. The only areas free from books were the plastic chairs and that was only because they were currently occupied by academics. Two vacant spots remained, in the corner furthest from the door. Carl and Nadia sheepishly made their way over to them.

'This is my/our newest member of staff: Nadia Behnam,' Carl said after they had taken their seats.

The assembled academics, a few of whom Nadia recognised from her student days, responded with nods, indifferent smiles and in one case a wink. She was the only woman present.

One of the indifferent smilers appeared to be chairing. He was younger than the others. There was something about the shape of his face that reminded her of a cartoon insect, possibly Jiminy Cricket, but she couldn't be sure. 'So has everyone had a chance to look at the course structure and reading lists,' he said in a voice that indicated he was already bored of the meeting.

'Do we even need another module?' an older, red faced participant asked.

'We've already decided that we do. We now need to go through the details, Richard,' the insect answered wearily.

'Have we, Dylan? When?'

'At the end of last term. You were here.'

'Richard has a point. Do we need this at all? Or perhaps we need to do something completely fresh,' another participant offered, the winker.

'William, we've spent a considerable amount of time discussing this module. We're already behind schedule. There have been several emails back and forth which everyone had the opportunity to contribute to, and indeed did. I hardly think now is the time to debate it again,' Dylan said, determinedly keeping his eyes fixed on the agenda on his lap.

'Dylan, but did we discuss whether we actually need another module?' Richard again.

A few others made suggestions for alternative modules. Nadia stopped listening, preoccupied only with her bladder. She began to psyche herself up for her exit.

She turned to Carl, who had been one of the few to say nothing. He was staring at a stain on the rug. She stood up and made her way across the cramped gathering, bumping into knees and dislodging piles of books as she went. When she reached the door she realised the room had gone quiet. She smiled apologetically before rushing out and down the corridor.

On completing her mission, euphoric relief turned immediately into worry. They were probably discussing her now, she thought, saying she was typical of her sex, unable to handle robust discussion, intellectually weak. She inhaled deeply. She would simply resume her place without a word and at the appropriate moment make an incisive comment that would gain their respect and plaudits. If she found that she had no insights she would simply sit out the meeting and deal with the anguish later on.

As she turned a corner on her return journey she almost bumped into Carl again. He looked worried.

'I'm so sorry, Nadia. I should have warned you. Are you alright?'

Nadia reddened as she realised her full bladder had prolonged her time away.

'Yes, I'm fine. I was on my way back. I just needed the loo,' she said, immediately regretting the last sentence.

'They get like this sometimes, especially at the beginning of term. They like to practice the art of filibustering and cause a bit of mischief.'

'No need to apologise. It was interesting.'

Carl looked doubtful. 'Dylan's got us back on track with the agenda. We'd love to hear what you think, as a recent student.'

As they walked back to the meeting, Nadia strained to think of constructive ideas.

William leaned over to her as she took her seat. 'Sorry about that mischief, my dear.' He smelt of Vicks.

'It's fine, really. It was coffee that got to me, not the meeting,' Nadia said, raising her voice a little, glad for the opportunity to explain.

'It has that laxative effect on me too,' William smiled.

'Item 3 – Photocopying Allowance,' Dylan said, before Nadia could correct the misunderstanding.

*

Nadia was better prepared for the next meeting, though was in no doubt of the pointlessness of it.

She found herself involuntarily gazing at Carl on a number of occasions. She immediately looked away when she caught herself doing it, hoping desperately that she hadn't been gawping too obviously. She tried to focus on various items in the room to prevent her eyes from straying, finally settling on a small triangle of the rug that was visible under all the academic debris. As she scrutinised its various stains, the voices around her became vague and her eyelids heavy. She eventually let them close, then as she felt her head fall forward, jolted upright. In front of her Carl was looking up at the ceiling, biting his lower lip to suppress his laughter. Dylan glared at her. No one else seemed to have noticed. One person was snoring.

Nadia was embarrassed to have been caught looking foolish by Carl. Though she refused to fully acknowledge to herself that she had any feelings for him, she took measures to mitigate any potential heightening of affections. In preparation for private meetings with him she would deliberately eat food that made her feel bloated and uncomfortable. This worked to a degree, as did her tendency to maintain a good distance from him as they sat alone together in his office. But it was when he stood right behind her at her desk that she felt unable to prevent the heat rising from her neck to her ears.

*

Nadia looked at the time on her computer. She was due to meet Carl in five minutes. She had eaten her lunch and checked her emails. There was no point starting anything new, so she picked up her files and walked to his office.

Carl's door was ajar but not fully open as it usually was when he wasn't taking a tutorial or in a meeting, so she gently knocked, then pushed it open. Carl was at his desk, facing the window, with his back to the door. He was on the phone and evidently hadn't heard her knock. Nadia knew she should leave but her feet remained planted to the spot when she heard him speak.

'Have you? ... I know, sweetheart, but it's to help the wound heal. It'll come off soon... Yes, the tooth fairy will definitely still visit you.'

Nadia turned, knocking into the door frame as she left.

In the privacy of a toilet cubicle, she allowed tears to flow liberally, then scolded herself for crying. As she passed Carl's office on the way back to her desk, she resisted the urge to glance through the now open doorway.

'Carl was looking for you, Nadia,' one of her colleagues said as she sat down. 'He said he'll have to reschedule your meeting but will catch up with you before he leaves.'

Nadia managed to write four words in the next half hour before being conscious of Carl standing behind her. She could always tell when it was him. She didn't turn around immediately, so he started speaking to the back of her head.

'Nadia, could I talk to you please? In my

office.'

She sluggishly rose and followed him into the next room.

'I'm sorry about cancelling our meeting. I know there are various things we need to clarify before you can move forward with that funding application,' Carl said as he took his seat. Nadia remained standing. 'My daughter had a bad fall at school. Managed to graze her chin badly and lose a tooth.'

'Poor thing,' Nadia said.

'My wife collected her from school, but has to get back to work for some training thing or other and my mother-in-law's visiting her sister, so I'll have to go back and stay with her.'

Nadia was sure she had physically crumpled at 'wife'. She realised that Carl had deliberately called her into his office to break this news to her. He could easily have said it at her desk.

'That's fine,' she whispered, focussing on the window. 'I hope she feels better soon.'

Nadia passed the next hour imagining Carl's home life. His wife, she was certain, was a perfect balance of glamour and intellect. She wondered why Carl had never mentioned her or his daughter before. Amid the familiar clutter on his desk were no photographs to suggest their existence. There was nothing in his office that gave any hint of his personal life, apart from a cricket bat signed by men she'd never heard of. She left work early saying she had a migraine and slept for the rest of the afternoon and into the evening, waking only at ten to make herself some toast. She had reacted to Sasha's death in the same way.

Before returning to bed, she switched on her computer and drafted a brief resignation letter.

*

The next day Nadia arrived at work determined to be cheerful. She had decided against handing in her notice immediately, wary of making a sudden decision.

When she met Carl later that day, she used all her energy to appear relaxed and breezy. She did not let her eyes remain on his for more than a second. But while she tried to sound light, Carl was serious, his usual quips and wry smiles absent. Perhaps he felt guilty for leading her on by withholding key information about himself, Nadia wondered, before forcing the thought to the back of her mind. He was probably worried about his daughter.

By the end of the day Nadia's head was pounding from the effort of concealing her hurt. This continued over the following days. Carl, she noticed, had definitely become tentative around her, as though he was uncertain of what was appropriate.

Two weeks later she dated and printed her letter of resignation. She read through it several times, before placing it in an envelope and sealing it. She poured herself a large glass of Rioja and enjoyed the best night's sleep she'd had in a long time.

*

Carl's door was often closed these days, Nadia thought, as she stood in front of it. Except when they were meeting - then he left it wide open, whereas before he had always made sure it was shut.

She knocked.

He looked tired, she thought, as she approached his desk and handed him the envelope. She briefly caught his confused expression before fixing her eyes on the corner of his desk. She could feel him staring at her and when she quickly glanced up was taken aback by how dejected he looked.

Nadia carefully gave her prepared statement, about enjoying the work but that it would not be appropriate for her to stay. She had been certain he would understand what she meant and would not press her. But now he seemed unpredictable, so she rushed away to a lecture she would not be able to concentrate on. As she crossed the car park, she was certain of his eyes following her from his window. It took all her determination not to turn and look.

CHAPTER SIX

May - August 2004

F lora was grateful to discover it was the Indian Ocean that lapped her feet, not electric-tongued komodo dragons as she had dreamt, but snapped into panic when she realised where she was. She frantically scanned the beach for Iris. Clumsily dislodging herself from the plastic garden chair in which she'd been ensconced, Flora desperately called her granddaughter's name, her voice husky from sleep, 'Iris! Iris! Darling!'

'I'm behind you, grandma.' Iris was kneeling in the long shadow of the chair, crafting a sand turtle. 'Did you have a nice nap?'

Flora had to catch her breath in relief, but was annoyed with herself. If anything had happened to Iris she would never have forgiven herself.

'Tide's coming in, darling. We should move back,' Flora said, picking up the chair.

'Now you're awake, can I go back in the water?' Iris asked hopefully.

At Flora's nod, she bounded eagerly into the surf, before there could be any change of mind.

They had been warned that the sea's undercurrents at Bentota could take people by surprise. Iris, yet to master any of her swimming strokes, had been told she was only to go into the sea if there was a responsible adult around. She had evidently decided that a slumbering version did not count.

Flora wondered if her obedience would last. Would she go off the rails as a teenager? Or would her adolescence be like that of her mother's, full of angst, but little rebellion. Her greater concern was that her granddaughter's sweet nature made her vulnerable to the conceits of others, as had been the case with Lily. She hoped Iris was more robust.

Flora watched as Iris ventured further out than she was comfortable with. She said nothing though. She had been too protective of Lily and didn't want to make the same mistake with her granddaughter. The sun was beginning to sink into the horizon, but Flora felt she had short-changed Iris of play so allowed her a little longer.

She felt sad as she thought about Iris being short-changed when it came to having a father. Nearly three months had passed since Carl left.

*

Flora felt uncomfortable walking through the empty house. When she received the call from Lily at lunchtime she had immediately started to panic. While relieved to find it was just a request to take Iris's PE kit to school, she had been unable to shake off the feeling of unease.

She found Iris's bag packed and ready by her bed, but as she left the room, instead of turning left to go downstairs, she turned right, towards Carl and Lily's bedroom.

She saw the note immediately. She was not normally a nosy person, but without hesitation picked it up. She glanced at the clock. She needed to get to school before the class started, so put the note in her handbag and left.

After dropping off Iris's kit with the sour school receptionist, Flora went to the library and pulled out the note. She read it several times and though the contents didn't particularly surprise her, they crushed her afresh with every reading.

Flora tried to remain composed as she collected Iris from school, but it was too much to hope that her intuitive granddaughter would not notice something was awry.

'Are you alright, grandma?'

'I think I might be getting a cold, darling.'

As she watched television with Iris and fixed her snacks, Flora's mind was on how she would help them get through this.

*

Iris waded out of the sea. She was a sturdy child, fond of food, like her grandmother, though not as fussy. Flora embraced her with a towel and they walked towards the beach cottage, which was emitting a welcoming glow. The aroma of garlic and spices informed them dinner was nearly ready.

They had been in Sri Lanka for nearly a week. After a day in Colombo, Flora's cousin Mervyn had organised a driver to take them down south to his company's holiday bungalows. He had arranged a cook, which they had particularly appreciated.

Lily had spent most of the time sleeping. At first Flora and Iris had tried to coax her out and onto the beach, but soon accepted the futility of their efforts and embarked on their own mini expeditions while she rested. Flora had looked forward to the opportunity to use her long dormant Sinhala, but discovered most of the locals were fluent in English and preferred to use that rather than wait for her to decipher their sentences. She noticed most were able to converse freely with the German tourists too.

On entering the bungalow, Flora and Iris found Lily asleep in a cane chair by a window, *Sense and Sensibility* lay open on the floor.

'Mummy, wake up. Uncle Rohan is making something yummy for us,' Iris said as she gently rubbed Lily's arm.

Lily smiled at her as she slowly opened her eyes. 'You smell of the ocean.'

Later on, as they ate freshly caught crab in the dim light of the veranda, dark waves lapping comfortingly in the background, Flora noted that Lily's appetite had improved. She decided it was best to say nothing of it.

*

'I looked so nervous, the nurse had to hold my hand. It was embarrassing!'

As Lily shared with them her experience at the dentist, Flora wondered how she would break the news of Carl's departure.

'I think I have a wobbly tooth.' Iris demonstrated said dental issue by pushing her tongue against a tooth that appeared immovable to her audience.

As Lily went into the kitchen to put the kettle on, Flora followed closely behind and handed her the note. 'I found this when I came to collect Irie's bag.'

She braced herself for the impact of Carl's scrawled words.

As Lily read, she bit her lip and quietly said, 'It must be that young research assistant of his.' When she had finished, she let the note fall from her fingers.

Flora held her tightly, absorbing her sobs. 'You're too good for him, always have been,' she said into Lily's hair.

'The kettle's whistling.' Iris had walked in, wondering how they couldn't hear it.

Flora had sometimes doubted Carl's love for her daughter, but had been certain he loved his own. She found it incomprehensible that he would leave Iris. To compound her resentment, she realised she would have to restrain herself from criticising him.

'What's wrong?' Iris's eyes started welling up in sympathy with her mother's.

Flora looked at Lily, unsure of who should break the news.

'Mummy's sad because...her tooth hurts,' Flora volunteered.

'Darling, daddy has had to go away,' Lily interrupted.

'That's why you're sad?'

'Yes.'

'Why didn't he tell me?'

'It was sudden.'

'When is he coming back?'

'I don't know, sweetheart.'

'How come?'

'He didn't tell me,' Lily said, wrapping her arms around Iris's head.

Flora stayed with them that night and got Iris ready for school the next day while Lily slept. When she returned, Lily was still in bed. 'Darling, you need to call your office and tell them you're not coming in.'

There was no response, so Flora called them, saying Lily had suddenly taken ill. She felt this was not untrue.

She spent the morning plumping cushions and dusting already clean surfaces before reluctantly starting on the kitchen. As she was examining the back of the oven she was startled to hear Lily's voice.

'I'm going to the university to speak to him. I'll tell him that I understand why he left me, but I need to know how he could leave Iris.' Lily looked up at the ceiling but failed to stop a tear spilling.

'I'm not sure that's a good idea, darling.'

'I need to know.'

'Hasn't he humiliated you enough already? Do you really want to make a scene?'

'So I should just leave it? Accept the end of my marriage?'

After half an hour of persuasion, they reached a compromise. Lily agreed to allow Flora to go on her behalf, providing she asked a set list of questions and got Carl to agree to meet her in a less public place.

As Flora sat on the bus, she tried to think of anything but the errand she was on: what she needed to buy for dinner, the plot inconsistencies of the novel she was reading, the jobs that needed doing in the garden. She would start well, but then her son-in-law's infidelity would come crashing in, which invariably brought to mind her husband.

It was only when she alighted at the university that it occurred to her that she had no idea of where to find Carl. She walked towards a map of the campus, doubtful it would help her.

'Are you lost, madam?' asked a smiling young woman with candy floss pink hair and an assortment of facial studs.

Flora tried not to look disapproving. 'I'm looking for Professor Carl Jansen.'

'Do you know his department?'

Flora had never bothered to grasp the details of Carl's job. 'History of some sort. Maybe even archaeology.'

'I believe they're in the same building and I'm heading that way so I can walk you there.'

Flora was grateful for the young woman's assistance but wasn't keen on being accompanied by her.

'Are you a student here?' Flora's guide asked.

At first Flora was unsure if this was a joke, but looking at the earnest face of her inquisitor realised it was not.

'No, I'm too old for that!'

'Not at all. You can never stop learning. My nan has just taken up Japanese. She's 64.'

Flora smiled, impressed by this information.

'I'm Charlie, by the way. Second year Social Anthropology.'

'Lovely.' Flora had no intention of offering her name.

'Do you mind if I ask you where you are from originally? What your heritage is?'

'Sri Lanka. I'm a Tamil.'

'Fantastic! My boyfriend was there last year, saving turtles in Trinc-o-mani.'

'Trincomalee.' Flora smiled again, wondering how long it would take to reach Carl's building.

'Have you lived here all your life, or have you spent time in Sri Lanka?' Though annoyed with the persistent questioning, Flora admired the fact that the girl had picked up her pronunciation of 'Lanka'.

'I was born there and came here in my early thirties.'

'Wow, that must have been massive for you.'

'Is it much further?'

'Just down here. Sorry, I'm just really interested in people's stories, you know.'

'Well, that's good if you want to be an anthropologist.'

'So, what languages do you speak?'

Flora was surprised at how quickly the girl returned to her questions and wondered if she was being appraised to be the subject of a study.

'Well English, of course. Tamil, a little Sinhala, and school girl Latin.'

'That's amazing! What was that one – "Sinhala"?'

'It's what the majority of people in Sri Lanka speak.'

'Oh, sorry, I didn't realise.'

'Is this the building?'

'Oh, yeah it is.'

'Thank you so much, Charlie. All the best with your studies.'

'No worries. Thank *you*. That was really interesting.'

Flora shook hands with the second year anthropologist and hurried into the building.

There were groups of students milling about in the high-ceilinged entrance hall, their conversations creating an echoey murmur. Flora looked around for someone official, or at least who was above the age of 22.

A man with an exceptionally high forehead was scowling at a sheet of paper. He turned it over, sighed melodramatically and turned on his heels. As he appeared to be not only over 22 but was possessed of a shirt so crisp and white that no student could possibly attain to it, Flora felt he was her best hope.

'Excuse me!'

He turned and regarded Flora indifferently.

'Do you know if Professor Carl Jansen works here?'

'Yes,' the man said impatiently and started walking away briskly.

Flora was annoyed but persisted. 'Where's his office?' she shouted, prompting raised eyebrows from passing students.

'First floor, left, fourth right.' His voice trailed off as he disappeared into a corridor.

Flora could feel her neck getting hot, flustered at the social incompetence she was encountering. She had tried hard to remain calm, but wondered how she would react when she saw Carl. She slowly ascended the stairs, then took out her spectacles so she could read the names on the doors.

When she arrived at his, she took a deep breath and breathed a prayer for composure before knocking. There was no response, so she tried again, hurting her knuckles. She tried the handle, only to find it locked.

Flora walked further along to a room with an open door. Inside were a number of desks, but only one resident - a young woman putting files into a satchel. Her back was to the door. Flora wondered if she was the one, and coughed. The young woman stopped her packing and turned to face her.

'I'm looking for Professor Jansen.' The young woman's eyes widened and Flora knew her suspicions were correct. 'I'm his mother-in-law.'

'I don't think he's coming in today.'

'Are you...*her?*' Flora asked.

Nadia nodded and looked down. 'I'm so sorry.'

'My daughter's life has been destroyed,' Flora said. 'And my granddaughter has lost her father overnight.'

Nadia looked up, confused. Flora continued, 'Perhaps you could pass that on to him. Is he lying low today? Didn't want to face his colleagues, I suppose.'

'Um...'

'It's not that I want him back in their lives. Good riddance. But at least he provided some security.'

'I'm so sorry for all the trouble I've caused,' Nadia whispered. 'I don't know how I could have behaved like that.'

Flora listened. She had not expected The Other Woman to be so contrite or so modest in demeanour. 'Well, it's not just your fault. He's as much to blame, if not more so.'

'I don't know where he's gone. I thought he'd returned to the family. Obviously not.' A tear rolled down her cheek.

Flora had wanted to hate this young woman, but found she could not.

'He left a note admitting the affair. We thought he was with you.'

Nadia shook her head.

Flora turned to leave. She stumbled at the door as she felt a twinge in her left leg. Nadia instinctively reached out to her, then retreated as Flora reached for the wall to steady herself.

'I'm so sorry. For everything.'

Flora continued out the door and down the dusty corridor, without looking back.

When she returned to the house, Lily was sitting at the bottom of the stairs. She looked at Flora expectantly. 'What did he say?'

Flora slowly lowered herself onto the step

next to Lily, her large posterior next to her daughter's slight frame.

'He wasn't there. But the girl was. He's not with her anymore. She doesn't know where he is.'

'What?'

'She thought he had come back to you. She seemed...remorseful.'

'Was it his assistant? Young, middle-eastern looking girl.'

'I think so.'

Lily nodded sadly. 'Is that worse? If he's not with her it means the push to leave was greater than the pull.'

'What it means is: he's a coward.'

Lily pulled the note from her dressing gown pocket. 'He says he'll be in touch.'

As they sat silently on the stairs, Flora wondered if that would be helpful. She thought of the impact on Lily of her father's few appearances when she was a child. Carl was not as reckless, but certainly as feckless.

*

When Flora saw Mrs Stanford, Iris's teacher, at the school gate her heart started pounding.

'Where's Iris? Is she alright?'

'Iris is safe. I was wondering if I could have a quick word with you, Mrs Ratnam.'

Flora followed her down the corridor, decorated in multicoloured hand prints and paintings of giant insects, to Iris's classroom. Iris was in the reading corner looking glum, as a teaching assistant attempted patient conversation.

'Iris, your grandma's here.'

Iris slowly walked towards Flora, and wrapped her arms around her comforting hips.

'Iris has been very sad today, which is very unlike her. Usually she's my bubbliest, brightest girl,' Mrs Stanford said, ruffling Iris's already dishevelled bob. 'She mentioned something about her daddy going away?'

'Yes, her father's gone away,' Flora said deliberately, looking Mrs Stanford in the eye, hoping she understood the euphemism. 'We're not sure when he'll be back.'

The teacher nodded in comprehension and looked down at Iris, whose face was buried in Flora's cardigan pocket. 'Poor poppet.'

'It was sudden,' Flora added, as explanation for why the school had not been informed of the change in circumstances.

'I see. Well if Iris needs some time at home for a few days, just let us know.'

When they returned to the house, Iris was in no mood for her programmes and headed straight for her bedroom. Flora gloomily emptied the untouched contents of Iris's lunchbox and took up some hot chocolate.

'Grandma, will you stay here with me?'

'Of course, my darling.'

She sat by the bed, unable to concentrate on

her novel, imagining instead what the future would look like. When Iris was finally asleep, she walked into Lily's room. Finding her also asleep, Flora went downstairs and ate supper alone.

*

The fact that it was Friday was for some reason a relief to Flora. Neither Lily nor Iris had surfaced from under their bedcovers, so she brought breakfast to them, in the hope they would take some sustenance.

By the time she returned from buying her newspaper, the post had arrived. There was just one piece of mail. She recognised her son-in-law's handwriting.

She put the kettle on, waited impatiently for it to boil, and steamed open the envelope.

Inside were two letters. One addressed to Iris and one for Lily. She read them:

'Dear Lily,

I am so very sorry for all the hurt I have caused you, not only now, but throughout our marriage. I have been a bad husband to you and a cowardly father to Iris.

I realise now how selfish and foolish I have been. I honestly don't know what I was thinking when I started this ~~affair~~ situation. Perhaps it was a mid-life crisis. I am entirely to blame for it. Don't blame Nadia. I took advantage of her. It's over now anyway.

I don't expect you to forgive me. I am convinced

that you will be much happier without me – that is my only comfort.

Of course I want to ensure that you and Iris are both provided for financially. I have already arranged standing orders into your account (formally our joint account) and into Iris's trust account.

I've resigned from the university, but am hoping to find a post initially somewhere in the north west so I will not be very far. Please tell Iris I love her. I'm not sure what you've said about my leaving. I'm sure you know what's best. I only ask, please don't let her hate me (I know I'm asking for what I don't deserve).

Sincerely,
Carl'

Flora put it in her pocket and then read the note to Iris.

'To my darling Irie,

Sweetheart, I am so sorry for leaving without saying goodbye. Please don't be cross with me. I'm sure mummy will have explained why I had to do that.

I have been thinking about you all the time and miss you so much. I hope to see you very soon. I am not very far away. I will call you tomorrow (Friday) and we can chat properly.

I know you will do well in life, my brilliant girl. I'm sorry this is a short note, I want to catch the 12 o'clock post.

I love you so much. Please remember that.
Hugs and kisses,

Daddy'

Flora put down the letter and took off her glasses. She again thought of her husband and his interactions with Lily. Carl's letter appeared loving, but also cowardly, expecting Lily to fill in the gaps. How dare he ask her to make sure Iris didn't hate him? She put Iris's note back in the envelope and placed it in her handbag. She would take up Lily's. She knew she needed to see it. She would think about what to do with Iris's.

'There's a letter from Carl,' Flora announced to the bedcovers.

Lily sat up immediately and took it from her.

'You've read it already, haven't you?'

Flora said nothing.

'Where's the envelope?'

'In recycling. There's no address on it.'

Lily started to get up.

'I'll get it,' Flora said, surprised at her daughter's lack of trust. She clambered downstairs, retrieved the envelope, emptied it of its content and heaved herself back up again.

Lily was looking hopeful. 'He'll be in the north west,' she said.

'You wouldn't take him back, would you?'

Lily shrugged. 'For Iris.'

'He's let down two women in as many days, not to mention his daughter. Darling, I think you need to think carefully about what you'll do.'

Lily looked deflated and Flora knew she had

said the wrong thing. She tried to recover. 'You deserve so much better. You can get on without him.'

Lily let go of the letter and slipped back under the bedcovers.

Flora spent the rest of the day reading and gardening while Lily and Iris stayed in bed, consuming only tea and toast. She felt she should be helping them take their minds off their sad situation, but was at a loss for what to do.

She managed to coax Iris down at four o'clock to watch her programmes. As they settled, the phone rang.

Flora anxiously went to answer it.

'Hello?'

'Hello, it's Carl.'

Flora had expected it to be him, but was unprepared so there was an awkward pause, before both starting talking.

'I'm so sorry...' / 'How could you ...'

Silence.

'How could you do that? Have you any idea of the mess you've caused?'

'I'm sorry. I thought...things would be better without me.'

'You left because you were chasing after a young girl. This has nothing to do with making things better for your family.' Flora was conscious of her voice getting louder so stopped abruptly.

After another pause, Carl said, 'You're right.

I'm pathetic...But I do think things will be better for them now. I'm a useless husband and father.'

Flora sighed, feeling that though she had won the argument, there was no victory in it.

'Could I speak to Iris?' Carl asked tentatively.

'I'm not sure that would be a good idea,' Flora said hesitantly. 'She's been in bed all day and has only just come down. It might disrupt things.'

'Oh,' Flora could hear the disappointment in Carl's breathing. Why hadn't he insisted? she would later think. If he'd asked again, she would have relented. Why did he give in so easily? 'If you think that's best, then I'll leave it for now. I don't want to upset her. When do you think would be a good time?'

'I don't know. It's too early to tell,' she replied. 'Do you want to speak to Lily?'

'I'm not sure that would be a good idea at the moment.'

His reluctance to speak to Lily convinced Flora that her decision to deny him access to Iris was the right one.

'Fine.'

'I've set up payments into their accounts so-'

'Are you going to divorce her?'

'I think it's too early to think about that.'

'So would you consider returning to her?'

After another pause Carl said, 'I really don't know.'

Flora put the phone down. Her heart raced, as the only other people she had ever cut off like that were double glazing sales reps and her husband. She waited a moment to see if it would ring again. It did not.

*

As Flora watched Iris and Lily ahead of her, gathering shells on the beach, she knew she should feel happy. Here they all were, the most relaxed they'd been in months, yet she was uneasy. Buying postcards for her friends had reminded her of the mound of post that would be waiting for them when they returned, which in turn reminded her of the mound of lies she had told. She would have to make sure she got to the post first when they returned so she could weed out anything from Carl. How could she undo this? she wondered.

'Look, grandma, a cruise ship!' Iris pointed to the horizon. Flora caught up with them and smiled.

Iris took hold of her arm. 'Grandma, you look tired.'

CHAPTER SEVEN

April - May 2004

Nadia recognised Carl's footsteps in the corridor. He wore the rubber-soled shoes common to most of the university's professors of a certain age, which muffled their steps on the stark concrete. But his were distinguishable by their pace, which to Nadia was surprisingly hurried and at odds with his generally laidback demeanour. Even the uptight department head, Dylan, didn't walk so speedily. She minimised the job advertisement she had been looking at on the computer and braced herself for Carl's imminent arrival.

'Lily wants to come to the dinner,' he said to the back of her head.

'I'm sure it will be fine,' she said, without turning around. She didn't think she would be able to so quickly disguise the look of horror on her face.

*

The intercom buzzer startled Nadia, causing her to spill wine on her pyjamas. She ignored it, assuming it to be drunk students. It buzzed persistently. She continued to ignore it. After a pause her phone started ringing.

'Where are you? I'm at your door.' It was Carl.

He had established a routine in the last semester, visiting her on Tuesday and Friday nights, having told his wife he was taking evening lectures. In the early days of their affair they had gone out, for dinner or drinks - once to the theatre, but now they always remained at her flat. She would provide dinner, then they would retire to her bedroom, or occasionally another spot in the flat. This, however, was a Thursday.

'I just got back from London and thought I'd pop in,' Carl said when she opened the door. She smiled weakly. 'I haven't yet eaten,' he continued, pecking her on the cheek.

As Nadia rummaged through her freezer, Carl took her place on the sofa and changed the channel from a re-run of 'Friends' to a documentary on Amazonian amphibians.

'Won't your wife have prepared something for you?' she asked from the kitchen doorway. 'All I've got is pizza.'

'She may have. Pizza's fine. Anyway, come here, I've got something for you.' Carl patted the space next to him. Nadia wearily shoved the pizza in the oven before joining him.

Carl reached into his case and after some fumbling, produced a small velvet jeweller's box, which he held out on his palm. Nadia's eyes widened and she felt her heart plummet into her stomach.

'Hope you like them.'

Nadia opened the box, fearing what she would find inside and laughed in relief when she found a pair of antique silver filigree earrings.

'Early birthday present, as I can't see you on the actual day.'

'They're very nice,' she said, desperately hoping Carl wouldn't ask her to wear them. It would be embarrassing to tell him now that her ears were not pierced. 'I haven't got your birthday present yet.'

She had been seeing Carl for five months and had spent the most part regretting her decision, wallowing in the guilt of adultery and the foolishness of being involved with her boss. She was not certain how she had let herself get into such a situation. Yet she had not ended it, partly because she didn't know how to and partly because she enjoyed his company and the way he looked at her conspiratorially at work. She knew it couldn't last. That had become increasingly clear to her. She planned to see out the rest of the academic year, then be on her way.

Carl glanced at his watch and stood. Normally this would be Nadia's prompt to lead him to the bedroom or start removing her top, but as it was a Thursday and not part of their normal routine she wasn't sure what to do.

'We've got a while before the pizza's ready, haven't we?' he asked, with a wry smile.

Nadia got up and shuffled to the bedroom, wondering if Carl had heard her sigh of frustration.

*

Carl hadn't asked Nadia not to attend the university anniversary dinner, but she knew he would rather she didn't. She had RSVP-ed immediately, after reading the menu, but after his revelation about his wife's attendance, knew it would probably be unwise to go. As she gazed at the paltry contents of her fridge, she thought about the possibility of meeting Lily, whom she was very curious about. Was she the whimpering creature Carl portrayed? The promise of a good meal and a strange desire to punish him prompted her to snap shut the fridge. She marched to her bedroom to hunt for a suitable outfit. Twenty minutes later, dressed, powdered and fortified with a generous measure of rum, she set out.

By the time Nadia arrived at the hall, most of the history department were already there, though Carl was not. She headed straight for the canapés, realising she was over-dressed in her best outfit – a coral bridesmaid dress. Most of her colleagues had gone to the pub after work before turning up together for the dinner. It was evident from the tone and volume of their laughing that a fair amount of alcohol had already been consumed. She quickly downed two glasses of Prosecco to catch up with them, then fixed her eyes on the door.

'Carl's bringing his wife. Did you know?' William made her jump.

'So I hear,' she answered without looking at him.

'For a long time I didn't even know he had a wife,' William continued. 'He kept her very quiet. He's a dark horse, isn't he?'

Nadia stuffed a blini in her mouth, then nearly choked when she saw Carl and his wife appear at the door.

'Oh, here they are. She's quite a cutie,' William said, advancing towards them.

Nadia watched from the safety of the drinks table. Carl had caught her eye immediately. He looked serious, while his wife was beaming. They both were distracted by William, who had bounded over and was kissing the right hand of Carl's wife. Nadia turned away and refilled her glass. She was desperate to get another look at Lily, but controlled herself. 'Well presented' was how Carl had condescendingly described her, but it seemed an appropriate term. She was neat, there was nothing ungainly about her. Her hair was tidy, her clothes tasteful. Nadia had ascertained from Carl that she was not the glamorous career woman she had initially thought she would be. She was a finance officer for a medium sized company and had remained in the same role for twenty years.

'Hello, Nadia?'

Nadia turned and almost spat out her mouthful of drink at Carl's wife, who was smiling uncertainly at her.

'Sorry to interrupt you,' his wife continued, looking genuinely concerned at the disturbance she had caused.

'Sorry, I was miles away,' Nadia said, dabbing her mouth with a napkin.

'I'm Lily – Carl's wife.' She offered her hand. Nadia's was sticky from handling canapés clumsily, so she wiped it before taking Lily's.

'Carl's always saying what a great help you are,' Lily said, her eyes eager.

'Oh.' Nadia had no idea how to respond.

She looked good for her age, Nadia thought. She could definitely pass for younger, her skin was smooth. There was a childishness to her voice, but it was not as grating as Carl had described.

'I hope you don't mind me hovering around you. I feel a bit out of my depth here, so was just looking for a friendly face,' Lily said.

'Not at all. I would love you to hover by me.' Nadia wanted to hug her and apologise for stealing her husband. She was touched by the look of gratitude Lily gave her, but then immediately wondered if this lack of confidence could become cloying. She glanced across the room and found Carl staring anxiously. She grabbed Lily's hand. 'Carl talks about you all the time. It's lovely to finally meet you.'

Nadia spent the rest of the time before dinner talking animatedly to Lily about their recently published paper, *Misogyny and mischief in early modern Lancashire*.

'It mainly focuses on two individuals. A woman named Agnes Piper, who wanted to be a coachman. She loved horses, you see, and thought it would give her the opportunity to travel the country. But she couldn't, because she was a woman.'

'Of course.'

'So, she dressed as a man.'

'Goodness!'

'And not only did she become a coachman, but within five years she was running her own coach company. And in ten, she was running for mayor of Lesterbury. Then it all fell apart.'

'What happened?'

'One day a maid caught her removing her binding corset, and spread the rumour that she was a Hermaphrodite. She was burnt at the stake.'

'That's awful. The poor woman.'

'On the other hand, there was Benjamin Stutterbridge, who in the belief - the mistaken belief

- that women had easier lives than men, passed himself off as one, and found work as a milk maid. Of course he discovered the work was hard and the hours long and was on the verge of giving up when he attracted the attentions of the lord of the manor, the Earl Rufflesthorpe.'

'Rufflesthorpe?'

'Yes. Benjamin was said to have had exceptionally soft skin and a "ripe mouth". No doubt his artificially impressive bosoms were also a factor.' Nadia suddenly realised her hand gestures were more exaggerated than normal, so gripped the edge of the table to stop herself.

'Are you alright, Nadia?'

'Yes, I'm fine. Anyway, Benjamin was forced to confess his schemes, but because he was an artful blagger, he managed to pass it off as a social experiment and somehow got away with it, without any adverse consequences. He became a regular at Henry VII's court. Everyone enjoyed his bawdy milk maid stories.'

Nadia wasn't sure how to respond to Lily's uncertain smile so an uncomfortable pause hung between them for a few seconds, which was gratefully broken by an announcement asking guests to take their seats for dinner.

A problem with printers meant the seating arrangements for dinner had gone awry and Nadia found herself sitting next to Lily, at her insistence. Carl was on the other side. Though they were sitting with colleagues from another department, Nadia was deeply conscious of the awkwardness of the situation. She was grateful when Carl and Lily left soon after the main course but sat in quiet shame, ignoring the speeches. When a plate of tiramisu was placed in front of her, she felt a sudden lurch of nausea at its unashamed creaminess. She rushed out of the hall, uncertain of where to find the toilets in the unfamiliar building.

Locating them just in time, after passing of all people the head of department Dylan, Nadia vomited the contents of the evening. She walked home briskly, eyes brimming. She would tell Carl the next day that it was over.

CHAPTER EIGHT

May – July 2004

Iris was surprised at how readily her grand-mother accepted her claim of illness.

She had lain awake late into the night trying to figure out why her father had left without a word, and was in no mood for school. Additionally, Flora's snoring, which she normally found a comforting reminder of her presence in the room, had irritated her, disturbing her thoughts and sleep.

She was also annoyed when her grandmother had opened the curtains in the morning, so that sunlight streaked across her face and illuminated her yellow walls, making sleep impossible. She was too lazy to close them, so turned on her side and again started to go over the likely reasons why her father had left, hoping she would uncover something that she had earlier missed.

On the morning that he left, he had kissed her on the top of her head while she ate her corn-flakes, just as he usually did. She had looked up at him and he had held her face in his hand, which he didn't normally do. He had looked sad, she remembered.

The night before, he had gone with her mother to a special dinner at his work. They had dressed up for it. Her mother had seemed happy even though she had toothache, but her father had looked worried. She wondered if something had happened at the dinner. Had someone been horrible to him?

Iris could hear the radio downstairs in the kitchen and her grandmother opening and closing cupboards and drawers. She strained to listen, trying to work out her movements.

Eventually, after the distant flush of the downstairs toilet, she heard Flora getting ready to go out. The sound of rustling fabric as she put on her coat, her handbag being unzipped and zipped, the jangle of keys, and after a loud blow of her nose, the opening and closing of the front door. After she heard the keys double locking it from outside, Iris slipped out of bed and went into her parents' bedroom.

Her mother was laying on the far side of the bed, with her face towards the window. The breakfast tray had been left on the side of the bed nearest the door – her father's side. She walked around so that she could see Lily's face. Her eyes were open. She stretched out her arms and Iris was glad to let her hold her.

'Where's daddy?'

'I don't know, darling.'

'How come?'

Lily released Iris from her embrace and turned to face the other way. Iris started to cry quietly and walked back to the door. Lily reached out again, but Iris didn't stop.

She continued walking to her father's study. She had always liked the smell of it.

*

Iris had tired of her bed by the next day, Saturday, and got up at her usual time to watch her morning programmes. Her mother stayed in bed. She accompanied her grandmother on her various errands in the morning and they spent the afternoon playing Scrabble and watching her favourite movie, *Aladdin*. It had been a diverting day and had partly taken her mind off her father, but when the film ended happily, she thought about her own situation and how sad it was. Just a week ago, while she helped her mother bake fairy cakes for the church picnic, her father had been in his study. She had felt safe knowing he was there.

'Grandma, why didn't daddy tell me he was going away? Why hasn't he even called?'

Flora took off her spectacles. 'He's not well. He's gone away so he can get better.'

'What's wrong with him? Is he in hospital? Can't we visit him?'

'He's not in hospital and we can't visit him, but when he's better you can see him, Irie.'

'When?'

'I don't know, darling.'

'Why won't anyone tell me anything?'

'Because we don't know anything more.'

'How come you don't know?!'

Iris jumped down from the seat and was about to storm out of the room, when she suddenly became anxious about her mother.

'Mummy won't go away, will she?'

'No, no, darling! Of course not!'

'But how do you know?'

*

Iris had been told that she didn't have to go to school the following week if she didn't want to. She was happy to take Monday off, but by Tuesday was keen to return. Although she enjoyed the presence of her grandmother, she didn't like the sad atmosphere of the house. Her mother had remained in her bedroom for much of the weekend and when she did come out, hardly said a word.

Iris was also keen to speak to a girl in her class called Cerys. She had once gone to her house for tea and Cerys had told her that her father lived in Spain. She wanted to question her further and at lunchtime rushed to get behind her in the dinner queue.

'You know your daddy?'

'Mmmm...' Cerys was distracted by a felt tip stain she had just discovered on her blouse.

'Does he live in Spain?'

'Yeah, I'm going to visit him in the summer holidays!' Cerys looked up, now animated.

'How come he doesn't live with you?'

'Because him and mum got divorced.'

'Oh.' Iris felt she should know what this meant and was embarrassed to display her ignorance.

'They've just bought a puppy, so I'll get to play with him.'

'Do you miss him? Your daddy?'

'Yeah.'

They had reached the servery, so Iris was no longer able to continue her questioning. She kept in mind the word Cerys had used, writing it in her general work book as soon as she returned from lunch.

*

'Grandma, what's "divorst"?' Iris asked as soon as Flora came to pick her up.

'Where did you hear that?'

'Someone at school. What does it mean?'

'I don't think you need to be worrying about those big words, darling.'

'But I want to know what it means. I'll just look in the dictionary if you don't tell me.' Iris hoped this would persuade her grandmother as she was uncertain she had got the spelling right to be able to find it.

'Why do you want to know so badly? There are lots of words you don't know. When you get older you'll learn the meaning of them.'

'Cerys said her mummy and daddy got a divorst and that's why her daddy lives in Spain. Is that why daddy has gone away?'

'Oh no, darling. When people get divorced it means they're not married anymore. Your mummy and daddy are still married.'

'So daddy won't go and live in Spain?'

'That's not something you have to worry about.'

*

As Iris sat in front of the television sipping milky tea, she could hear creaking floorboards above as her mother slowly walked from the bedroom to the bathroom. She had not come down since Iris had returned from school.

'Darling, how would you like it if I moved in?' Flora asked.

'Forever?'

'Well, not forever, but just for a little while. Mummy's not well and it's difficult for her to look after you properly at the moment.'

'How long until she gets better? She won't go away, will she? You said she wouldn't!'

'No, no, I told you, darling – mummy's

not going anywhere. But until she's better we thought it would be good for me to stay here.'

'I would like that, grandma.'

Iris had assumed her grandmother would stay while her father was away, just as she'd done before when he'd gone away with work for a week or two. It felt strange to be told formally.

The reason became clear the following weekend, as she was asked to help pack away her father's books from his study. Flora would be using it as her bedroom. As the walls became more visible and the room looked less like her father's, Iris started to cry.

'Darling, this is only for a short time. We'll put your daddy's books in the attic. We're not getting rid of them.'

'When is he coming back, grandma? I miss him.'

Another week passed. Then another. Her mother did not return to work, nor her father home. She missed them both, but the absence of her father and the ghostly presence of her mother began to feel almost normal and the ache in her chest dulled - either that or she had got used to it. Sometimes her mother would comb her hair and ask about her day, but she seemed a smaller, quieter version of herself.

She found her grandmother's presence reassuring and appreciated the steady stream of homemade treats, from sweet milk toffee and coconut ice to crunchy patties and *palaharam*.

Plus she was a ready, if not always willing, companion for board games. Sometimes the sadness would go away, but then the game or programme would end, and it would come back.

*

It was the final fortnight before the summer holidays. Iris had been selected to narrate the Lower School's end of year production, a modern urban retelling of *Hansel and Gretel*. Her grandmother had confirmed her attendance, but nothing had been said about her mother.

'Grandma, is mummy coming to my play?' Iris asked the evening before the first performance, as they tended their newly planted herb garden. She loved inhaling the rosemary, even though Flora was constantly warning her to beware of bumble bees.

'Have you asked her?'

'Well, she knows I'm in it.'

'I think you should ask her if she's coming. Why not do it now?'

'Really?'

Flora nodded.

Iris stood up, took off her oversized gardening gloves and walked to the house. Flora followed. They removed their gardening shoes before going inside, then walked purposefully upstairs to Lily's room. The door was open so Iris walked in. Flora stayed by the entrance. Lily was reading a diary.

'Are you coming to my play tomorrow, mummy? You know I'm the narrator.'

Lily glanced at Flora via the reflection in the wardrobe mirror. Flora remained impassive.

'I don't know, darling. You know I'm not well.'

'Mrs Derbyshire says I'm the best reader in the Lower School.'

'I'm sure you are.'

'How are you sure when you've never heard me?'

Lily turned to Flora for help. When none was forthcoming she turned back to Iris. 'Darling, we'll see.'

*

Iris stood alone on the stage, desperately scanning the hall. The room was quiet as the audience waited expectantly for the play to begin. Iris continued to systematically check each row and the silence turned to uncomfortable murmuring and coughing.

'*Iris!*' Mrs Derbyshire whispered loudly. Iris automatically started reading.

At the next opportunity, Iris resumed her search of the room and this time spotted her grandmother, uncomfortably wedged between two people, neither of whom was her mother. Flora was gazing at Iris sympathetically, paying no attention to the rest of the play. Iris felt the ache in her chest spread to her throat. Unwelcome tears threatened to spill over. She became aware that the room had gone quiet again and turned to find her classmates glaring at her from the centre of the stage. She struggled to find her place in the script.

'Hasan and Georgia followed the trail of bottle tops home,' Mrs Derbyshire prompted.

'Hasan and Georgia followed the trail of bottle tops home,' Iris repeated and continued reading haltingly, grateful it was a relatively short section.

Iris decided not to look up again, but was conscious of Flora's eyes on her. She had been looking forward to the production, but now couldn't wait for it to be over.

At the end of the evening, while her classmates giggled excitedly in the classroom-turned- dressing room, giddy from the applause, Iris quietly gathered her belongings and went in search of Flora. She made her way through the crowds of parents holding plastic cups of wine and silently took her grandmother's outstretched hand. As soon as they were clear of the building she released her tears.

'I'm sorry, darling. You were excellent. You were the only one I could hear.'

'Did you even listen to the others?' Iris asked between sobs.

'No, because I couldn't hear them.'

The house was silent when they returned, as it so often was now.

'Sit there, I've got something for you.'

Iris perched herself on the tall stool in the kitchen, while Flora opened her handbag and produced a small gift bag, pale blue with multi-coloured polka dots.

Delighted already with the bag, Iris peered inside and found a jeweller's box. She carefully retrieved it and prised it open. It contained a small gold heart-shaped locket.

'That's for being the best and most talented granddaughter in the world.'

Iris got down from the stool and silently hugged her grandmother. They said nothing about her mother's absence.

As she settled into her cool bed, she could hear her grandmother's voice in her mother's bedroom. She seemed to have two tones for speaking to her mother these days: very gentle, like she was soothing a baby, or sharp, like she was scolding a naughty toddler.

'You're not helping yourself. You won't take the medicine, you won't eat, you won't make any effort. What do you want to do, just melt away?'

Lily said nothing.

'You have a child, remember. Don't you care about her? She's lost her father. You want her to lose her mother too?'

It took Iris a long time to fall asleep, but when she did, she dreamt of being on stage with her grandmother. The only people in the audience were her mother and a man, whose face was unfamiliar, but she knew was her father.

The next morning as Iris ate breakfast and Flora made her second pot of tea for the day, they were surprised to hear movement on the staircase. Lily sheepishly sat down at the table and pushed over a folded piece of file paper. On the front was a love heart and inside it read: '*I'm so sorry my darling Iris. I love you more than you can know. Lots of love and kisses Mummy*.' There was an abundance of kisses. Iris looked up at her mother's anxious face, got down from her chair and embraced her tightly.

*

Iris scanned the seats before going on stage. There was no sign of either her mother or her grandmother. She tried to contain her anger as she slowly walked up the steps to take her place. Just as she was about to start reading there was a distant cough. She looked up. Flora was standing at the back. Lily was next to her. Behind them a teacher was busy trying to find extra seats. Iris smiled. Another cough, this time from Mrs Derbyshire, reminded her of her cue.

That evening, her mother joined them downstairs to watch television for the first time since her father's departure. They had left school hastily in order to avoid small talk with other parents. As her mother stood up to collect their empty mugs, Iris noticed that she had pinned in a large portion of her skirt at the waist. It was the new one she had bought for her father's special dinner.

*

'I've got a surprise for you,' Flora said to Iris as they walked home from school. It was the last day of term.

'Is it another present?'

'Yes, but not one you can open.'

'Is it a puppy?'

'You'll see.'

As they approached the house, Iris felt Flora's grip on her hand tighten.

'What is it, grandma?'

'Nothing, darling. Just a bit of cramp.'

Her mother was in the kitchen making tea when they returned.

After Iris had sat at the table with her juice, Lily placed an envelope in front of her. In it was a handmade card, this time of better quality paper than the last one. On the cover was a simple drawing of three people of varying heights and builds, recognisable as Flora, Lily and Iris. On the next page they were standing outside a house holding suitcases. On the next they were standing by a plane. On the final page they were standing next to a palm tree and a sand castle – the words 'Sri Lanka' written underneath.

'What do you think?' Lily asked.

'It's a bit too short for a story, mummy, and needs a few more words. I can read, you know.'

Lily laughed, which sounded strange to Iris. 'It's my silly way of saying that the three of us are going to Sri Lanka in the summer holidays.'

'Really!' Iris turned to look at Flora, but she was missing. 'Grandma?'

'She's probably gone to the bathroom, darling.'

A few moments later Flora appeared, looking flustered.

'What's wrong?' Lily asked.

'Nothing, just a little wind.' Flora said, sitting down.

This had satisfied Lily, but Iris was not convinced and gently put her hand on her grandmother's arm. 'Are you worried about going on a plane, grandma?'

Flora smiled. 'You know me too well.'

Just then, something clattered through the letterbox. Iris felt her grandmother's arm tense before she sprang up to retrieve it. She returned a moment later. 'It's just a pizza flyer.'

Iris noticed her mother looking uneasy, as though the arrival of the pizza flyer had somehow spoiled her newly found happiness.

'It'll be OK, mummy. We'll all look after each other,' Iris said.

CHAPTER NINE

July 2004

From the front room window, Carl watched the progress of the postman as he went from house to house, considerately closing gates behind him. As soon as he arrived at theirs, Carl sprinted to the door and grabbed the two envelopes dangling from the letter box. One was a charity appeal, the other a final reminder to pay the gas bill. Nothing from Iris, just as there had been nothing from Iris in the 61 days since his departure.

Carl chewed his left thumb. He had bitten his nails right down, leaving only painful stubs for him to nibble at. He walked desolately to the kitchen. After filling the kettle, he sat down at the rickety table and started sobbing.

He had not returned to Nadia that day in May. Instead he had gone back to his office and written her a note, which he left on her desk. He had then typed a resignation letter and left it in Dylan's pigeon hole. He had apologised for not giving any notice and requested they dock his pay accordingly.

He had been grateful that he had been able to carry out his tasks undisturbed. It was only as he had crept out of his office with a boxful of books that he encountered one of the administrators. He had passed her silently, smiling nervously. It was only when he was several metres down the corridor that she had called after him, 'Be careful, Carl.'

He had not given himself time to think about what he was doing, aware it was reckless, feeling only a need to punish himself and get as far away as possible from the mess he'd made. He had since wondered, on a daily basis in fact, if he'd acted too hastily. Dylan would probably take him back if he asked, but he couldn't face the humiliation. Nadia probably wouldn't appreciate it either.

He had spent the night in a bed and breakfast on the outskirts of the city, convincing himself that the lives of those he had left would be better without him. He was ashamed at how he had behaved with Nadia. He had been tempted before by flirtatious students and lascivious colleagues, but had resisted. He hoped he had not ruined her career by his indiscretion.

Carl had been reluctant to think too deeply about the impact of his departure on Lily and

Iris, focussing only on the benefits of being rid of him. His mind, though, kept playing over the scene of Iris's sixth birthday, of her running towards him, Lily smiling gratefully. How could they love him? he wondered.

The next day he had driven to his brother Edwin's. He had never been close to his brother, who was ten years his senior and a confirmed bachelor and alcoholic, but hadn't known where else to go.

Edwin had left home when Carl was eight, apparently to go to university, but within a couple of months he had written to their parents informing them he had gone into business. They heard very little from him over the following years, receiving only sporadic postcards and dutiful Christmas gifts. A series of watches arrived for Carl and his father, with different components missing each time, while his mother received necklaces and bracelets of unspecified material that were twisted, tarnished or had broken clasps. They never deduced if these were a reflection of the quality of goods Edwin was trading in or if they were merely seconds he could not sell.

Carl only saw him again at their parents' funeral, four years after Edwin had left home. Carl was sent to live with his mother's sister and her husband, who had no children of their own. They were academics, and while they adequately provided for his needs, neither was particularly warm towards him and he did his best to not disturb their quiet life. Edwin made more of an effort to stay in touch with Carl during this period, dropping in unannounced once or twice a year, like an unwieldy rock shattering the still pond of their existence.

Like Edwin, Carl moved out at 18, choosing a university a fair distance away, returning home only for Christmas. He was therefore surprised when his aunt contacted him about the prospective match.

He was 41 at the time, with one long term relationship behind him, which had been with a university friend. It had continued halfway into his doctorate, at which point she had expected him to marry her, asking him plainly when he had failed to take her hints. He had not been ready to settle so she had looked to his closest friend for solace. He had subsequently withdrawn into his work, engaging occasionally in short-lived dalliances.

As Carl sat in Edwin's grimy kitchen, staring into his mug of tea, he thought about the day his aunt had called him at work. His first reaction was to think his uncle had died, but it was soon apparent from the awkward pleasantries that it was not to be that kind of news. His aunt was clearly uncomfortable with what she had to say and he had often wondered what had prompted her to take this action, but had never felt it appropriate to ask.

He had surprised himself with his response. A characteristic answer would have been that he was busy and not comfortable with the arranged marriage method, but he had been feeling particularly lonely at the time.

Lily turned out to be exactly as he expected. She was pleasant to look at, nothing outstanding. Her temperament matched her looks. She was no great wit, but well-informed and a good listener. He decided straightaway that she would make a good wife. Someone to come home to and provide for his needs, yet amenable enough to let him lead his own life. He smiled bitterly as he thought about his approach to their marriage. Lily deserved better. As he thought about her gentle eyes, he acknowledged for the first time that he missed her. Her unassuming, accepting nature, that he had come to scorn, had once soothed him. He wished she was with him now, earnestly asking him if he was OK. He would say 'no' and she would comfort him.

He reached into his trouser pocket for his wallet and pulled out a small photograph of the three of them, taken a year earlier. He and Iris had the same eyes and shared the same mischievous smile, while Lily's was placid, content. He stood up suddenly, banging his knee on the table leg. He winced as he stumbled over to the telephone by the front door. He took three deep breaths and dialled his old home number.

'Hello,' Flora answered, as he had expected. He had called a few times before and without exception she had answered and he had hung up.

'Do you think Lily will take me back?'

There was a long pause. 'Have you already started drinking for the day, Carl?'

'I've not touched a drop. Tell me what I have to do for her to take me back.'

'Have you any idea what you've done to her?'

Before Carl could respond, Flora continued. 'It destroyed her. Broke her into pieces. Anyway, why are you suddenly interested in her now? You've not sent one letter to her since the beginning. Does your bed feel cold?'

'No, no, that's not it,' Carl started to protest. 'I've been stupid. I didn't know what to say to her before. I thought she would be better off without me...'

'Well, you're right,' Flora said and put down the receiver.

Carl threw the phone on the floor. A bit of plastic flew off. He knew he would be fixing it later but was too frustrated to focus on anything now. He launched his fist into the flimsy wall, leaving a small dent, then went in search of whisky.

He had not been much of a drinker before, but could see how his brother had fallen into the habit through boredom and loneliness.

Carl had managed to line up some summer lecturing through an old college friend who was now head of department at the local university. It was not as prestigious as his former place, but would do until he heard back on some offers he was following up on that he had previously rejected. The university didn't have the budget to take him on as a staff member so he worked freelance, which meant he had much more time on his hands but less cash, especially as he continued to pay into Lily's and Iris's accounts. He did not want them knowing of his strained circumstances.

Edwin had only asked for a small contribution from him, in addition to requesting that he occasionally clean the house, though had not pressed him on the latter. They lived off tinned spaghetti, fish and chips, whisky, and the occasional apple as a token gesture towards a balanced diet.

Edwin was verbose as some who live alone can be, when given the opportunity. He was full of anecdotes and Carl found him unexpectedly good company. He was surprised to learn that he had almost married on a handful of occasions.

The first was as a young man, while lying low in a small Peruvian town, having upset a crime lord in Lima. He had taken lodgings with a middle-aged widow, who lived alone in a vast villa. Enamoured by her charm, as well as her property, he had wooed her with his best trinkets and soon proposed. Delighted, she had enthusiastically agreed and prepared a feast to celebrate their engagement. As they dined at her great table, laden with Peruvian delicacies, a rattling at the door caused her to take fright. She ran from the room, leaving Edwin bemused and alone with their half-eaten banquet. Moments later, a smartly dressed man had burst in brandishing an umbrella and an ornate pistol. It transpired that Edwin's fiancée was in fact the housekeeper. She had been charged with keeping watch of the house while the family sojourned in Europe for a few months. She had muddled their return date.

'Never saw her again after that. Shame. She was a looker. I would have forgiven her,' he told Carl. 'Though perhaps best off not getting hitched to her, eh?'

He had finally given up on marriage when he discovered his last fiancée was in fact a man. 'So convincing, Carl. Those Thai boys really are beauts. Lovely hands and hair, but all the wrong paraphernalia.'

Carl found his brother's honesty drawing out his own confessions, though none were as bizarre. They would laugh and drink, then he would wake up miserable, only to repeat the process a couple of days later.

Carl had a rule that he would not drink before lunchtime, but on this occasion he felt he needed to be flexible. He grabbed a bottle of *Teachers* (in honour of their parents, Edwin would say) from their stock in the kitchen and took it into the front room. He switched on the television, poured the whisky into his tea and gulped it down, finding the combination not unpleasant.

Edwin had gone out. There were only two places he could be: the bookies or the pub. Carl was disappointed, as he was keen to discuss with him ways of reclaiming his wife and daughter. He topped up his empty mug so that it was half full. The main barrier to his happiness, he thought, was his mother-in-law. He needed to side-step her and get straight to them. If Lily was so unhappy, surely she would welcome him with open arms.

He would go to them, he decided. He finished the contents of his mug, sat back in the grubby armchair and closed his eyes, pleased with his plan.

He was woken by the front door slamming shut.

'I'm going to go and get them,' he announced to his brother, whose large frame soon loomed above him.

'That's my boy!' Edwin said, falling into the settee.

'It's my mother-in-law that's the problem. I need to…circumvent her,' Carl said.

'Why not bump her off once and for all?' Edwin said, reaching for the whisky bottle.

Carl threw a cushion at him, which knocked the bottle over, causing it to spill some of its contents onto the carpet.

'Watch it, son,' Edwin said, quickly rescuing it.

Edwin's cat, You, appeared from under the coffee table and started licking the spilt liquid from the carpet. Both brothers watched, stupefied. Carl suddenly stood up, which gave him a head rush. His movement startled You, who turned to flee. Instead, she bumped headfirst into the sofa and remained stunned for a few seconds. Carl fell back into his seat. Edwin started chuckling. So did Carl.

Some hours later, in the tired light of early evening, he found himself still in the armchair, slightly dazed. Edwin was asleep on the sofa, You splayed across his stomach. They snored in unison.

Carl resolved to return to his family as soon as possible.

*

The next morning Carl woke with a grinding headache, but forced himself out of bed. He had decided he would go back that very day before he lost his nerve. When he caught sight of himself in the bathroom mirror, something he generally avoided, he started to get cold feet. His eyes were bloodshot, his hair overgrown, with significantly more greys than he remembered. His stubble, at least, could be easily dealt with. After a hasty coffee he made his way to the barbers, stopping first at the chemist for eye drops.

Post-trim, Carl felt a little better about him-self, but was self-conscious. He had always veered on the side of slim, but now looked gaunt, his cheeks sallow. He had aged consider-ably in the last couple of months, after being temporarily invigorated by Nadia.

He stood in the hallway facing the front door. The easiest thing to do would be to take up his usual position in the front room to watch day-time television. He peered into the lounge. You had taken his preferred seat, her head under a cushion. Carl grabbed his car keys and strode out, squinting at the brightness of the July sun.

He hardly used the car these days, taking the bus to the university and rarely going anywhere else, so was surprised when it started at the first attempt. He fiddled with the radio and settled on a station playing eighties rock and power ballads. Not something he would normally lis-ten to, but had always had a fondness for. Plus he wanted to be distracted from the task ahead, fearful he would bottle out if he thought about it too much. It was only when he was just a few miles from the house that he switched off the radio and started to plan his approach.

It occurred to him that he had brought noth-ing with him, so he stopped at a florist and pur-chased an expensive bouquet and a dainty card. He struggled to think of what to write to Lily. After several minutes of mental composition, he drafted something on the paper bag in which the card had been packed, before transcribing it as neatly as he could.

His heart raced as he pulled into the familiar road. He parked across the street from the house and glanced at his watch. He hadn't planned it, but he had arrived in time for Iris's return from school. He looked in his wing mirror and waited. Eventually two figures emerged, making their way slowly towards him. He was transfixed by them. As they gradually got nearer, he could make out Iris busily chatting to her grandmother. He wanted to leap out of the car and instinctively opened the door. He then wondered how his mother-in-law might react and closed it. Better to do this privately.

He turned to look at them directly and was shocked to find Flora staring at him. He now had no choice but to see through his task.

He watched them enter the house and took a moment to compose himself before making his move. As he placed his hand on the door handle, he caught sight of Flora striding towards him across the road. He rolled down the window, afraid to open the door.

'What are you doing here?'

'I've come to see my wife and daughter.'

'You think you can walk back in, just like that?'

'Can't you let them decide that?'

'You have no idea of the damage you've

caused, have you? If you come any closer to the house, I'll call the police. I'm only thankful Iris didn't see the car.'

Carl said nothing. Flora stared at him, waiting for a response. He blinked at her. She sighed and turned to go back to the house.

Carl sat in the car for a moment and reasoned that the police would not arrest him for visiting his own family. Of more concern was what effect his presence would have on Lily and Iris. He was hoping they would accept his grovelling apology and overrule any objections from his mother-in-law. With this in mind, he got out of the car and walked towards the house.

The door opened before Carl could knock. Flora's stern face greeted him. She stepped outside before he could say a word.

'Why didn't you listen to me?'

Carl held out the flowers. 'I want Lily and Iris back. I will do anything. I know I've been useless. I want to make amends.'

Flora's face softened slightly. 'Your timing's lousy. Why did you wait so long?'

'I don't know. I'm an idiot.'

'I can't let you in today. Of all days, you chose today. I can't let you disrupt things, not when Lily's come so far.'

'When then?'

'Grandma?'

Carl's heart leapt at the sound of Iris's voice. Flora started moving back inside the house. She looked at him with frustration, then closed the door. Carl remained on the doorstep, straining to hear what was going on inside. He was surprised when the door opened again.

'Please don't ring the doorbell or try to come in,' Flora whispered. 'I'm asking you politely to go. It will spoil everything if you're seen today.'

'Has Lily got someone else?'

Flora's expression turned bitter. 'She's not like you,' she said, and closed the door on him.

Carl didn't move. He knew he would not be ringing the doorbell, though he didn't know why.

He walked back to the car and threw the bouquet onto the passenger seat. He then noticed the card which he had forgotten to pick up before. He grabbed it and walked briskly across the road again, not wanting to give himself time to think. He posted the card through the letterbox and sprinted back to the car. He drove off immediately.

CHAPTER TEN

August 2004

T he ceiling fan whirred noisily above Lily as she lay in bed. She had always been nervous of its wild gyrating, fearing it would spin loose any moment and slice her to pieces. In over thirty years it had neither been fixed nor fallen. She wasn't sure if this should worry or reassure her.

She turned onto her side. The other beds were empty. Her mother's neatly made, her daughter's unkempt, but she knew soon to be tidied after breakfast. Its mosquito net flapped under the fan, and occasionally ballooned, inflated by the breeze coming in through the window.

They would be returning to England in less than a week. Her mother had seemed distracted throughout their three weeks in Sri Lanka. Probably worried about her, Lily thought. But Iris had thrived, willing to try anything. Making them anxious with her desire to wade deeper, climb higher and pick up anything that looked interesting, oblivious to the possibility it might harm her. Lily smiled at the memory of Iris triumphantly presenting a sea cucumber to Flora, who responded by running off, scolding her as she went.

Lily's last visit to the island had been as a newlywed with Carl, when they had duly completed the tour of relatives. She had felt self-conscious, embarrassed at being such an old bride, particularly when they met cousins a decade younger who already had two or three children. She was grateful to have been spared the ignominy of having to visit everyone this time round. Of course they all, no doubt, knew of her situation.

She had almost managed to discard the awkward memories from the trip with Carl, focussing instead on the pleasant ones. She'd think about sitting next to him in an open top Morris Minor, as he manoeuvred the winding roads to Nuwa Eliya, through the verdant tea plantations. She did not dwell on how nauseous she'd felt to begin with, remembering only the efficacy of the pills her aunt had given her. When she had commented on the lush scenery, Carl had said that it was probably a shadow of what it had looked like before the British came and made the whole island a tea estate. Lily recalled that when she went quiet, Carl, aware that it had sounded like a rebuke, placed his hand on her knee and agreed that despite this it was still beautiful.

They had stayed in this room on that trip, her aunt and uncle graciously giving up their bedroom then as they had now. She wondered if the bed her mother slept on was the one she had shared with Carl, the springs creaking with every move. She remembered how they had giggled, wondering if the whole household was aware of their nocturnal activities, occasionally tiptoeing downstairs to continue undisturbed on a quiet settee.

Over the past few weeks she had spent hours contemplating whether Carl had ever loved her, but she was certain that in those early days at least, she had held some appeal. His interest had gradually waned, reinvigorated only during his sabbatical, when she conceived Iris. She had wondered whether Carl had embarked on other affairs, whether it was only because these distractions were not present in America that he had been forced to focus his attention on her.

She closed her eyes. She could hear birdsong and shuffling footsteps along the dirt road outside the house. She looked up at two geckos on the peach walls that seemed on course for a collision. Nothing seemed to have changed from her childhood, yet everything had.

From the road below she heard the fish man announce his wares, his cry of '*Malu*' getting louder as he approached the house. Her stomach tightened. It was an evocative sound, which she had once associated with happier more innocent times. Teenage days that had been filled with possibility. She got up and walked over to the window where she watched him make a sale, before pushing his bike down the lane, a hopeful cat in his trail.

The previous day her mother had told her that in 1983, when mobs had come to the town looking for Tamil houses to ransack, the fish man had given them information for a couple of bottles of Arrack and a few rupees.

Lily wondered if anything was really as it seemed, or whether she was just blind to the obvious. Even this house, rich with memories of birthday parties and lazy holidays, had a veil of sorrow around it. Her aunt Meera and uncle Thomas had bought it from her grandfather when he left the country. It had been torched in '83 and most of their heirlooms, as well as the antique furniture left by her grandfather, had been looted or burnt. Her aunt would occasionally reminisce about a favoured bureau or painting they'd lost, but give thanks that they had escaped with their lives and some of their photographs. The building had survived the flames, but repairs and whitewashing could not erase its sad history.

After her mother had spoken about the *malu* man, Meera had mentioned that her wedding sari had been destroyed in the fire, and how sad she'd been as she had wanted to give it to her daughter to wear at her wedding. Flora had scolded her, saying a marriage was more than a sari. Lily knew her mother had said it for her benefit, but had been saddened at how hurt her aunt had looked.

She walked away from the window and started rummaging in the suitcase for something to wear. She would not allow herself to be pulled into misery again.

CHAPTER ELEVEN

October 2004

C arl sat at the kitchen table and stared at the bottle of whisky, lost in its amber depths. His left hand was clasped around a bottle of sleeping pills, two years out of date, which he'd found in Edwin's bathroom cabinet. It felt strangely comforting.

He thought of Nadia. She had told him of the night she had forced her sister to regurgitate the tablets she had taken. He imagined the scene, her desperation. He let go of the pills and grabbed the whisky. He poured himself a generous measure and downed it before shuffling to the front room where he flung himself on the sofa.

His mother-in-law had said he'd only called

the house that day, those weeks ago, because his bed felt cold. He acknowledged that this was partly true. He pictured his wife, with her kind face and well-maintained hair. She had been obliging but not imaginative, not like Nadia. He allowed himself to think of Nadia, something he tried but often failed to avoid doing. He would deal with the guilt and hangover in the morning.

It was the middle of the night when Carl woke. He hazily surveyed the room, disoriented. The rays of the streetlamp were artfully bathing its grubbiness in orange light. It occurred to him that he had seen neither his brother nor the cat for some time.

He sat up, prepared for the headrush. After a moment's stupor he fashioned himself upright and carefully walked upstairs to Edwin's room. The door had been left wide open. He stepped inside hesitantly. It was difficult to ascertain whether the bed had been slept in recently as his brother was not in the habit of making it. It was, however, vacant. Naked hangers jangled as he yanked open the wardrobe. He started to panic as he pulled out drawers and found them emptied of most of their contents. He stared at the bed, feeling a sense of *déjà vu*, then sloped to his room, anxiety filling his stomach.

On his pillow was a gas bill still in its envelope, which Edwin had scrawled across: '*Sorry bro. Needed to leave sharpish. Owe quite a bit. You may want to lie low. Will be in touch. E.*'

Carl sat down heavily on the bed, prompting the cat to run out from underneath.

'So he's left You, has he?' he said, picking her up.

Carl lay down on the bed, still holding the cat. He closed his eyes and drifted off, his head too foggy to contemplate any action.

He was woken by aggressive knocking at the front door. You had been lying across his stomach and dug her claws in as he bolted up. He glanced at his alarm clock – it was 5:58am. He rushed downstairs and pulled open the door, fearing bad news about his brother. A large, suited man, whose nose suggested he'd been either a boxer or rugby player, stood before him.

'Edwin Jansen?'

'No, he's not in.'

'Who are you then?'

'I'm his-' Carl stopped himself just in time, '… lodger.'

The man looked down at a piece of paper in his hand, then squinted back at Carl.

'When will he be back?'

'I don't know. Shall I ask him to call you when I see him?'

The man's expression of barely concealed disdain remained unchanged.

'I'm here on behalf of a creditor of Mr Jansen.'

'How much does he owe?'

'One thousand two hundred and fifty-eight pounds, forty-nine pence.'

'Right, well if you give me a bit of time, I'll get it for you.'

'I thought you were just a lodger?'

'I am but...What are you going to do?'

'I'm here to recover the debt. Time's run out.' The man folded the piece of paper he'd been holding and slid it inside his suit jacket. He then stepped over the threshold, forcing Carl to retreat into the house. Only then did he notice another vast man standing at the end of the path, dressed in a Fair Isle sweater and chinos. Carl closed the door.

'Don't do that!' the first man barked.

Carl quickly opened the door and found the other man directly outside it.

The first man sighed and walked into the living room. Carl followed him, embarrassed by the squalor in which he lived, the stench of stale carpet seeming more fetid than usual.

'Two sofas and a television,' the suited man said to his colleague waiting in the hallway, who then pushed past Carl to look around. The first man moved into the kitchen, screwing up his nose.

'Anything?' the other man said from behind Carl.

'Nah. The microwave and fridge are probably health hazards.' He shouldered past Carl again and continued upstairs. Carl followed, while the Fair Isle man remained by the front door.

The suit man strode into his bedroom and

picked up Carl's fountain pen, then put it down again before pulling open the wardrobe and drawers.

Carl was paralysed as the debt collector proceeded into Edwin's room. He soon came out and jogged downstairs.

'Don't even think we'll get hundred from this lot,' he said to his assistant.

'The house then?'

The first man shrugged.

'I'll get you the money. I can write you a cheque now,' Carl offered, from the landing.

'We don't do cheques.'

'Cash then. I'll go to the bank as soon as it opens.'

'Interest'll have gone up by then.'

'I'll cover it.'

The first man glanced at the second. 'Alright. We'll be outside so don't get any ideas,' he said and walked out the door, leaving it wide open.

Carl walked down, closed it and imagined punching his brother. He went back upstairs and sat on the edge of his bed for twenty minutes before eventually getting up to shower.

Once dressed, he went into Edwin's room and peered out of the window. He could see their red van. The Fair Isle man was leaning against it, smoking and vigorously picking his nose. The other one was probably inside. Their radio was blasting out Phil Collins.

Carl wondered if he was getting what he deserved. If he paid for his brother's mess, perhaps that would go some way towards making up for the mess he had made? There was still time before the bank opened, so he resumed his place on the bed and continued to reflect on the series of mistakes he had made that had brought him to this place. Something that had become a regular pastime.

At 8:30 he wearily descended the stairs, concerned that the cat was missing again.

Both men were in the van but alighted immediately when they saw him emerge from the house.

'How far's your bank?' the lead man asked.

'About a fifteen minute walk.'

'Alright. Get in.'

Carl was made to sit between the two men. He compared the size of his thighs with theirs and wondered how long it would take to inflate his to their enormity. Their pungent aftershave, combined with his hangover, made his head throb. The pain dulled his fear. He told himself that the episode would shortly be over and he could soon lie down again.

They reached the bank in five minutes, school traffic only mildly hindering them. Its doors were resolutely shut.

'Why d'you come out so early?' the Fair Isle man asked.

'I thought...' Carl started, then shrugged.

They waited for ten minutes, staring at the

bank's closed doors. Carl willed time to speed up and wondered why they had switched off the radio.

'Might as well go now, so you're first in the queue,' the suit man said. They walked together to the bank and stood by the entrance. They waited in silence: Carl hunched, biting the side of his left index finger; the debt collector broad-chested, hands behind his back, face like granite.

When the doors opened - six minutes late, Carl noted - he rushed to the first clerk who smiled at him brightly.

'How can I help you today, sir?'

'Can I withdraw one thousand, two -.'

'One thousand, five hundred,' Carl's companion interjected.

'One thousand, five hundred pounds, please,' Carl said, handing over his bank card.

'Certainly, sir,' she smiled, then glanced at Carl's chaperone, before looking back at him.

'And how are you today, sir?' the clerk asked, looking intently at Carl.

'Fine, thanks. I'll have that in fifties I think.'

Both men watched as the money was counted out. When the notes were finally passed under the counter, the debt collector grabbed them. 'That should cover our time this morning.'

'Thanks very much,' Carl said before the cash-ier could say anything more.

When they reached the van, Carl continued to walk past it. 'Bye, then,' he said as cheerily as possible.

'We'll drop you home.'

'It's fine. I can walk.'

'We'll drop you home.'

Carl wondered if he should run, but instead did as he was told, seeing as they could easily find him. When they reached the house, Carl was relieved that suit man got back in the van after letting him out. He walked briskly up the path and fumbled in his pocket for the keys before dropping them, hands trembling. As he pushed open the door, he became aware of someone by his shoulder. He turned and found Fair Isle man behind him.

'Did you still want the sofas?' Carl asked nervously.

The man said nothing, but moved closer towards him, forcing Carl forwards and clumsily over the threshold.

'Please. You got what you came for, didn't you?' Carl asked, turning so that his back was against the banister.

'I was asked to deliver something to your brother, but as he's absent, you'll have to receive it on his behalf.' With that he delivered a sharp jab to Carl's right eye, then turned and left.

Carl staggered about the hallway, one hand over his eye, the other rubbing the back of his head which had hit the banister with the impact. He then managed to slowly lower himself onto the steps. He had received punches from

Edwin as a child, but nothing compared to this pain. He was afraid his eye had been crushed. The front door was wide open but he thought he would vomit if he tried to stand. He felt movement by his feet and could blurrily make out the cat squeezing herself behind his legs.

'And where have you been? It's too late now.'

Eventually Carl stood and gently closed the front door before going into the kitchen in search of frozen vegetables. He found the freezer completely bare, apart from a packet of Yorkshire puddings. He grabbed it, wrapped it in a tea towel and sat down to nurse his eye, keeping the other shut in sympathy.

Drowsiness began to overwhelm him. When he heard himself snore he knew he had to try and open his wounded eye in case he fell into blind unconsciousness. He wondered for a moment if that wasn't such a bad option. As he felt himself drifting off again, he jolted upright. Bracing himself for a fresh wave of pain, he tentatively attempted to raise his heavy lid. Gradually coming into focus on the table in front of him, left from the night before, was the bottle of sleeping pills.

CHAPTER TWELVE

July 2006

I ris lowered herself into the depths of the beanbag with Mrs Chicken, a toy rabbit that had been a favoured companion since infancy but only recently named. Having settled into a comfortable position, she carefully tore open a fun-sized *Mars* bar. Unlike her classmates who had elaborate ways of consuming said confectionary, tackling the sides first, caramel last or some other variation, Iris ate conventionally but slowly, savouring each mouthful. She did not understand how people could enjoy such a messy way of eating. Such sensibilities in an eight-year-old had led to her best friend Amma nicknaming her 'Grandma', which annoyed Iris greatly.

After taking a prudent bite, Iris opened her book, *First Term at Mallory Towers*, recently given to her by a previously unknown relative. It had clearly been grabbed from a shelf as a last minute gift as the edition was more than thirty years old, its cover faded and dusty. This had annoyed her grandmother considerably.

Iris was enjoying it though. She looked up at Flora, ensconced in her chair, watching *Countdown*. She suddenly thought about how sad it would be if her grandmother died. Filled with grief at the notion, she walked over to protectively hug her. Flora, on the verge of dozing off, was initially startled but soon reciprocated.

'Grandma, you must never die.'

'Darling, I shall do my utmost to avoid it.'

Flora had been living with Iris and Lily for the past two years, ever since Carl had left. Iris sometimes wondered if this had been a good swap.

Prior to her father's departure, Iris had seen her grandmother almost daily, as she was the one who picked her up from school and stayed with her until her mother returned from work. At that time, she also had a father. She had vague memories of him reading bedtime stories to her and giving piggybacks. Now she had an ever-present figure who doted on her, cooked her favourite Sri Lankan delicacies, taught her to knit and planted herbs with her in the garden. It sounded like a good deal, yet she still sometimes cried into her pillow at night.

No one had ever told Iris exactly why her father left. Her grandmother had said he was unwell. Her mother changed the subject whenever she brought it up, so she stopped asking her.

He had not been in touch since. When she asked her grandmother how he could love her when he couldn't even be bothered to contact her, she was told that his mysterious sickness prevented him from doing so.

Iris curled up on the sofa next to Flora's armchair. 'Is daddy dead?'

'No, darling, of course he's not dead.'

'Is he in a coma then?'

'Where did you get that word? No, he's not in a coma. Irie, you should stop worrying about him. I'm sure he's fine.'

'But if he's fine, why doesn't he come back?'

'Darling, I don't know.'

Iris hoped one day to catch her grandmother off guard, certain she knew more than she was letting on. As she was about to declare her intention of finding her father, the phone rang. For a moment she wondered if it could be him, but soon heard her grandmother saying that she didn't want a mobile phone before abruptly hanging up.

'I thought we had registered with that Telephone Preference Service,' Flora said before heavily landing back in her seat.

That evening, as Iris worked on her homework at the dining table, she could hear her grandmother in the kitchen speaking to her mother in Tamil. It was the low voice she used for secrets.

Her mother answered in English, as she always did. This, combined with the fact that her grandmother's Tamil was liberally sprinkled with English, meant she had learnt the meaning of several Tamil phrases. She stopped colouring so she could hear them better, picking up sections of their conversation like a badly tuned radio.

'Tell her...know... man her father...Move on with your life [in English]....Clever girl...know.'

Her mother was silent.

'She deserves to know the truth,' her grandmother said in English.

'What she deserves is for her father not to have left in the first place.'

Lily then emerged from the kitchen, so Iris quickly resumed colouring in the giraffe she had been asked to draw for her homework, representing her favourite animal.

Lily kissed her on the top of her head. 'That's lovely, sweetheart.'

Iris smiled, hoping her mother would not say anything that required a verbal response as she felt unable to speak. Flora joined them at the table, looking sullen. They ate in near silence, the only things audible were the munching of salad and Flora's gulping.

Iris replayed the conversation several times

that night as she lay in bed. Her father had 'left' them. It sounded like he had made a decision to leave, not that he had been forced into it through illness or whatever. What was the 'truth' her grandmother had referred to? Was he a criminal? She longed to see him, but wasn't sure how she'd feel if he had done something really bad. She had to know the truth and would force them to tell her by threatening to run away. She would then search for him. Iris decided she would announce this to them the next day.

The journey to school the next morning was in silence, Iris preoccupied with her plan. When they arrived at the school gates, Flora held her hand to Iris's forehead. 'Are you alright, darling?'

Iris nodded and walked away. After five metres she returned to kiss Flora goodbye.

'I'm OK, grandma. I have a test so I'm a bit worried,' Iris lied, feeling wretchedly guilty as she said it.

'You'll be fine. You're my bright star,' Flora said as she moved stray strands of hair out of Iris's eyes.

Iris dwelt on her plan for most of the morning, hoping her teacher would not ask her any questions about giraffes. Her lie was also playing on her mind and she planned to apologise for that. At lunchtime she decided to stop thinking about it as there was nothing more she could do until her mother returned from work.

The first lesson after lunch was maths. Iris completed the set exercises within twenty minutes and started doodling her father's name in her general work book. She would normally have asked for more sums but was enjoying day-dreaming about a reunion with him. She had temporarily banished the possibility that he might be horrible.

A knock at the door disturbed her thoughts. It was the school secretary, whose appearance always resulted in an anticipatory silence. She whispered something to Iris's teacher, who then looked straight at Iris and beckoned her to the front.

This was not good news she had immediately surmised from the anxious looks on the adults' faces. All the class watched her as she walked to the desk.

'Iris, your mum's here for you. Pack up your things and follow Mrs De Souza,' her teacher said quietly.

'Why? What's happened?'

'Your mum will explain it to you. Don't worry.'

Iris avoided eye contact with her classmates as she returned to her desk to pack away her belongings. She wondered why adults were so secretive. Why were children always kept in the dark about things? As she walked to the door, she slipped on a rogue pencil, but only the naughtiest boy in the class laughed.

Mrs De Souza's heels were loud as they clipped along the otherwise silent corridor. She was a tall woman and Iris found it difficult keeping pace with her.

Her mother was waiting at the school reception, in the middle of a phone call. She looked like she was on the verge of tears, which made Iris feel sick. She ran over to her and Lily held her with her free arm. When the phone call ended, Iris looked up expectantly, dreading the news.

'Sweetheart, you have to be a brave girl for me, OK?' Lily sighed. 'A lot has happened today.'

Iris nodded, though was uncertain she could keep her promise.

'You know how grandma lights a candle to get rid of strong cooking smells? Well, today it seems to have fallen and caused a fire.'

Iris gasped.

'Mr Masih noticed it and called the fire brigade before it spread.'

'But what about grandma?'

'Grandma wasn't in the house at the time. She had left the candle and gone to Mrs McKenzie's for her Thursday women's fellowship meeting. The police called me at work. I called Mrs McKenzie to tell grandma. After she took my call, in all the rush she seems to have slipped and hurt herself.'

Iris gasped again.

'She's been taken to hospital.' Lily's voice started to break. 'I need you to be a good girl for me. Like you normally are.'

Iris nodded, her heart pounding with fear.

They drove to the hospital in near silence, apart from sporadic uncharacteristic muttering from Lily at motorists who failed to indicate or were deemed incompetent for other reasons. Though Iris was filled with questions, she held back, worried she might say something that would further upset her mother.

They had to drive around the hospital car park a couple of times before a space was found. Lily swerved into it and stamped off to find the parking meter before Iris had a chance to remove her seatbelt.

By the time they reached the unwelcoming sliding doors of A and E, Iris could feel her mother's hand shaking, so tightened her grip in an effort to stop it.

'I'm here to see Mrs Flora Ratnam,' Lily told an impassive receptionist.

'Flora?'

'Yes.'

'What's the surname?'

'Ratnam. R.A.T.N.A.M.'

'Slow down please. R.A...'

'T.N.A.M,' Lily said impatiently.

'Rat Nam?' the receptionist mispronounced.

'Yes,' Lily sighed, in no mood to correct her, though Iris was sure her grandmother would have.

'Take a seat.' The receptionist nodded in the

direction of the waiting room.

As soon as they sat down, Lily's phone started to ring. She looked at it wearily and declined the call before closing her eyes. She had only recently purchased it, reluctantly, after a clampdown on all personal calls to the office phones at her workplace, even incoming ones.

Iris sat quietly beside her mother, wondering why her hands felt so cold when the waiting room was so hot.

After about ten minutes, a round smiling male nurse appeared in front of them, temporarily blocking the harsh fluorescent light. 'Hello, are you here for Flora?'

'Yes,' Lily said, standing.

'Follow me. We've bandaged her up for you.'

He makes her sound like a present, Iris thought.

The nurse took them through to the emergency ward, whipped back a curtain and presented them with Flora.

'I'll be back in a sec. You OK there, my darling?'

Flora blinked at him.

'Excellent,' he said, then disappeared.

Iris had never seen her grandmother look so pathetic and lonely. She was sitting on the edge of the bed, her head and ankle heavily bandaged. Lily and Iris went over to gingerly embrace her. She responded with a sob.

The nurse reappeared with a clipboard and

paper bag.

'OK, so we're just looking for a wheelchair for you, Flora, then you're good to go. Here are your meds and you've got to promise me, no rugby for a few months. You've got to keep your weight off that ankle and rest up.'

Iris appreciated his attempt at humour, but knew her grandmother would not. Nor would she appreciate someone that young addressing her by her first name.

'Could I have a quick word?' he said to Lily.

As they disappeared, Iris propped herself up on the bed next to Flora, then placed both arms around her grandmother's sturdy waist.

'We'll take care of you, grandma, like you've taken care of us,' Iris said. Flora responded by placing her papery hands over Iris's. They sat in silence until Lily appeared a few minutes later.

Iris recognised her mother's strained smile that indicated stress, and wondered what the nurse had said.

'I'm sorry, Lily. I can't believe I left the candle burning. I'm too old,' Flora burst out.

'Shhh, mummy. It was an accident. It could have happened to anyone.'

'That's not what you said earlier.'

The nurse appeared before Lily could respond. All three of them looked at him expectantly.

'OK, guys, the good news is: we've found a wheelchair. The bad news is: we kind of need the bed, so I'm going to have to ask you to wait in reception,' he said, turning down his mouth to do a sad face.

'Can't you just bring the wheelchair here and then we'll go straight home?' Lily asked.

'We just have to disinfect it. Won't be long,' he said.

'Has someone pooed in it or died in it?' Flora asked. 'If it's the latter I'll just jump in, no need to clean it. We can do that at home.'

The friendly nurse smiled, then left.

Lily sighed heavily. Just as she was about to sit down on the solitary plastic chair left in the cubicle, two porters arrived. The first smiled mischievously, the other looked angry at life.

'Can you jump off the bed for me, love,' the cheerful one asked Iris. She did so at once. Then without warning, both men approached Flora and lifted her off the bed.

'What are you doing?' Flora and Lily protested in unison. Both men continued in their task undeterred. They took Flora into reception and manoeuvred her into the nearest available seat.

'Light as a feather,' the friendly one winked at Iris before walking away. The morose one left without a word, wiping his hands on his jumper. No one else in the waiting room battered an eyelid. Flora breathed deeply, dealing quietly with the humiliation.

'Mummy, I'm sorry about what I said earlier,'

Lily said after a while, when Flora's breathing seemed to have regulated. 'I was in shock. It just came out.'

'You were right. I was careless. You've told me not to use the long candles, to make sure there's nothing nearby. It's my fault.'

Iris was surprised her mother had said this to her grandmother and wondered whether she had still been angry from the previous evening.

'Is the house OK to sleep in?' Iris asked. Until then, she had temporarily forgotten the other dramatic incident of the day.

'Oh, the insurance!'

Lily searched through her handbag for the paperwork she had grabbed from the house. After getting through the labyrinthine call system, she explained her situation to someone, who evidently put her through to someone else to whom she explained it again.

After making a few more calls, Lily threw the phone into her handbag and leaned forward placing her head in both hands.

Iris was keen to know the sleeping arrangements for the night as she hadn't been able to ascertain this from the phone conversations, but thought it best not to disturb her mother.

'How long does it take to disinfect a wheelchair?' Lily said eventually, emerging from her hand cave.

'They probably need to get half a dozen people to sign off for the disinfectant,' a voice nearby said. Iris and Lily turned and found it belonged to a slim older lady, in a turquoise velour tracksuit.

'Where are we sleeping tonight?' Iris braved the question again.

'At home. We need to get the kitchen windows boarded up.'

Iris was relieved, but a little disappointed. She generally did not like sleeping anywhere but her own bed, but had wondered if there might have been the possibility of a hotel stay. She had never stayed in one before and had wondered if this might provide the opportunity.

Iris turned to Flora who had closed her eyes. 'The house is still OK to sleep in, grandma,' she said loudly.

Flora opened her eyes and looked at Iris, before they rolled back and she brought the lids down again. Lily reached behind Iris and shook Flora's arm.

'Don't sleep, mummy. It's not good if you're concussed.'

Flora looked at Lily and blinked slowly several times.

'Let me go and find out about this chair. Read to her, Irie. Don't let her sleep.'

Iris started to read *Mallory Towers*, punctuated with several shakes to keep Flora awake. She was not sure if this was necessary but did not want to disobey her mother.

While making a regular attention check, Iris

found Flora looking surprisingly alert. She followed her grandmother's gaze. It was fixed on the menacing porter, who was pushing a wheelchair towards them. Her mother followed. Before he could lay a hand on her, Flora tried to stand, grabbing the armrest of the waiting room chair. Iris and Lily tried to assist her. The porter seemed content to watch them complete the transfer into the wheelchair without his assistance. As Flora let her weight fall into the chair, it rolled onto Lily's foot, causing her to cry out in pain.

A couple of heads turned. Disappointed at the lack of entertainment, they immediately turned back and resumed their stoical waiting.

'I'm sorry, Lily,' Flora said.

'It's OK, mummy. Let's go.' Lily winced as she pushed Flora to the exit, the porter watching them dispassionately. As they reached the door, he called after them, 'You should probably let someone know you're leaving. We'll want that chair back, you know.'

Lily looked at him contemptuously, before hobbling over to the reception desk. The porter smirked before fading into a corridor.

'Fascist,' Flora said.

The operation to get Flora into Lily's two-door hatchback, and the wheelchair folded and into the boot was a display of quiet determination. When they finally arrived at the house after a glum journey in rush hour traffic, they found the policeman assigned to watch over the house, waiting in his patrol car. He immediately stepped out when he saw them pull into the driveway.

'I've kept it safe and sound for you,' he said smiling at Iris, who was unable to hide her excitement at meeting a real life policeman.

'The insurance company haven't turned up yet?' Lily asked, less impressed.

''fraid not. A couple of people have been round with food though. I told them to leave it on the front step.'

'Must be church people,' Flora said. 'Julia must have told them.'

As Lily wheeled Flora towards the house, the policeman followed them. 'It all smelt very nice,' he said.

Lily unlocked the door and heaved Flora and the wheelchair backwards over the threshold. After Iris was in and they had retrieved the food, she turned to the policeman and said, 'Thank you so much for your help,' before closing the door.

Iris was surprised at her mother's behaviour. 'Don't you think we should have offered him a cup of tea or something, mummy?'

'How would you suggest I make it?' Lily answered abruptly, and Iris felt foolish.

Yellow tape had been placed across the kitchen doorway, forbidding them to enter. Lily tentatively pushed the door open so they could survey the damage. Everything had been blackened by the smoke and was still dripping from the fire brigade's hoses. Broken glass and assorted debris were scattered across the floor.

'They said it was a miracle it didn't spread. Good thing you closed the door, mummy,' Lily said.

CHAPTER THIRTEEN

September 2006

F lora watched Iris pace up and down the living room, memorising her lines for the school Christmas production. She would occasionally pause and adopt an expression of deep concentration, before checking her script in frustration. It was only mid-September but the drama teacher, keen to erase memories of the previous year's shambolic offering, had started rehearsals early. Flora knew that Iris had been given the lead role, but couldn't remember the name of the play, despite having been told several times.

She was reluctant to interrupt her grand-daughter, but having already waited twenty minutes for a suitable interlude, her bladder felt like a cannon ball. She feared the outcome of further delay, so called out, ashamed at how needy she sounded.

Iris halted immediately. 'Grandma?'

'Darling, I need a number one.'

Iris walked over to Flora and helped her lift herself off the sofa. Flora was aware she had gained weight in the two months since the fall and had deliberately avoided scales. She had made half-hearted attempts to diet, but boredom and inertia were against her. She leaned on Iris, embarrassed by the load she was placing on her eight-year-old frame. Iris was strong for her age, but Flora feared this burden would do her long-term damage.

They hobbled together to the downstairs toilet, where Iris helped Flora lower herself before making a tactful retreat. Flora closed her eyes in relief, then started sobbing.

'Grandma?' Iris called from the hallway.

'Nothing, darling. Not finished.'

Flora was unsure if she was crying in self-pity or self-loathing. She often wondered if she'd been selfish in refusing a catheter. She had reduced her intake of fluids to lessen the burden on others, but had still been dependent on her granddaughter's goodwill throughout the summer holidays and now when she returned from school. Iris had never complained nor been anything less than loving and sweet-natured, but Flora hated the disruption to a childhood already pockmarked with disappointments.

She vowed to reduce her sugar intake and dig out the exercise sheet the doctor had given her.

Once re-installed on the sofa, Flora watched Iris resume her memorising. She searched for traces of resentment, but found nothing obvious. She wanted to tell her granddaughter how wonderful she was, but knew it would be more of a hindrance than encouragement at the present moment.

She searched for her book among the cushions. The Women's Fellowship had passed on various paperbacks, but they were mainly romances which she had disdainfully discarded, disappointed they didn't know her better. She occasionally flicked through the puzzle books, but mainly focussed on the Christian writers, having reconciled herself to the fact that they could be edifying, if treated as written sermons. Her pace was slow as she often dozed or daydreamed, then lost the thread of what was being expounded.

With no activities to look forward to or plan, she often found herself reminiscing about the past. She had been thinking about her husband a great deal, something she normally tried to avoid. But she was finding it almost pleasurable to wallow in the bittersweet memories. Invariably, unsavoury episodes clamoured for attention, but a couple of days later she would start again from the beginning. Resetting her memory bank. If only life could be like that, she thought. If only she could reset things.

CHAPTER FOURTEEN

March 1951 – July 1952

F lora sat in her father's cane rocking chair, in a corner of the veranda.

It was Saturday afternoon and it had been raining all day, even though it was not yet monsoon. She was alone, a rare occurrence.

The dark skies meant the house was dimmer than usual and felt oppressive, so she had gone outside to read. She liked the smell of wet soil and the way her mother's flowers, particularly the lilies and bougainvillea, seemed somehow luminous in the muted light. Her book, *Bleak House,* taken from her father's study, lay open in her lap as she gazed at the heavy clouds, when a cough startled her.

A man, who she had never seen before, was

standing at the gate. He was unlike the other young men she knew. His thick wavy hair was not greased back but almost wilfully dishevelled. He did not have a moustache, but clearly hadn't shaved for a day or two. His eyes would have looked sad if not for his wry smile.

'What's so mesmerising up there?'

'Everything,' she replied, though her attention was now firmly earthbound.

He regarded her for a moment through the tall iron gate, his hands gripping the bars like a prisoner. Flora was not used to being appraised in this way and was grateful that her blouse collar was hiding her neck, which was flushed with embarrassment.

'I was wondering if Dr Selvan was around.'

'He's not here, but he'll be back soon,' she said, even though she knew her parents were at least an hour from returning. 'You can wait for him if you like.'

Flora allowed the words to spill out, aware of the risk she was taking. As the stranger proceeded to open the gate and approach the veranda, she straightened her posture and pulled her stomach in, attempting composure.

He paused. 'Are you sure? I don't want to disturb your cloud watching.'

'Of course. Can't leave you standing out in the rain,' she said, trying to sound confident and worldly, though as a sheltered 22-year-old she had no experience in the art of coquetry.

'Well, alright. Thank you. I'm Reuben, by the way.'

'Flora.' She stood as he stepped up to the veranda. 'Sit here. I'll bring some cool drinks.'

Flora walked carefully into the house, worried that adrenaline might cause her to trip. She found some chilled cream soda bottles, but started to panic about what she was doing when she couldn't locate a bottle opener. She eventually pulled off the bottle tops with her teeth, so that when she emerged with her tray of refreshments, her lips were bleeding.

Reuben pointed to his mouth, concerned. Flora raised her hand to hers and tried not to gasp at the blood on her fingers.

'I bit my lip. It's nothing.'

This seemed to reassure Reuben, who immediately relaxed into his chair.

'So, Miss Flora, when you're not studying clouds, what do you get up to?'

He lit a cigarette. Flora did not protest even though she detested them.

*

By the time her parents arrived, Flora had discovered that Reuben had studied at King's College London and travelled Europe. He was worldly, a little boastful and she disapproved of many of his reported antics, but she had never before been so urgently fascinated by someone. He had shown an interest in her, asking questions and listening intently, that no one else ever had. He was also very pleasant to look at. She sensed it was probably dangerous, but couldn't help herself being drawn to him.

Within a fortnight he had asked if he might court her; within three months he had asked for permission to marry her. Her father was enthusiastic, having taken a shine to his latest protégé at the newspaper. Her mother did not approve. She was more devout than her father and would have liked Flora to marry one of the young men from church. Not this alcohol-drinking subversive, who was over a decade older than her daughter and claimed only a nominal faith. Flora's older sister Frieda shared her mother's concerns.

Flora hated being at odds with them and tried to convince them of Reuben's attributes. When that failed, she tried another approach, declaring he was the first to show any interest in her and that she risked being left alone if she rejected him.

She had always felt ungainly, too tall and too wide, and resented the fact that clothes passed down from Frieda always had to be taken out for her. She wanted to look like the other girls, slim and petite, despite her mother's assurances that she was the one whose figure they envied and who their brothers wanted to marry.

But Flora believed Reuben was special because he accepted her for who she was, not caring that she stood out.

Within six months of their first meeting on the veranda, they were married.

*

Flora followed Reuben through the doorway, bracing herself for the cigarette fumes. It was another Saturday evening, another party. Little had distinguished one from another in the six months of their marriage, apart from the addresses. The lighting was always low, the food ordered in. The latest jazz records that had somehow made their way over from America would be passed around and admired before being reverently placed on the turntable.

Reuben was known for being late, even though she was always punctual. She eventually got used to his timing and stopped getting ready so early.

'Ruby, you need to buy a watch, darling.' One of Reuben's friends, Nomi, the current party host, stood up to greet them. Flora was always bemused by people's preference for sitting on the floor, conversations taking place at her knee level. She watched as Nomi held Reuben in a long embrace and whispered something to him. She was wearing three-quarter length trousers and a sleeveless blouse. She finally turned to Flora and blew her a kiss. 'Hello, darling. Can I steal your husband for a moment?'

Before Flora could answer, Reuben was led

away. She stood alone, self-conscious, wondering what to do. It was a familiar predicament. An older woman in a black sari, holding a martini glass, tapped the seat next to her. Flora lowered herself carefully, her voluminous skirt fanning out around her.

'Are you Reuben's girl?'

'Yes.'

'Aren't you a beauty. I can see why he chose you,' she said as she stroked the side of Flora's face. 'Exquisite skin.'

Flora looked desperately at Reuben, who was in a far corner of the room surrounded by a small grinning group. Nomi's arm was draped over his shoulder.

'You want one of these?' The woman held up her martini glass.

'No, thank you.'

'You're not a teetotaller?'

'I don't drink, no.'

The woman looked disappointed, then turned to speak to someone perched on the armrest on the other side of her.

Flora was used to this. She knew she just had to bide her time, listening to conversations around her, trying to understand. Her mother had told her that she was just as clever as them and needed to speak up. Yet when she did, she found herself sounding childish and naive.

Eventually, towards the end of the night, Reuben returned to her, as he always did. He kissed her neck before resting his head in her lap, fully aware of the feelings he was stirring in his admirers. Flora knew she should punish him for abandoning her, for flirting shamelessly with other women, but instead she stared blankly ahead as she ran her fingers through his hair. She didn't know what else to do.

*

'You're happy aren't you, Flo?' her father asked as she opened the car door to leave. 'Your mother's worried about you.'

'I'm alright, *uppa.*'

Flora was afraid to look at her father in case he noticed her damp eyes. Returning to the apartment after her Thursday evening visits to her parents was the part of the week she dreaded most. It meant the weekend was near, which meant another miserable party followed by a moody hung-over Reuben.

She reluctantly ascended the newly polished steps to their first floor flat. Her marriage was six months old and already she was wondering if she could cope with a lifetime of the same. She loved Reuben and there had been some exhilarating times, but she wondered if it could stay the course.

When she opened the front door of their apartment, Nomi was standing in the lounge, buttoning up her blouse. Flora dropped the bags she was holding, which contained food parcels from her parents, and ran back down the slippery stairs and out of the building. She continued down the lane towards the beach, grudgingly grateful for the light of the full moon.

She walked southwards along the shore, oblivious to the passing of time. Anger overruled fear as she strode defiantly past drunk, leering men, holding tightly to the stones she'd picked up to use as weapons if needed. Anger gradually morphed into despondency. And despondency into exhaustion.

Eventually she decided to turn back, walking up an unknown lane to the dizzying lights of Galle Road, uncertain of what she'd find on her return.

As she reached their apartment she lingered in the dark corridor, staring at the strips of light that came from within, illuminating the edges of their front door like a neon frame. If the woman was still around, she would pack a few belongings and take a taxi to a hotel.

When Flora opened the door, she found Reuben sitting alone, a bottle of arrack in front of him. He stood as she entered.

'Flo, I can explain. Why did you run off? I was worried about you.'

Flora had discarded all but one stone. She flung it at Reuben, hitting his arm as he shielded himself. 'What's wrong with you?!' he shouted.

She marched past him to their bedroom and slammed the door behind her, noisily turning the key so that Reuben knew it was locked. Sleep did not come easily. When she woke the next morning, Reuben had gone.

Flora spent the day in a state of numbness, wondering if her marriage was over. She was for the first time resentful of Reuben's modern willingness to let her continue working after marriage, but thankful for her manager's tacit indifference. She was in no mood to either share what had happened or to feign cheerfulness. For the same reason, she was grateful for a slow day at the bookshop, something she usually found tedious. She didn't have the energy to assist people in finding suitable gifts for their nephews and nieces.

In the quiet hours she tried to pray, but struggled to find the words. She wondered if God would listen to her anyway, when she had been so foolish, allowing lust to rule her rather than common sense. She desperately wanted to confide in her mother but was afraid of hurting her, knowing she would be heartbroken to hear of how badly her daughter had been treated. Flora had neglected her friends during her courtship and was ashamed to call on them now. She decided to see what awaited her that evening before speaking to anyone.

As Flora made her way up the stairs to the apartment after work, she held the railing to stop her hands trembling. From the stairwell she could see a note had been taped to their door and could make out the word '*Sorry*' in Reuben's elaborate script. Surrounding it were sprays of flowers - frangipanis, lilies, orchids, jasmine, even roses – just like the day of their homecoming. The rich fragrance took her back to that first night in the apartment. She tore the note from the door and started sobbing with relief.

Inside, she allowed Reuben to hold her, as she held the note limply in her hand.

'I'm so sorry. I swear it won't happen again,' he said into her hair. 'She came by last night. I know I shouldn't have let her in. It was the first time, I swear, Flo. She seduced me. I know I shouldn't have let her. I was weak.'

Flora listened quietly, doubting this was the full story, but chose to accept it, as she didn't want to hear anymore anyway. When Reuben suggested they take a break from their circle, she found herself more grateful than she could have imagined.

*

The following months were filled with visits to relatives, during which they took pleasure in talking about the mundane things that made them feel like a respectable couple: which floor polisher to use, interest rates, the price of dal. They took day trips down south, packing thermos flasks of tea and consulting train timetables.

Just as Flora began to feel optimistic about

her marriage, she noticed Reuben's enthusiasm waning, as the novelty of domesticity wore off. When one Saturday afternoon he sheepishly mentioned a party, it was no great surprise to her.

'I thought we'd finished with all that, Ben.'

'We don't have to stay long. You don't expect me to give up all my friends do you, Flo?'

'No, but I thought...'

'She won't be there, I promise.'

Though she wanted to, Flora did not know how to refuse him, but she decided that she would not allow things to continue as they had. Word had got round of Reuben's infidelity and she had to appear strong.

When they entered the smoke-filled gathering that evening and a slender, trousered acolyte tried to lead Reuben away, Flora followed. When anyone was too tactile, she glared while smiling sweetly, and watched hands retreat awkwardly. She found it exhausting.

Reuben was silent on the drive home, swigging liberally from a whisky bottle. When they reached their apartment block, he hurried up the stairs, knocking into walls as he went. Flora followed at a distance and watched as he fumbled with the keys. As soon as they were inside, he turned to her.

'Why can't you just let me have a little fun, Flo? Or are you going to be my chaperone from now on?'

'I'm your wife, Reuben. And you're my husband.'

'So, you want me to sit on my hands from now on, like your nice church boys? Is that what you want? We'll just go to Bible studies from now on?'

Flora had never seen Reuben so drunk or angry before. She edged past him towards their bedroom.

'They're my friends. Do you want me to stop having fun altogether? Is that it?'

'If your idea of fun is to bed your friends, then yes!'

CHAPTER
FIFTEEN

September 2006

L ily woke with a sense of disappointment heavy on her chest. She was familiar with this feeling as it had engulfed her in the months following Carl's departure. She had thought she was free of it, but since the day of the fire and her mother's fall, it had crept back into her life, making its presence felt in the quiet moments. It was like claustrophobia. The inability to escape the clutter of her circumstances. The feeling that grief would always follow her.

She sat up in bed and stared at her reflection in the mirrored wardrobe. She had always looked younger than her age, but now the years seemed to have caught up with her. Her hair was still thick, but there were now too many greys to pull out as she had previously been doing. She'd had the same mid-length cut since her twenties, with occasional mild variations. Perhaps she should look up what styles were appropriate for fifty-two-year-olds, try something different.

As she got out of bed she was grateful that she didn't have to go to work that day and hoped the installation of her new kitchen would be straightforward.

Another task for the day was to cancel the half term holiday to Euro Disney that her mother had pressed her into booking for just herself and Iris. She had assured them she would be fine by herself for a few days and had even agreed to wear a catheter. But it was now obvious she had not made enough progress in her recovery to be left alone for that long, even with friends checking on her.

Iris had tried to mask her disappointment when she was told, saying quickly that she wouldn't have been able to enjoy it as she'd be worrying about her grandma. But Lily had heard her crying in her bedroom later that evening. The thought of her daughter's disappointment brought another wave of sadness. She got up and walked into Iris's bedroom. She was relieved to find her looking peaceful.

'Time to get up, sweetheart.'

Lily sat on the edge of the bed watching Iris struggle to wake up, stretching and squirming with eyes firmly closed. The sight cheered her and she kissed her on the cheek before going downstairs to make breakfast.

Flora was already sitting up and staring into space in the dim light of the living room, which had become her temporary bedroom.

'Good morning, mummy.' Lily kissed the top of her head, then opened the curtains.

'Good morning, darling. Could you help me to the loo?' Flora asked quietly.

Lily found Flora's weakened state unsettling. She didn't feel she had the stamina to be the strong one and feared her mother's stubbornness might be setting back her recovery. During the summer holidays, after she had returned to work after a fortnight of caring for her, she had reluctantly left Iris and Flora to look after one another. On the very first day she had received a mid-morning call from Iris. While still in bed she had heard a thump and raced downstairs, to find Flora in agony on the floor by the front door. She had apparently heard the postman and hobbled over to retrieve the mail, losing her balance in the attempt. The fall had further torn the ligaments in her ankle. When asked why she didn't wait for Iris to pick up the post, her mother had remained silent.

As Lily waited for Flora to finish, she tried to occupy her mind with her new kitchen, so as not to allow space for any gloom.

*

'Are you feeling alright, sweetheart?' Lily asked Iris as they reached the school gate. She had been unusually subdued and Lily feared the strain of the past few months were taking their toll.

'I'm OK,' Iris replied before solemnly kissing her goodbye. She looked so much like her father, Lily thought. Those eyes she could never read.

When she returned home, the kitchen installers were waiting by the front door, having already unloaded most of her new kitchen on the lawn. They were half an hour early. As she opened the door she heard her mother calling faintly. She rushed inside and found Flora sitting on the floor by the sofa, wincing.

'Did you try and get up to answer the door? Haven't I told you just to wait, mummy?' Lily tried to heave Flora back on to the sofa. One of the fitters noticed her plight and came to give assistance. Flora bore the humiliation in silence.

'Have you hurt yourself? Do you need a pain-killer?' Lily asked.

Flora shook her head.

'Don't you want to get better, mummy? You really must do as you're told,' Lily said before going to instruct the workmen. She tried to ignore the tear running down her mother's cheek.

When she returned, Flora was dozing. Lily sat down next to her and gently rubbed her arm. Her mother's eyes slowly opened.

'I don't know how you can sleep with their radio blasting.'

'It makes a nice change from silence.'

Lily got up and pulled out a couple of photo albums from a bookshelf then settled back next to Flora.

'Is it a good idea to look at those?' Flora asked.

'It's OK.'

The album contained photographs from her engagement to Carl and their early years of marriage. She hadn't looked at them in years and was surprised at how young she looked. She hadn't thought herself young at the time.

Lately she had been thinking about Carl more than usual. There had been a period when he was almost constantly in her thoughts. Time had lessened the intensity, but it had flared up again in the summer, when out of the blue they received a postcard from him. It was the first communication they'd received since the first brief note in the immediate aftermath of his departure.

It had been addressed to Iris and sent from America. He had said that he missed her and asked her to write to him, as well as giving bland details of some old cargo ship he'd visited. It had upset and confused Iris, as no return address had been given. She had wondered how he was well enough to go visiting a ship in America, but couldn't come and see her.

Lily had tried to talk to her mother about it. To find out what she thought it meant, but Flora had just shrugged and said she didn't know and that it was better not to read anything into it. But Lily couldn't stop herself thinking about what this sudden incursion into their lives meant. Carl had referred to her only in passing, asking if she was well. She had started to wonder what life would be like with him back in their lives, something she hadn't dare think about in a long time.

Lily thought about how she'd felt in the weeks leading up to The Phone Call to her aunt Frieda, which seemed a lifetime away. Two colleagues had got engaged that year, both much younger than her. She had been happy for them, but it had brought her own disappointment to the fore. At the age of 36 she had never had a boyfriend, never been out on so much as a date. When conversations steered towards the subject of relationships she would remain conspicuously silent, ashamed at her lack of experience.

There had been a couple of admirers. One, a widower from her church, 25 years her senior, whose attention she had found intimidating. He would make a beeline for her after services, standing too close and mentioning exhibitions that 'would be more interesting with a companion'. She had always been polite, avoiding eye contact as much as possible, determinedly ignoring his hints.

The other was someone from work, from the post room. At first she had found his compliments flattering, having rarely received that kind of attention before. They seemed harmless: 'what a lovely smile', 'that colour really suits you.' After a few weeks, he had started leaving her magazine cuttings of baby animals and Postit notes of inspirational quotes.

She began to find his attention oppressive. She felt guilty admitting to herself that she found him repulsive. She could hear him breathing as he approached her desk, sweat shadows under his arms. She had chided herself for judging someone on their looks, but reasoned that if he'd had a winning personality she would have overlooked this.

While she had initially thanked him for his compliments, she began to ignore him, continuing with her work when he dropped off her post. She would be aware of him lingering at her desk and would silently urge him to move on. He failed to take the hint, and replaced the photos of kittens with photos of himself, slipped in with her post. The first few were fairly innocent - a picture of him standing by a steam train, and at various tourist destinations, but when he included one of him at the seaside in vest and shorts she feared what might come next. She had thought about telling her manager and even considered resigning to escape his attentions.

After a weekend praying and looking at job

adverts, Lily returned to work having resolved to tell him not to leave her any more photos. Bracing herself for his post round she had been surprised to find someone else doing the deliveries. She braced herself again the next day and the next, before discovering through an overheard kitchen conversation that he had been sacked. He had been caught watching a pornographic film in the store room adjacent to the post room, using a company television and video player.

She had felt guilty at the time that her overwhelming feeling was one of relief rather than disgust. She had wept bitterly that night at the thought that it was only desperate men that were attracted to her.

She had only really fallen for someone once, prior to Carl. She attributed this to lack of opportunity rather than fussiness. She had gone to an all girl secondary school and there had been a dearth of eligible males in her church and workplace.

It was at sixth form college that someone caught her eye, as well as those of many others. She would never have considered herself in his league if not for his friendliness and apparent interest in her. He often sat next to her in their weekly tutorials and would enquire about her weekend, remembering what she had said the previous week and referring back to it. It caused some anxiety, as while his evenings and weekends were filled with parties, gigs and drinking, hers were invariably quiet. She was ashamed to have, on a few occasions, turned a trip to the supermarket with her mother into a shopping trip with a friend.

She thought he must be a good person to be willing to give someone like her the time of day, when he was sought after by so many. She convinced herself that while he was gregarious and spoke to most people, he gave her special attention.

She was eventually disabused of this notion. One afternoon she had walked into the tutorial room and found him sitting languidly on a desk at the back of the room, whispering and laughing conspiratorially with a girl from her English class. She had instinctively stepped back out of the room, but he had spotted her and jumped down from the table to greet her. She felt dowdy as she compared her appearance with his pretty friend's. She used all her self-control to answer his questions in her usual not quite relaxed manner, conscious of her adversary grinning in the background.

She had been ashamed of her reaction. Of course he would have attractive female friends. Of course she was not special to him. She had been stupid to think she was. She tried hard not to think of him, but bought some eyeliner and new jeans, all the same.

A couple of weeks later, she had discovered through overheard conversations that a party had taken place at the weekend, at which a number of new couples had formed. She was used to hearing gossip from events she had not been invited to, but when it became apparent that he had been the host, she was unprepared for the disappointment that swallowed her. It was made worse when she discovered that Lizzy, one of the prettier more outgoing girls from her small group of friends, had been invited.

As Lily looked at her engagement photos she remembered how excited and happy she had been that day and tried to analyse it objectively without getting emotional.

She'd had doubts about Carl's affections from the beginning and had wondered if he was the marrying type. Even during their courtship he had not shown much interest in what was going on in her life. She had deliberately put these anxieties to the back of her mind.

She tried to imagine what her life would be like if she had decided not to go ahead with it. It was impossible. She could not contemplate life without Iris.

There were relatively few photos from the years before Iris's birth. A few awkwardly posed shots from rare day trips, interspersed with several landscape shots that Carl liked taking. Then a spate from their time in the US, just before Iris's birth.

She had been surprised at how Carl warmed to fatherhood and how he doted on Iris. The first few years of Iris's life were probably the happiest of their marriage. Lily couldn't understand how he could then walk out on his daughter, never to contact her again, save for a pathetic postcard. She snapped shut the album and stepped outside to get some air. Flora had closed her eyes again.

Lily started to mull over the last months of married life, something she had done countless times in the immediate aftermath and had deliberately avoided since. She had been unable to read Carl and was wary that everything she said seemed to annoy him. She had often wondered what she could have done differently. Whether she should have been more aloof, given him more space, wore more make up or suggested they go to America. It had done the trick last time. She started to get annoyed with herself for thinking this way and went back inside, switching on the television.

Lily was disappointed with how quiet her mother was. She was keen to talk things over with her, but now she slept for most of the day and when she was awake often seemed distant.

She had not allowed herself to contemplate the possibility of her mother not recovering. Perhaps she needed to be more insistent in getting her to exercise and eat healthily, she thought. Maybe she should pay for a nurse. She placed a blanket over Flora and went upstairs to do some cleaning.

*

Lily gently rubbed Flora's arm to wake her.

'Mummy, do you want to come with me to collect Iris? I'll push you there and she'll love to push you back.'

'I'm tired, Lily. You go.'

Lily knew her mother hated the wheelchair but that she also valued any opportunity to go outside so was surprised at her response.

Iris was still subdued when Lily picked her up, giving only monosyllabic answers to her questions. When they reached home she ran upstairs immediately.

Lily walked into the living room where she found Flora slumped forward in her seat.

'Mummy?'

The left side of Flora's mouth was dragging downwards. Her eyes looked pleadingly at Lily.

CHAPTER
SIXTEEN

October 1990 – July 2006

L iz scanned the restaurant in search of Lily. She found her in a corner, waving excitedly. Opposite her was a man, Carl presumably, his head down studying the menu. Lily stood when Liz reached the table, her smile bright.

'Not late, am I?'

'No, no! Liz, this is Carl. I'm so glad you can finally meet.'

'Lovely to meet you, Liz,' Carl said, standing up to shake her hand.

Carl was not as Liz had imagined him to be. She had expected a shy, gawky crustacean of a man, but here he was, confidently holding her hand and gaze for a little longer than necessary.

Lily had told her he was handsome, but Liz had taken this with a pinch of salt as Lily was too sweet-natured to view anyone as ugly. But on this occasion she was right. Liz had dated many men with faces inferior to Carl's.

'And you, Carl. I've been dying to find out who's making an honest woman of Lily.'

As they took their seats, Liz noticed that Carl had not yet averted his eyes from her.

'Well, anyway, how's the wedding prep going? What's the colour scheme? I've told Lily the colours to avoid, as there are quite a few that clash with my hair and/or make me look like a corpse.'

'I can't believe any colour would have the gall to do that to you,' Carl said, before taking a sip of his wine.

'I'm not like Lily, Carl. She can wear any colour and she glows.'

Liz had been keen to meet Carl ever since Lily first mentioned him, curious to know who her friend had finally fallen for. She had rescheduled a meeting with a potentially lucrative client in order to join them for dinner. When she had visited Lily soon after the proposal, it had been obvious from her mother's faint praise that Carl did not live up to her expectations for her daughter. Having now met him herself, Liz feared for Lily.

As she climbed into bed that night, all Liz could think about was the way Carl had looked at her throughout the evening, as Lily sat guilelessly by, clearly happy that they seemed to be getting along.

*

'Well, what do you think of him?'

Liz had been expecting the phone call all day and had been mulling over what to say to Lily, but now felt sick at the possibility of hurting her.

'Well, he seems nice.'

'Do you think he looks nice?'

'Yes, he looks nice.'

'I know you've been out with models and the like, but I think he's lovely.'

'Oh, Lily, sweetheart.'

'What?'

'Do you really think he's the one?'

'Well, he's asked me to marry him, Liz. No one else has.'

'Just because a man asks you to marry him, doesn't mean he's right for you.'

'It's easy for you to say that, Lizzy. You've had lots of...options. Anyway, that's not the only reason. I love him.'

'What makes you love him?'

'Because he's been good to me. He's a good man. I never imagined that someone like him could be interested in someone like me.'

'What do you mean, Lily? Why do you keep putting yourself down? He's the lucky one.'

'You sound like my mother.'

'Well, she's a very sensible woman.'
'Please be happy for me, Lizzy.'
'If you're happy, I'm happy.'
'Well, I am.'

*

March 1994

Liz slammed shut the taxi door and smoothed down her skirt, which she now felt was too short, something she never usually worried about. She continued tugging it down as she walked up the drive to Lily's front door.

'Hello, Liz.'

As expected, Carl answered the door.

'Carl. Your lovely wife ready to roll?'

'No, but you look like you are.'

Liz stepped forward to enter the house. Carl retreated only slightly, meaning she had to brush past him. She could smell alcohol on his breath.

'So what have you got planned for this evening?'

'We're planning for Lily to get her mid-life crisis out of the way in one evening, so she can relax for the rest of her forties. I've lined up a selection of indulgences.'

'So just a regular night out for you, but please don't break my wife. If you do, you'll have to organise a replacement.'

'What's this about replacement wives?' Lily

said as she walked down the stairs.

'Carl's worried I might break you with too much fun.'

As they sat in the back of the cab on the way to Lily's fortieth birthday meal, Liz was disconcerted with how Carl always disconcerted her. It was not a feeling she was used to.

*

July 2004

'Thanks for coming,' Flora said as Liz stepped into the house. Liz had always admired her as she had seemed so formidable and robust, but in the three months since her last visit, Flora had aged and seemed to have somehow diminished.

'Why didn't she call me?'

'I don't know. She barely says anything these days.'

'I'm glad you got in touch.'

'Aunty Lizzy!' Iris appeared from the kitchen.

'Hello, gorgeous girl. Come here, I've got some pressies for you from The Big Apple. Your grandma won't approve of most of them of course.'

Flora raised her eyebrows. 'Come, have some tea. And let me vet these items.'

'Thank you, Mrs R, tea sounds wonderful. Is she upstairs?'

Both Flora and Iris nodded.

Liz slipped off her heels and made her way

up the immaculate beige-carpeted stairs. She had tried introducing colour and contemporary art to the household over the years, with carefully selected, often expensive, Christmas gifts. While some had been politely displayed for a while for her benefit, they had all eventually disappeared and the house returned to its tasteful inoffensive decor. She had tried something similar with Lily's wardrobe, but had encountered a similar response so eventually gave up on her endeavours.

Liz stood at the door of the bedroom. She had been in this position before, after Lily's miscarriages, tentatively waiting to enter, wondering what to say that would sooth.

'Hello, sweetheart.'

Lily turned towards her.

'Lizzy?'

'Why didn't you call me?'

'He's gone.'

'I know.'

'He left me for a pretty young thing.'

'He's a fool.'

Liz walked over to Lily's side of the bed and kissed her on the forehead. 'You were too good for him.'

'Maybe that was the problem,' Lily whispered.

*

'She was almost defending him.'

'I know.'

Liz and Flora sat at the kitchen table in silence for a while.

'Do you think she should take him back?' Flora asked eventually.

'Absolutely not. Were you...surprised?'

'What do you mean?'

'I don't know. Could you see any signs? She's always been blind to his faults.'

'I didn't see it coming, though I suppose in some ways it wasn't a great surprise. I thought he loved Irie though.'

'Yeah.'

Flora pulled out some envelopes from her handbag. 'These are from him. I haven't shown them yet. I didn't think it would be helpful.'

Liz took them from Flora and glanced through them. 'No, I don't think it would be either.'

'So you agree, it's better to keep these from them? For now?'

'Yes.'

*

July 2006

Liz watched Carl from a discrete corner of the room, as he listened patiently to a man talking animatedly. His hair was completely grey and his eyes more sunken than she remembered, but he still retained a boyishness to his demeanour.

She took a swig of the cheap white wine that had been laid on for the post-grad reception. When she next looked in his direction, Carl was staring straight at her. She turned away and desperately tried to find her fiancé in the crowded room.

'Liz?' Carl had made his way over surprisingly quickly.

'Oh hello, Carl.'

'What are you doing here? Are you working here?'

'No, no. My fiancé, Brech, is picking up his doctorate.'

'I see.'

'You?'

'Yep, back in Boston, working. Just temporarily. I'm heading back in a few weeks' time.'

'Right. Good.'

'You well? Business doing alright?'

'Um, yes to both.'

'Good.' Carl nodded, then stared at the wall. 'Have you, have you seen Lily lately?' he asked, turning back to Liz.

'I saw her, and Iris, a couple of months ago. When I was last in the UK.'

'How are they? Are they well?'

'They seem to be getting on OK. Iris is thriving at school, of course. You know she's been moved up a year?'

'Has she? Of course, she's always been bright. I'm so glad.'

Liz had never seen Carl look so desperately

sad.

'I expect she's pretty busy with school work. I haven't really heard from her,' he continued.

'Oh.'

'I'm glad they're doing well though.'

'I better go, Carl.'

'Please give them my love when you see them.'

Liz hurried away, again disconcerted by Carl.

CHAPTER SEVENTEEN

October – November 2006

After a hearty burst of singing, the robin looked towards Flora, as if for approval. She was certain it perched on the cherry tree by the window just for her benefit. In the two weeks that she'd been at the rehabilitation centre, the area by the bay window in the TV lounge had become her favoured spot. And there was an implicit understanding that it should be kept free for her. Unlike the other patients who stared passively at the television, she wanted to face outward, towards the garden and the world outside.

She was finding the days unfathomably long. It reminded her of the early period of Lily's marriage when she'd first moved into the sheltered flat, when she didn't have anyone's company to look forward to in the evenings. But this was worse, as now even reading was difficult and gardening out of the question. Infirmity had crept up on her so suddenly, she thought.

As she gazed out, Flora could see someone approaching through the reflection in the window pane. The robin flew off, just as she felt a hand on her shoulder. She turned and gasped.

It was a care assistant who Flora had never seen before. He looked so much like her husband she'd thought it was a ghost.

'Hello, Flora. I'm Jude. I've come to give you your medicine.'

Flora looked at him more closely. He hadn't sounded like her husband and his nose was different. But the eyes and the hair and the mouth were uncanny. She desperately wanted to find out more about him but was embarrassed of her clumsy words, so just stared.

She took her medicine compliantly and was rewarded with an encouraging smile. Her husband's smiles were always tinted with mischief, never innocent, she thought. What did this boy, Jude, think of her, she wondered. Another old prune? She did not want him taking her to the toilet. That would be an indignity too far.

Flora expected Jude to leave immediately after feeding her the tablets, but instead he lingered by the window, looking out at the robin who had returned, though Flora's attention was now on him. She was unable to take her eyes away from his face.

'Lovely garden, isn't it?' he said, touching her arm before taking his leave.

Flora spent the next hour chiding herself for being flattered by the attentions of a man probably young enough to be her grandson. How pathetic she was, she thought, and how foolish.

At dinner time, Flora reluctantly plunged her spoon into the bowl of tasteless, tepid slush. She had requested chilli powder, but had been told that it was unwise for someone in her condition. She managed to bring the spoon to her lips, but as she was yet to fully regain control of them after her stroke, it deposited only half its content in her mouth, while the rest made its way slowly down her chin and onto the bib she was made to wear.

Flora was then aware of someone by her side. Jude gently wiped her chin, then retrieved the spoon from her loose fingers and started feeding her. She finished the bowl of sludge even though it made her want to retch, purely to please him, though she felt the humiliation like a python around her chest, slowly crushing her.

The next morning, Flora was woken by a knock at the door. She was momentarily disorientated. Believing herself to be in her daughter's house she looked towards the window, expecting to find the door. She was disappointed when she realised where she was.

She was tired of being so restricted. She hated the wheelchair. She wanted to be able to go for walks when she pleased, to the library, to her church Women Fellowship, even to the supermarket. She was so frustrated with her situation that she thought she might implode, like Krook in *Bleak House*.

She shifted her gaze towards the door, which then opened. It was one of the younger carers.

'Mrs Ratnam, your visitors are here.'

Her heart lifted as she realised it was Saturday, which meant a visit from Lily and Iris. How could she have forgotten, when it was the highlight of her week. Iris came bounding in and planted a kiss on her good cheek. She held her close, her eyes welling up, which they seemed to do far more often these days.

Lily walked over and kissed her on the forehead. 'Good news, mummy! We've got permission to take you to the park!'

Since moving to the rehabilitation centre from the hospital, Flora had been wheeled out into the garden on a few occasions, but it felt like she had been deprived of the sky for months.

'Wonderful,' she said, as clearly as she could.

With the help of Lily and the carer she was washed and dressed for the excursion.

'I had to sign a disclaimer saying I take full responsibility of you while we're off the premises,' Lily said as she combed Flora's hair.

'No doing cartwheels down the hill,' the care

assistant said, as she probably had a million times before.

It was a bright autumn day, unseasonably clement. Though Lily was diligent in checking the blanket was tightly wrapped around her, Flora enjoyed feeling the breeze on her face and neck, when it occasionally slipped. It offered a hint of exhilaration and reminded her of being a young girl in Ceylon, running along the beach with her sister. Though Frieda was older, Flora would always win.

'Are you enjoying it, grandma?' Iris asked.

Flora managed a nod and a wonky smile. She had been told she needed to smile more as that would strengthen the muscles in her face. She found it easy to oblige for Iris.

'How's school, da?'

'Alright,' Iris shrugged.

A family walked by; their young son unable to hide his curiosity of Flora's skewed features. Flora attempted to smile at him, which caused him to impulsively grab his father's legs in fear. The father smiled apologetically.

'Stupid boy,' Iris muttered.

'Iris!' Lily rebuked.

They continued to the peak of the park's small hill and stopped by a bench.

'Did you bring any *kaju*?' Flora asked, knowing what the answer would be.

'Mummy, you have to stop being so stubborn and do what they ask if you want to get out of there soon. They said you've not been trying very hard at physio.'

Flora's reflex was to grumble at Lily, but instead she nodded meekly. She knew Lily was right, but found the physiotherapy sessions tiring and boring.

They sat in silence, taking in the birdsong, punctuated occasionally by the distant thud of a football being kicked and playful shouting. Flora soaked in the cloudless blue sky and the brilliant green of the grass. She hadn't remembered them being so luminous.

'We better head back,' Lily said, after what seemed to Flora a very brief period. 'Jane has fit in a physio session today as she's away on Monday and Tuesday.'

Flora said nothing.

'She didn't have to come in today, mummy,' Lily persisted.

'Are you leaving me then?'

Lily squeezed Flora's hand and shook her head, to Flora's relief.

*

The therapy room was dark compared to the blazing brightness outside.

'Can I stay and watch?' Iris asked.

Flora was not keen on her granddaughter seeing her at her most cantankerous but didn't know how to refuse, so nodded when the physiotherapist looked her way for approval. She wondered if this was a ploy to make her more amenable.

As the session commenced, Flora grimaced and strained. She was certain most of her energy was being used in exercising self-control. She was desperate to complain. Iris uttered regular encouragements, which would briefly lift her, but by the end of the twenty minute session she was exhausted.

'Grandma, you'll be running around in no time.' Flora tried to accept this as a statement of truth.

Afterwards, Lily fed Flora the indeterminate lunchtime offering. She had hoped Jude might appear, keen for him to see she had loved ones, but he did not.

By the time the plates were cleared, Flora's eyelids were heavy.

'Mummy, you should take a nap.'

'Please don't go.'

'Don't worry, grandma, I've brought some homework to do,' Iris reassured her.

Once deposited on her bed, Flora closed her eyes and listened to Iris colouring followed by her sums, which she calculated under her breath. Soon she could hear herself snoring.

When she woke, it was dusk and the room was empty. She felt a pang of loneliness. She slowly turned towards the clock on her bedside table. She had slept for a solid three hours. A note was propped up by the reading lamp. She could tell it was Iris's handwriting deliberately writ large: there was a church harvest meal that evening and they would be back on Sunday afternoon. She was annoyed they hadn't woken her to say goodbye.

Her bladder felt heavy. If not for this discomfort, she would have attempted to go to sleep again, until someone came to fetch her for dinner in half an hour. She doubted she could hold it in 'til then.

She had been offered incontinence pads, but refused them, saying they were for incontinent people, which she was not. She had control of her bladder, it was the rest of her body that rebelled against her.

Eventually Flora pressed the button for assistance. She hated the ignominy of it. Within a couple of minutes, there was a knock at the door. Her heart plunged when she saw it was Jude. She started to protest, which he seemed to understand as he immediately retreated. Calling for another assistant, she hoped.

The shock of seeing him had increased the pressure and Flora felt warmth under her. She was dismayed at what was happening. Why were they taking so long? After what seemed like an inordinate amount of time, an assistant arrived. It was the one who had offered her the incontinence pads, known throughout the centre as Blink. Jude followed behind.

'You should stop being so fussy, or else start

wearing the pads.'

Jude looked at the floor.

'I'm afraid everyone else is busy and I need help lifting you, so you're going to have to put up with him being here. He won't stay in the loo.'

Flora felt like crying, but knew this would make the leak worse.

As she was lifted from the bed into the hoist, Flora was conscious of the wet patch on her skirt that would be visible to them.

She relieved herself in misery. After she had finished, she sat for a while, willing herself to die.

'Are you done?'

Flora nodded meekly.

After they had both helped her into a chair, Jude left.

'I wish you lot wouldn't wait until the last minute to call us. We've got to change you and your bedclothes now.'

Flora sat hunched forward.

'What do you want to wear?'

Flora shrugged.

'For crying out loud!'

Blink starting rummaging through Flora's wardrobe, then roughly dressed her in new bloomers and a skirt that clashed with her blouse. Flora remained listless throughout. She could understand why Blink hated this job, but couldn't help being filled with resentment.

*

It was the last Saturday of the month, which meant karaoke night. In theory it was for patients to sing their favourite songs, as part of their rehabilitation. In practice, employees of the facility used the opportunity to perform ballads to a captive audience. Helpless, the patients looked on, mostly blank-faced, some visibly pained. A few would heckle in the vain hope it would make them stop.

Flora normally asked to be wheeled back to her room straight after dinner, where she would listen to one of her cassettes. This evening she was forced to join the ranks, as her request hadn't been heard.

She noticed that Jude did not join in with the singing. He leaned on a table at the side of the room. It was apparent he had already caught the eye of some of his co-workers, who kept looking his way for approval. At first he humoured them with flirtatious smiles back, but soon he became weary and started flicking through an old TV guide. He did not look her way. Flora wondered if this was for her benefit, or because he was disgusted by her.

After what seemed like an unreasonably long time to Flora, the patients were offered hot drinks and asked whether they wanted to go to bed. She gladly took the offer.

As Flora's head hit the pillow, she prayed for

eternal rest and for the Lord to provide for Lily and Iris.

In the early hours of the morning she dreamt she was outside Lily's house with a suitcase. A taxi arrived, but she was reluctant to get in as she felt certain she had forgotten something. She woke up, breathless. She knew exactly what it meant.

*

Flora stared at her reflection as the young assistant gently combed her hair.

'You're looking much better, Mrs Ratnam.'

Flora liked this girl and appreciated the respect she showed, not using the over-familiar 'Flora' like all the others, including Jude. She was right, there was an improvement. The left side of Flora's face still sagged, but not quite as markedly.

It had been a week since the dream. Realising the urgency of her task, when Lily and Iris had visited the following day she had asked them to bring the holdall that she kept under her bed, on their next visit.

Flora had then made a concerted effort to work on her speech that week, reciting Psalms and poems she had memorised from childhood. It had exhausted and frustrated her, but she persevered as she feared the consequences if she did not.

There was a knock at the door.

'They're here!' the assistant said, putting down the comb. 'I'll leave you to it.'

Iris ran in.

'Grandma, you're ready!'

Flora's heart quickened. She was fearful of losing her granddaughter, but knew she had no choice but to see her task through. She did not want to deal with that yet, though. She wanted to enjoy their company for as long as possible.

'I thought we could go to the garden. It's such a lovely day,' Flora said slowly.

'Grandma!' 'Mummy!' Iris and Lily said in unison.

'Your voice!' Iris continued.

'I've been practicing,' Flora said, glancing at Lily.

'Well done, mummy! We can't wait to have you home.'

Despite her improved speech, Flora said nothing as Iris enthusiastically relayed the details of a police raid in their *cul-de-sac*, managing only a mild look of astonishment at the culmination of the story, 'They were growing drugs in their dining room, grandma!'

After lunch, Flora suggested they sit in the conservatory. 'First, Lily, can you fetch that bag I asked you to bring.'

'What's in it, grandma?'

'You'll see,' Flora said, sick with anxiety.

Lily brought the holdall and placed it on a coffee table. As she did so, Flora closed her eyes and prayed for forgiveness.

'Are you alright, mummy?'

'Lily, Iris, I am so sorry for what I've done,' Flora's voice quivered.

'Grandma, don't be silly!' Iris got up and hugged Flora. 'You don't have to be sorry.'

'Darling, I do. I need to tell you both something. I can only pray that you will forgive me.' Flora's throat ached.

'Mummy, don't upset yourself. I don't think this is a good idea.'

'Lily, unzip the bag. There's another bag inside. Take it out.'

Lily did as Flora instructed and retrieved a crumpled carrier bag. Iris took it from her and passed it to Flora.

She sat for a moment with the bag in her lap, tears falling heavily.

'Grandma, don't cry. We're here, it's OK.'

'My darling, I have done something very bad. These are letters from your father. I kept them. He's been writing...' Flora's voice trailed off.

Flora looked down, afraid to see the reaction. Soon she felt her lap free from the weight of the bag. She looked up. Lily was rubbing her forehead, her eyes brimming. Iris was walking back to her seat with the bag. When she turned, her face was upset and confused.

'Why did you do this?' Lily said eventually.

Flora shook her head, unable to speak. Iris started rummaging through the bag.

She looked up at Flora dolefully as she picked out a letter.

'Can we go now, mummy? I want to read daddy's letters.'

'Perhaps we should. We'll see you, mummy.'

As they walked away, Iris held the bag protectively close to her, like a hot water bottle.

'I'm so sorry,' Flora called after them, her voice breaking. They didn't turn back.

Flora shrunk into her wheelchair. She felt as if a ton of earth had been dropped on her, burying her alive. Even her husband's repeated betrayals didn't compare to this loss.

As she sat alone, something distracted her and she looked up. In the garden was another inmate - Ted. He was staring at her from his wheelchair, though Flora thought it unlikely his eyesight was good enough for him to actually see her. Towering above him was Blink.

'Ted, I know you can hear me!' she barked.

Ted winced at her voice, but continued to stare into the distance, his mouth slightly open.

'Why didn't you use the alarm? We gave it to you to make it easy for you,' Blink continued. 'You keep doing this! Is it so you can get a sponge bath from Marie?'

Ted didn't respond. Blink slapped him on the side of his head. Ted raised his hands protectively.

'Don't do it again! We'll leave you to die in your own crap next time.'

Blink wheeled Ted away cowering in his wheelchair.

CHAPTER EIGHTEEN

June – July 1960

F lora sat on the edge of the bed, holding her mother's frail left hand in both of hers. She kept her eyes fixed on the bedcover, its peonies embroidered by her grandmother half a century earlier.

'I don't want to go, *umma*.'

Her mother's grip tightened. 'He's your husband. You have to go to him.'

Flora looked up at her mother. 'Why can't things stay as they are?'

'The longer you delay, the harder it will be for you to go.'

There was a gentle knock at the door, before Lily walked in solemnly. She embraced her grandmother, quietly crying into her shoulder.

'We need to make a move,' Flora's father said from the doorway.

'I love you both so much. The Lord be with you always,' Flora's mother said, and kissed first Lily's hand, then Flora's.

Flora cherished her mother's blessing, yet still feared letting go of her hand, as if doing so would cause her to plummet into darkness.

*

Mervyn, a 17-year-old cousin, had been permitted to drive Flora's father's Morris Minor to the port. Flora sat in the back with Lily on her lap, small for her six years. Mervyn's mother Rani sat next to them, the scent of her Yardley combining with the smell of the warm leather seats. As they passed the familiar street corner shrines and neighbourhood boutiques with goods hanging from the rafters, Flora wondered when she would see them again.

Reuben had been in London for the past nine months. One of his contacts had offered him a position on a new current affairs magazine. He had suggested that he first go and establish himself before Flora and Lily joined him. They, meanwhile, moved in with her parents.

When Reuben finally asked them to join him, Flora had been in no hurry to start making arrangements. Though she missed certain aspects of their marriage, she had noticed that while living with her parents her regular headaches had virtually disappeared. Lily also was less sickly and more outgoing. Flora had hoped it might turn into a more long-term arrangement. She knew of others who maintained long distance marriages and felt it might be the best way for hers to survive. She enjoyed Reuben's company, but living with him had been hard work.

She was surprised to receive another letter from him a fortnight after the initial request, practically pleading with her to join him as soon as possible. Though relieved at this apparent display of affection, she was anxious about the period of respite coming to an end.

Some things had changed since the uncertain early days of her marriage. The frequency of the parties had reduced as the number of participants gradually diminished because of new family commitments or migration abroad. Lily's arrival had provided a good excuse for Flora to decline joining Reuben when they did still occur. She tried not to think of what he got up to in her absence, returning in the early hours reeking of alcohol and other women's perfume. Initially she had questioned him, keen to show she was no pushover who would accept infidelity, but she grew weary of listening to his excuses and eventually stopped asking. She chose to believe his assurances that she was the only one he really wanted, only because she saw no alternative to acceptance.

Lily was born two years into their marriage.

Reuben's interest in her waxed and waned. He was fascinated by her in the first few weeks, but soon became irritated by her tendency to disrupt their sleep and was relieved when Flora suggested she move to her parents for a while. His interest piqued again as Lily started crawling. She had been a robust and giggly baby and in the evenings he would dance with her on his shoulder, often causing her to regurgitate her supper in excitement. Flora was reluctant to chide him, grateful for the attention he was finally giving their daughter.

Lily grew into a lively curious toddler, with a tendency to relocate or chew whatever she got her hands on. When, on one occasion, this had led to her emptying a bottle of his prized single malt whisky into a house plant, Reuben had called her a 'selfish little idiot' before storming out of the apartment.

He had returned penitent, but the following week, when Lily chewed pages of his early edition *Crime and Punishment*, he had picked her up and thrown her on to the settee. 'You need to discipline your daughter!' he had yelled at Flora. This time he did not apologise.

Flora would often think about the look on Lily's face. She had not cried immediately, but seemed to be in shock for several seconds before she started screaming in fear. She watched Lily become more cautious around her father, keeping out of his way. In the following weeks she would visibly tense when Reuben picked her up.

Reuben was never violent towards Lily again, but became indifferent, rarely playing with her or taking any part in her care. He insisted Flora put her to bed by 6pm and at weekends would arrange to play golf. If he was unable to get away, he would suggest Lily was taken to her grandparents. There were sporadic moments of paternal interest, when he'd again dance with her or teach her how to draw, but these were few and far between.

As Flora stood on the dock, Lily clasped around her legs, she wondered what London had done to Reuben. Which version of him could she expect? Would it be a completely new one altogether?

They had arranged to meet a young woman called Karthi before boarding the launch that would take them to the ship. She was the niece of her parents' neighbours, leaving to study at Cambridge. Flora had expected a cynical cigarette-smoker, like the slender creatures of the despised parties. Instead, Karthi had the wide-eyed enthusiasm of the head girl she had no doubt been.

'We'll look after each other,' she said, which Flora found strangely reassuring.

Her father and aunt joined them on the launch, while Mervyn stayed with the car. All but Karthi were silent as they made the short journey to the ship.

'You better hurry and get on,' her father said when they reached the vessel. He was no longer the jocular figure of her childhood. He looked old and feeble in his suit, which was now at least one size too big. Retirement had disoriented him and Flora knew he felt guilty about her marriage.

'God bless you, Flora,' he said and kissed her forehead. He bent low to embrace Lily. 'Darling Liliput, you'll look after your mama, won't you?'

Flora couldn't bear to turn back as she walked up the gangway, fearful that she might faint with sorrow if she caught sight of her father. The night before, as they held a prayer meeting in the house to send her on her way, he had wept as he prayed for her. The first time she had ever seen him cry.

*

Flora was unsurprised that Lily did not take to sailing. She had come prepared with smelling salts, ginger and, as a last resort, sickness pills, all of which had limited effect. It pained her to see her daughter lose what little weight she had. Lily would watch from the sidelines as other children took part in the specially arranged games, fascinated by what she saw but resolutely determined not to participate.

Karthi on the other hand was keen to experience everything the liner had to offer, signing up for dance classes and various tournaments. After breakfast she would leave Flora and Lily, returning to them only in the evening to share her experiences, including all the compliments she'd received from the Europeans. Flora resisted the urge to warn her, to advise caution, thinking that she would learn soon enough.

Flora and Lily had fallen into a modest routine: after observing the morning children's activities they would find a quiet spot, somewhere in the more stable central part of the ship, where they would read or nap, in between dealing with Lily's nausea. Flora would sometimes look for Karthi at mealtimes and, more often than not, find her on the other side of the dining room talking animatedly to a new group of friends. She would then search for a table and sit in silence, save for a few words exchanged with fellow diners about the weather, and encouragements to Lily to eat. She wondered how everyone else found it so easy to talk, when she could find nothing to say.

*

Lily had vomited without warning and Flora was desperately mopping up the royal blue carpet with her handkerchief.

'Here, use this.'

Flora looked up, uncertain on whether to accept the offer from the elderly white man holding out his handkerchief.

'Let me,' he said and got down on his knees to assist her.

'No, please. I'm fine. You don't have to.'

'I'm sure you're fine, but it's nice to feel useful now and again, so please let me help. There, just like new.'

Though it clearly wasn't, Flora was grateful for this act of kindness. She had been on the ship for five days and had not yet had any meaningful interactions with anyone other than Karthi and Lily.

'And what's your name, sweetheart?' the man asked Lily after hauling himself upright.

Lily looked at Flora, who nodded.

'Lily.'

'What a pretty name. I'm Jim. Jim Lewin, and this is Marjorie, my wife.'

From then on, Flora and Lily no longer had to face mealtimes alone. Afternoons were filled with card games and jigsaws with their new companions. Flora found their presence comforting. There was something about them - their turn of phrase, their committed Christian faith - that reminded her of her parents.

She was especially grateful when they reached Naples, the part of the voyage she had been dreading most. It was the first time she had sent foot in another country, let alone another continent. With their new friends guiding them, Flora and Lily were at ease as they strolled through the city, astonished by the wild differences and strange similarities to Colombo. They were persuaded to try the local ice cream, with the promise that it was even better than Ceylon's Elephant House. They were surprised to find it to be true.

*

It was the day of embarkation. Flora dressed Lily in the woollen socks and sweater she had knitted for her, even though it was June. She considered the possibility of staying on board and returning to Ceylon. She wondered how long she could keep that up, travelling between the continents, never having to face up to her marriage.

Karthi had come by the cabin in the morning to say goodbye before they got swallowed up by the crowds. Flora was sad to leave her and although they promised to keep in touch, was certain she would never see her again. She had said goodbye to the Lewins the night before, as their cabin was on the other side of the ship. They too had given her an address, but they lived in Edinburgh so she was not sure if anything would come of it. 'If we don't meet again here, we'll see you in Heaven,' they'd said.

As passengers bustled off the ship, Flora squinted at the sky, which was an unexpectedly vivid blue. Everything else though, even the air, seemed so different to Ceylon.

She had not previously noticed how many

Ceylonese were on the ship. Now they were contained in the same area, waiting to be processed by immigration officials, she saw that the majority were young Tamil men, hair slicked back, wearing their best shirts. They were all wide eyed with nerves or eagerness, none looked confident. She searched for Karthi among them but couldn't find her.

The officials were impassive as they scribbled and stamped her passport, looking down at her. Flora squirmed as a man with large hands routed through her belongings, seeming to take an expressionless pleasure in the feel of the silk saris and embroidered sheets.

One of the Brylcreem-ed young men helped her retrieve her luggage from the examination table, placing it on a trolley he'd acquired, leaving the porter to shrug and step aside. Though Flora was grateful, she was wary of his unsolicited help, especially as once through the arrival gate he hovered nervously by them. It was then that she noticed how young he was, probably still a teenager.

'Thank you so much for your help. My husband will be here soon.'

The young man nodded, then quietly retreated, soon lost in the crowd. Flora wondered if she should have tipped him or whether that would have been an insult.

In the distance she saw Karthi rush towards a board probably bearing her name. She scanned the crowd for Reuben and held tightly to Lily's shoulder. After fifteen minutes the crowd had thinned slightly, but Reuben was nowhere to be seen.

As another ten minutes passed, panic began to flood Flora's chest. She began to fear that Reuben had been given the wrong day. After another twenty minutes, most of her fellow passengers had gone. She took out her diary, in which she had noted the name and address of Reuben's workplace. She looked around for someone who might be able to help her. Lily waited quietly, accepting everything that was happening to her without complaint, safe in the belief that her mother was in control.

'Darling, do you think you can wait here with the bags for just a minute while I go and get some help?'

Lily shook her head. Flora sighed, then noticed someone jogging towards them.

'Flo, I'm so sorry. I missed the train and then there were some cancellations. I had to wait for over an hour. Have you been here long?'

Reuben looked different. He didn't seem as boyish as Flora remembered. His face seemed sharper. She wondered if his previously lustrous hair had also thinned slightly. He kissed her on the cheek, then bent down to kiss Lily but she retreated behind Flora.

'It's daddy, Lily.'

Lily regarded Reuben uncertainly as he ruffled

her hair.

On the train journey to London they chatted politely about the voyage and Reuben's work, in the manner that vague acquaintances might catch up on the intervening years. For the most part they were silent, watching the fields rush by the window.

Occasionally Flora would look at Reuben's reflection, wondering what secrets he might be hiding this time.

When they arrived at Waterloo, they hauled Flora's cases into a cab, unaided by the driver, who watched them as he finished his cigarette. The journey to Reuben's flat took less than twenty minutes, in which time both Flora and Lily tried to take in the abundance of new sights and sounds.

Flora had seen photographs and newsreels of London, so some things seemed familiar to her, though she couldn't quite believe she was now part of its landscape.

The taxi pulled up outside a smart Edwardian terrace. Checkered steps lead up to the front door. Flora looked up at the large bay windows and the sloping red-tiled roof with its towering chimney.

Reuben heaved a suitcase up the steps. Flora looked at the taxi driver and realised he had no intention of assisting. So, picking up a smaller case, she took Lily by the hand and followed Reuben.

'We're on the ground floor. I'll get the rest, Flo.'

'Reuben!' someone called from the pavement.

All three turned. A young English woman was standing by the remaining luggage.

Reuben sighed and continued into the entrance hall. Flora and Lily remained by the threshold looking at the woman, who had started making her way up the steps.

'Hello. You must be Reuben's wife.' The woman stood face to face with Flora. She looked down at Lily. 'And you're the daughter.' She then made her way into the building and through the open door into the flat. Flora followed with Lily, a quiet rage forming.

'I just thought I'd come and say "hello"', the visitor said before taking a drag of her cigarette.

Reuben came out of the bedroom and stared at her.

'I was just saying that I thought I'd come and welcome your wife to England,' she said.

Reuben walked to the front door. 'Can you leave please.'

The woman raised her eyebrows. Reuben did not move. After an awkwardly long silence she sulkily exited.

They heard the entrance door slam and footsteps on the steps outside. Both Flora and Lily stared at Reuben.

'She's from work, Flo,' Reuben shrugged.

'Darling, come here.' Flora stretched out her

hand to Lily. 'I assume that's the bedroom?' she asked Reuben.

He nodded and Flora made her way towards it.

The room was large, with a wardrobe and chest of drawers of dark mahogany that seemed to suck the light out. It was tidy apart from the unmade double bed at its centre. Flora closed the door and locked it. She spread the coverlet over the bed, careful not to touch the sheets with her hands. Then she and Lily lay on top of it, using their coats as blankets.

Flora was not able to sleep, but she could soon tell that Lily was dozing and was grateful for this small mercy. She didn't have the strength to think about what they would do, after this inauspicious start to their life in London. She heard the front door open. She wondered if Reuben was going after the woman, the supposed work colleague. She wanted to get up and throw things at him for humiliating her again, but didn't have the energy, or the boldness, to make a scene in this strange new land.

She was surprised to hear the door open again soon after, followed by noises that sounded like cupboards and the jangle of cutlery. She got up, careful not to disturb Lily.

She found Reuben in the kitchen. Three newspaper parcels had been placed on plates.

'Dinner,' he said. 'Thought you might like to try the local delicacy. It's nothing like Jaffna king fish of course.'

'Who was she?'

'No one, Flo.'

'You expect me to believe that?'

'I promise it will just be us from now on.'

'What you do is not fair. I won't tolerate it anymore, Ben. I mean it.'

Reuben looked down. 'I know.'

*

That night, Flora made Reuben sleep on the settee as an initial punishment and changed the bedsheets, despite his insistence they were clean. She lay awake considering her options, wondering if she should return immediately to Colombo. It was only the fear of the humiliating pity that would await her that dissuaded her from that path just yet. She wanted to make him pay though, but the only way she could think of was to betray him just as he had done to her. And that went against her conscience.

In the morning she let Lily lie in as she went to prepare breakfast. Reuben was already in the kitchen drinking coffee.

She ignored his questions and apologies and exasperated sighs, feeling it was necessary but found the effort wearying. He eventually left for work. When she returned to the bedroom, she thought Lily looked so small in the middle of the bed, in the middle of the big room. Too small to have to deal with this nonsense in a foreign land.

*

Though it was summer, Flora carried cardigans for both herself and Lily as they took their first tour of the neighbourhood. As the rows of houses towered above them, Flora thought about how insignificant she and Lily were, in this city, in the world. She felt as if the buildings were judging her as she walked by. That they somehow knew she didn't belong. She was grateful when eventually the skyline opened up as they reached a park.

Flora was grateful to find a bench, suddenly aware of how tired she was. As they sat, Lily strained forward so she could see the ducks in the ornamental pond. Flora was relieved to see her take an interest in something.

'Go, darling. Just don't get too near the edge.'

Lily jumped down and walked towards the pond. As she watched her, Flora became aware of two figures on the other side of the pond - office workers on their lunch break. They were staring at her as they chatted to each other. They made no attempt to look away as she looked up, so she looked down at the cardigan in her lap, uncertain of how to respond to such bad manners.

As they continued their walk, Flora noticed a few more disapproving stares. The majority of people were indifferent, continuing their conversations or staring at unseen objects in the distance. She much preferred this anonymity. In her parents' neighbourhood in Colombo, people would often look at her with pity. Everyone seemed to know about her cheating husband.

As they made their way back to the flat, they passed a green grocers. In one of his letters to her, Reuben had written that the things they found exotic in Ceylon were in abundance here, while things they loved and took for granted were in short supply. Flora picked up a lettuce, impressed with how fresh it looked.

'Are you going to buy that? No one else is going to want it now you've had your dirty hands on it.'

An older woman with lilac hair and a pink raincoat was staring at her, behind her another pursed her lips disapprovingly.

'I'm sorry, I'm obviously mistaken. I had been under the impression that British people had good manners. I'm clearly wrong,' Flora answered, as she grabbed Lily's hand.

The pink-coated woman's nostrils flared almost imperceptibly before she turned to mutter something to her companion. Flora was determined to continue shopping though she found the experience excruciating. She willed the women to leave but they continued their conversation in the shop doorway, nodding regularly in her direction. She wasn't sure she had the energy to try and get past them.

'Don't mind them.' Flora turned to find a man with a beige overcoat and generous beard casually throwing apples into a brown paper bag. 'Years of disappointment have made them bitter.'

As Flora left the shop, the grocer's words felt like an unintentional warning.

*

They settled into a routine of sorts over the following days: reading, letter writing, cleaning and going on long meandering walks, but Flora still found it a challenge to fill the time. She had learnt to avoid eye contact, but if she did feel someone glaring at her, she would meet their eye, forcing most to look away. She learnt to contain her rage at utterances that she didn't quite catch and spit that would just miss her shoes. She was ashamed at how grateful she was when people sat next to them in the park.

Reuben had avoided writing to her about all this, careful not to discourage her from coming. He had failed to mention the signs in guesthouse windows stating 'No blacks, no Irish, no dogs', or the violence casually doled out on him by loutish men offended by his foreignness. It was only when Flora noticed a scar on his forearm that she discovered such people existed who could not be charmed by him.

Yet despite the hostility, she began to warm to London. The tall houses began to feel less threatening. She felt a freedom that she had not experienced before, there was something liber-

ating about not being known. She had also noticed a change in Reuben. It was obvious he was
making an effort. In their first week he returned
home earlier than he ever had in Colombo and
spent time playing card games with Lily and
reading to her. On their first Saturday he took
them by bus into Westminster and onto the
West End, revelling in their astonishment at the
famous landmarks. Flora was still not ready to
let him leave the settee though. She had experienced this before and was waiting for him to fall
into his usual habits.

*

'There was a letter from Frieda today. They're
back from Singapore,' Flora said to Reuben as he
dealt the cards for Rummy.

'Oh,' he said absently. Frieda had been less
effective than her mother at hiding her feelings
towards Reuben.

'She's invited me and Lily to come and stay
with them. They're somewhere near Manches-
ter. I thought it would be good for us to go for a
week or two.'

'But you've only just arrived!'

Flora had not expected any objection from
Reuben and was unsure whether to be pleased or
annoyed.

'It will only be for a short while. There's not
much for us to do here while you're at work.'

'Sweetheart, can you go and fetch a notebook

for us to keep score. There's one in my bag, on the kitchen table,' Reuben said to Lily.

As soon as she left the room he turned to Flora. 'Flo, if this is about what happened when you arrived, I promise you there's nothing going on now. Please stop punishing me for it. I need you here.'

'She's my sister. I haven't seen her in two years.'

Both adults smiled as Lily returned.

'Right, who's going to win this one?' Reuben asked her.

*

In the end, Flora persuaded Reuben to let them go, assuring him they would return in two weeks' time. She was perplexed at his reluctance, when he had managed without them for several months. She packed their warmest clothes, having been warned about the north.

Reuben accompanied them to the station before work. He looked sad, Flora thought, almost regretful. She spent the first hour of the journey wondering if she'd made the right decision.

An older couple shared their compartment. Both were engrossed in their heavy books, only occasionally looking up to take in the scenery. An hour into the journey, the man checked his watch, stood up and took down from the luggage rack his compact leather suitcase. He placed it on the seat between himself and his wife, carefully undid the clasps and retrieved a bag of humbugs. There was no rummaging around for them. He knew exactly where to find them, which quietly impressed both Lily and Flora. He returned the suitcase to the luggage rack and settled back into his seat before silently offering a sweet to his wife. Lily watched the whole operation unblinkingly, which had not gone unnoticed.

'Would you like a humbug, little girl?' the man asked with a formal but not unkind voice. Lily looked up at Flora who nodded. She reached out and took one.

'Madam?'

Flora reached in and took one herself, smiling gratefully. He then resumed his reading, to the quiet sound of humbugs being consumed. About an hour later, he checked his watch again. 'Lunchtime I think, Claire.'

This time, his wife put down her book and reached into a straw bag next to her, from which she produced two neatly wrapped parcels and a thermos flask.

'I'm afraid we can't offer you anything,' the man said to Lily, who again was making no attempt to disguise her fascination.

'That's quite alright,' Flora said. 'We've brought our own.' Flora had packed her usual refreshments of apples and tea, having not thought through the length of the journey. She was annoyed with herself for not having become as domesticated as she'd like to be.

When they finally arrived at the station, Flora was relieved to see Frieda waiting for them, though she looked strange with her western slacks and loose shirt.

'Oh, Flo!' She embraced them both tightly. 'Lily, haven't you grown so much, darling?'

'It's so good to see you, Fred.'

Frieda nodded, unable to hold in her tears.

'Fred?'

'Oh, Flo...It's *umma.*'

'What do you mean'?

'She's gone.'

Frieda began to sob. Flora struggled for breath.

Flora's mother had been bedridden for the two weeks before her departure. She had blamed her discomfort on a gastric condition. It had turned out to be a tumour in her stomach.

Their father had telegrammed instructing them not to return for the funeral, as the comfort he would receive in seeing them would be outweighed by the loss of them departing again. Instead he asked them to plan to visit in a few months' time, so that he had something to look forward to.

The fortnight was spent in mourning, as the sisters stayed up late into the night recounting childhood escapades. Both weighed down with guilt that neither of them had been by their mother's bedside. She had slipped away in the morning while their father had gone to buy his daily paper. Flora wondered how she would have coped if she had received the news in London, and was thankful for her sister's presence.

'Why is everything so sad now?' Flora asked one morning, as they sat in Frieda's bright living room. 'When we were young, everything seemed so light. Now it's heavy and sorrowful.' She looked out of the window. Lily was playing with the family puppy, and while she looked happy, Flora thought she cut a lonely figure.

As the day approached for them to return to London, Flora could feel the tension in her throat returning. Reuben had called her a few times via Frieda's husband's surgery. He had sounded edgy, she thought, but was pleased that he'd asked about Lily each time. She had tried not to think about what he might be hiding. The night before they were due to return, he called again.

'Flo, you are coming back, aren't you?'

'Of course. Why wouldn't I?'

'I need you here.'

Flora lay awake into the early hours pondering what Reuben meant. She was certain his words belied something more than loneliness. He was in trouble.

'Fred, would you mind looking after Lily today?' Flora asked the next morning.

'What?'

'I think Reuben's got involved in something

and I don't want her getting caught up in it.'

'What sort of something?'

'I don't know. I'll be back tonight and if all's well we'll both leave tomorrow.'

Though Lily was reluctant to let go of her at the station, Flora was convinced it was the right decision to leave her behind. As the countryside blazed outside in the midsummer sunshine, she tried to prepare herself for whatever Reuben had to say, considering various options.

He was waiting for her on the platform when she arrived. He looked anxious, but Flora felt strangely detached.

'Where's Lily?'

'With Frieda.'

'Why? I thought you were both coming back today.'

'Is there something you want to tell me, Reuben? I know there's something you're hiding and I'd like to know what it is. I won't return to you until you tell me.'

'It's nothing to worry about, Flo. Why don't we get something to eat?'

As they took a table at a station cafe, Flora was struck by how uncertain Reuben looked. He was normally so self-assured. It unnerved her but she was determined not to let it show. Reuben studied the menu intently, clearly taking none of it in.

'What's happened, Ben?'

'I can't keep anything from you, Flo, can I? You

know me too well,' he said, putting down the menu. 'I've got into a bit of a situation.'

'Does it involve a woman?'

Reuben nodded.

'The woman at the flat?'

'She's pregnant. I'm so sorry.'

It had been a possibility Flora had considered, but the words still seemed to punch her. She looked down at the menu, trying to remain composed.

'I don't know what to do, Flo.'

She glanced up at Reuben, who was looking imploringly at her. She still felt detached, though she was abundantly aware that his mistake would have massive consequences for her.

'What do you want me to say?'

'I don't know.'

'Are you sure it's yours?'

'She says it is. She's told her father it's mine. He's my editor. He's quite an influential man.'

'I see.'

'What should I do?'

Flora was getting increasingly irritated. She thought about what she might have left behind in the flat. She had taken most of her clothes to Frieda's. What was left could wait. She pushed her chair back, stood up and started walking towards the door.

'Where are you going?'

Reuben stood and grabbed her shoulder, but she continued walking onto the station concourse. He took hold of her arm, slowing her down.

'Please, Flo!'

Flora stopped abruptly and turned to face him. 'Reuben, you're making a scene.'

She turned and rushed away. She looked up at the departure board. She would just be able to make the train back. It was the one she had arrived on.

CHAPTER NINETEEN

July – August 1960

Lily sat on the stairs and strained to hear what her mother and aunt were saying.

This had become her regular practice since arriving at her aunt and uncle's house a month earlier. After being put to bed, she would wait a little while before creeping halfway down the stairs to try and listen to what the adults were saying. Her mother and aunt usually spoke in Tamil if it was just the two of them, with a liberal helping of English, as did most of her relatives. The first few weeks were full of stories about her grandmother, of the games and songs she had taught them, of her strong faith. They spoke of trips they had taken around Ceylon, with relatives known and unknown. Of people getting lost in the mountains, of tricks they had played on one another. They would laugh at the memories, then cry as they remembered their grief. She had desperately wanted to join in with their happiness and sadness, but never ventured further down the stairs.

Her father was often a topic of conversation, but their voices were low when they spoke about him and she struggled to hear them, catching only snippets.

Lily's main concern was their living arrangements. When her mother told her they would be staying with her aunt Frieda a while longer she had been relieved, but was keen to know exactly how much longer this would actually be. She feared the prospect of suddenly being uprooted again and did not want to return to the London flat. It had made her feel nervous and she had wondered if it was haunted. Her aunt's house, though, reminded her of her grandparent's place in Ceylon - full of family members, safe.

She felt sad about leaving her father alone in that place, yet had no desire to go to him. When her aunt asked her if she missed him, she had not known how to answer.

He had been kind to her in the London flat. He had read stories to her, putting on silly voices for all the characters. They had played games. These were things she couldn't remember him ever doing in Ceylon, but their life with him there seemed so long ago so she may have just forgotten.

One memory that had stayed with her was from shortly before he left for England. Her mother had gone out one evening, leaving her alone with her father, something that almost never happened. He had put her to bed soon after dinner, but had forgotten to leave her bedroom door ajar as normal, to allow light to come in from the living room until she was asleep. She had waited for a long time, fearful of getting out of bed in the dark, but eventually got up and pulled open the door.

She could see the back of her father's head on the settee. Another head, a woman's, was leaning on his shoulder. She could tell from the hairstyle that it was not her mother. She had watched them for a long time, listening to the low murmur of their voices, punctuated by laughing. The woman eventually stood up and Lily had quickly darted into bed.

She had asked her mother about it the next day. She had seemed surprised but told her it must have been one of her father's friends. For the next few nights, until he left for England, her mother had slept with her in her bed. She had assumed this was to comfort her.

*

Lily threw the ball halfway down the garden for Hampshire, the family puppy, to fetch. He duly chased it, then commenced barking at it.

'Lily, daddy wants to talk to you,' her mother said from the kitchen doorway.

She became anxious, not knowing what to say to him, but followed her mother into her uncle's surgery. It had a smell that was strange but that she quite liked. She picked up the receiver.

'Hello?'

'Hello, sweetheart. It's your dad.'

'Hello, daddy.'

'How are you? Do you like the north?'

'Yes. They have a puppy called Hampshire.'

'A puppy? That's pretty good. What would you say to a baby brother or sister?'

'I'd like that.'

'Well, soon you'll have one. What do you think of that?'

'Really?' Lily looked at her mother sceptically. Her mother, if anything, looked thinner.

'Yes, really! Are you excited?'

'But mummy doesn't look like she has a baby in her belly.'

Flora snatched the phone from Lily.

'What are you telling her?' Lily strained to hear her father's response, but was unable to.

'The truth?' her mother continued. 'You've got a nerve...' she turned to Lily and covered the mouthpiece with her hand. 'Darling, I just need to tell daddy something. You wait outside.'

Lily reluctantly shuffled out. She was used to being excluded from conversations between her parents. They would stop abruptly when she walked into a room, then continue in irritated whispers when she left. It wasn't long before her mother emerged from her uncle's office.

'Darling, you mustn't believe everything daddy tells you. He was teasing you because he misses you. I am not having a baby.'

'He made it up?'

'Yes. Exactly.'

The next day their evening meal was interrupted by the distant ringing of the surgery phone. Lily noticed all the adults exchange looks with one another, while her twin cousins continued eating. Her uncle wiped his mouth on a napkin, something she'd noticed him do at the end of every meal, then went to answer the phone. She stopped eating, waiting for his return. When he did, he looked nervous.

'It's Reuben.'

Flora pushed her chair back without looking up and went to take the call. Lily again watched the door.

'Aren't you hungry, Lily?' her aunt asked. Lily obligingly took a mouthful of mashed potato, which she had developed a taste for, then resumed watching the door. Her mother soon returned and took her seat without a word.

'All well?' Frieda asked.

'Mm hm,' Flora replied.

That night Lily listened for the creak of the stairs as her mother went down after saying goodnight. She waited for silence to descend from her cousins' room. They were older and slept later than she did. She could hear murmuring and giggling and the sound of their mattress springs as they settled, then eventually it went quiet. Her uncle would be in his study with his records and books and a glass of brandy.

She crept out of her room to the staircase then slowly slid down on her bottom, step by step, to minimise the creaks, until she reached her customary spot. It was frustrating listening in midway through conversations, like opening a book in the middle pages, but was better than nothing.

'He just doesn't want to be stuck with her. It's not that he wants me. She's a bit...'

'Unstable?'

'Unstable. Volatile. He's desperate. I don't know what he wants me to do. Does he want me to adopt it? Does he really think I'll agree to that?'

'No, of course not.'

'What is he doing then, Fred? I don't know what to do.'

'What are you doing there?' Lily looked up to see her cousin Vinod peering over the stair railing. He was eight and the spitting image of their grandfather, with his long forehead. 'Are you spying?' he continued.

'I couldn't sleep,' Lily said.

'What are they saying?'

'I couldn't hear.'

She stood and walked back up the stairs.

'I won't tell,' he said, smiling mischievously.

Lily got back into bed, her heart thumping.

The next morning she ate her porridge nervously, anticipating a scolding. As her mother sat down, she braced herself, enduring an agonizing wait as she poured her tea.

'Darling, do you want to see daddy? Do you miss him?'

Lily looked down, fearful of saying the truth. 'Darling, tell me honestly, where would you like to live? You won't get into trouble. Just tell me the truth.'

Lily looked up at Flora.

'Would you like us to go back to London to see daddy, or would you like to stay here for a little while longer?'

Lily felt a weight on her chest. She knew she should say her father, but it wasn't true.

'Can't we go to grandpa?'

'That's not possible right now.'

Lily had overheard her mother say, more than once, that she couldn't go back yet because of the shame, but hadn't known what she meant.

'I like Hampshire.'

'Hampshire?'

'The puppy dog.'

'Oh. So you like it here, darling? Tell me.'

Lily nodded reluctantly. Flora kissed her on the forehead. 'Then we'll stay.'

That evening when the telephone rang during

their evening meal, her mother stood before her uncle could. She was away from the table for longer than usual. In that time, her uncle and cousins finished their food and left, while Lily and her aunt remained. After the clatter of their plates being cleared away, the room went silent. Lily did not touch her food, but her aunt did not ask her about it.

'Your mama should tell your dad she's eating. Her food will be icy cold now,' Frieda said as she covered Flora's plate with another.

Lily said nothing. Eventually her mother came back. Lily could tell she had been crying, by her shiny eyes.

'Lily, do you want to go and give Hampshire his dinner while mama and I clear up?' her aunt instructed.

Lily reluctantly followed Frieda to the utility room that doubled as Hampshire's bedroom. He was asleep, but she picked him up. His soft warm head under her chin was comforting. Her aunt handed her a box of dog biscuits then left. After a moment, Lily followed her, cradling Hampshire, and stood by the doorway of the kitchen.

'What did he say?' Frieda asked.

'He took it badly.'

'That's to be expected.'

'I thought it would be a relief but it isn't.'

'This isn't the end, Flo. You just need a break. He has to learn to deal with the consequences of his behaviour.'

'It feels like the end.'

Hampshire stretched and as he yawned, let out a small whine. Lily ran to the other end of the utility room.

The next evening when the telephone rang, her mother shook her head as her uncle rose. He returned shortly afterwards looking uneasy.

The same thing happened the next day and then for a few days the phone didn't ring during mealtimes. Lily stopped listening on the stairs, afraid of being caught again by her cousin. Her mother had told her they would be staying for at least two months. It sounded like a long time to her and while this was what she had hoped for, it did not bring her the happiness she had thought it would.

*

Lily sat on the backdoor step with Hampshire and watched her uncle coat the garden fence in creosote, enjoying the smell even though something about it made her feel uneasy. The phone started ringing in the surgery. Kumar closed his eyes and sighed, before pulling off his gloves to go and answer it. Lily stood to let him pass then followed him, taking Hampshire with her.

'Hello?...Oh hello, Reuben...Yes, not bad, you know... I'll see if she's around but, you know, can't guarantee she'll take the call...'

Unaware that Lily had followed him, Kumar was surprised to find her at the door. 'It's your dad.'

Lily cautiously walked into the office, as her uncle went in search of her mother. She picked up the phone and listened. She could hear her father's breathing.

'Daddy?'

'Is that you, Lily?'

'Yes.'

'Did mummy put you on?'

'No, Uncle Kumar has gone to get her.'

'How are you, my little tiger lily? Do you miss me?'

Suddenly Lily felt she did miss him. 'Yes.'

'Would you like me to come and see you?'

'Here?'

'Yes.'

'I would like that.'

Flora came into the room and Lily slowly handed her the receiver.

'Reuben.' Flora kept her eyes on Lily as she listened.

'I don't know if that's a good idea...Well, you've never shown much interest before...Fine. I have to go now.'

Flora put the receiver down without saying 'goodbye'. Lily looked at her expectantly.

'Daddy wants to visit,' Flora said.

*

On being told of her father's visit, Lily immediately started making preparations, drawing a number of pictures outlining her activities over the past few weeks, real and imagined, all involving Hampshire. She drew a series of family portraits involving the three of them in various scenarios, again with Hampshire, whom she was certain her father would take to as he had a fondness for dogs. With her mother's help she made some butter cake, which she also iced. She began to think that it was just the location that had been the problem - the flat in Colombo that never felt cosy, the flat in London that always felt spooky. If they could live here, with everyone else, they would be safe and happy.

On the Friday night before his visit, Lily presented her mother with a list of possible activities they could do with her father.

'Let's see what happens, darling,' Flora said.

Lily woke at 7am on Saturday. She had been told that her father would be taking the eight o'clock train and she imagined him taking the bus to the station. She was impatient to see him and to show him their nice life.

At nine, the surgery telephone rang. She followed her uncle as he went to answer it.

'Hello...Oh...Right, I see... Do you want to speak to Flora?...Oh, right. The little one's here. Do you want to speak to her? She's been looking forward to your visit.' Kumar passed the phone to Lily. 'It's your dad.'

'Daddy, are you here already?'

'No, sweetheart. I'm so sorry, I won't be coming today. I'm sick.'

'But I was going to show you Hampshire,' Lily said, as she felt disappointment surge over her.

'I'll come and see you very soon, I promise. I'm really sad that I won't be seeing you.'

Lily was unable to speak. She put the receiver down on the table and ran upstairs to sob into her pillow.

Her father did not call again that week, or the next, but she kept the pictures carefully, so they would be ready for when he did eventually visit.

*

Lily watched Vinod and Veena wolf down their eggs. It was the first day of the summer holidays and she was looking forward to spending more time with them. Over the past few weeks she had waited excitedly for them at the front door to greet them from school each day, joining them at the kitchen table for tiffin and milk and watching them as they did their piano practice. When they played cricket in the garden she would field for them, self-conscious of her throwing, but happy to participate. Sometimes Veena even braided her hair or played snap with her.

Her cousins soon finished their breakfast and after piling their dishes in the sink, disappeared. Lily desperately blew on her milk to cool it, so she could down it and find them. After finally finishing, she wandered upstairs to their bedroom. They were not there so she traipsed around the house in search of them. She found her mother ironing and her aunt searching for stamps, but no sign of the twins.

Lily tried their room again, searching under their beds and in their wardrobes but they were not to be found. She went back out onto the landing, where she could hear laughing. Nervously, she went into her aunt and uncle's bedroom, then the bathroom and finally the room she shared with her mother. When she returned to the landing, she heard the giggling again. It was only then that she noticed a ladder, which led to an opening in the ceiling.

'Veena *acca*?'

The giggling continued. Tentatively she put a foot on the first rung. 'Are you up there?'

Lily climbed slowly, impeded by the ragdoll in her left hand. Eventually she reached the attic opening and peered around. Her cousins were playing draughts.

'*Acca*?'

Veena turned to look at Lily, then turned back to Vinod.

'This game is only for two players,' Vinod said without looking up from the board.

Lily remained on the ladder, unsure of what to do. She looked to her cousins for guidance, but they were absorbed in their game. She continued up another step, her stomach lurching with fear. She threw her doll into the attic and pulled herself up so that she was sitting on the edge, her legs dangling down. Her heart was racing. She clumsily hauled her legs up, hitting them on the frame, and went to join her cousins. They continued with their game.

She watched as they played, not fully grasping the rules. She wondered why they did not want to talk to her and what she might have done to upset them.

Eventually Vinod won. He stood up and flexed his muscles in victory, while Veena rolled her eyes.

'I'm going to get something to eat. You coming?' he asked Veena.

'OK.'

They both expertly descended the ladder, leaving Lily alone. She looked down, expecting Veena to wait for her and offer assistance, but instead she saw them gallop down the stairs. She looked around the attic, which was full of boxes, suitcases and cobwebs. The single light bulb was dim and flickered, creating sinister shadows. She sat at the edge of the loft opening and placed her right foot on a rung of the ladder. She was not sure what to do next. They had swung down onto it so quickly. She started to panic.

'Veena *acca*!' she called. After a moment she called again, louder, 'Veena!' She listened for movement. Nothing. This time she screamed, 'Mummy!' Panic had turned into exquisite fear.

Soon her mother was running up the stairs

towards her, then asking her to hold on to her tightly, as she descended the ladder. It was only as they reached the landing that Lily realised she had left her doll in the attic, but she said nothing.

*

Sunday afternoon was when Frieda and Kumar usually received guests. They seemed to know most of the Ceylonese families in the north west, who visited them on rotation, so that plans for a quiet snooze or stroll in the countryside were always scuppered by the doorbell as they washed the lunch dishes.

The children were only required to show their faces at the beginning and were then free to go. Depending on her cousins' moods, Lily would either join them for board games or cricket, or remain with the adults, half reading half listening to their conversations.

On one such occasion, when her cousins had quietly sloped off while an aunty held her cheeks for a prolonged period, Lily sat with a book by her mother's feet. She vaguely recognised these visitors but couldn't place them. She found the uncle's voice soothing as it reminded her of her grandfather's.

'Lily, why don't you go and play with *ana* and *acca*?' Lily was startled to hear her name as she had started to drift off, lethargic from the lunchtime rice. She knew there must be something they did not want her to hear as they were normally happy for her to be present.

She stood up and looked at the couple, who were smiling placidly at her. The lady's *thali*, hanging heavily around her neck, looked familiar.

'Do you remember it, darling?'

Lily looked at her mother.

'We went to Aunty Elsie and Uncle Theva's house for dinner, in London. Remember?'

She did and was now desperate to hear what they had to say, as they knew her father. She nodded and wondered if she could slowly sit down again without anyone noticing.

'You go and play, darling,' Frieda said insistently.

Lily slowly walked to the door, looking back at them. Once she had left the room, it was closed behind her. She stood with her ear against it. She didn't care if she was caught, she thought.

'You've seen him then?' her mother asked.

Lily held her breath, keen to take in every word.

'We went to see him before coming up here.'

'You knew about the situation?'

'Yes, he came to us the night you left.'

'*I* left? Did he tell you the full story?'

'Flora we're not blaming you,' Elsie said placatingly. 'We've known Reuben since he was a boy. We know what he's like. We're only sorry to see things turn out the way they have.'

'You know about this woman?' Flora asked.

'Yes, the baby is due in September,' Elsie replied.

'September! So he knew she was pregnant all along. That's why he called us over!' Flora sounded almost triumphant at this realisation. 'He's been lying from the beginning! I can't believe I didn't notice it that day. He thought we would provide an escape for him!'

There was a long silence. Lily felt her chest heaving. Though she didn't fully grasp all that had been said, she understood that her father had lied.

'Eavesdropping again?' Lily turned to find Vinod on the stairs.

She turned back, desperate to hear what they said next.

'You're like a little fly. Just a nuisance.' He came up behind her. 'Bzzz. You don't know how to do anything. Just hang around, listening and staring.' He started to pull her hair, a few strands at a time.

Lily turned suddenly and pushed him with all her strength. Taken by surprise, Vinod fell backwards into a side table, knocking over a jar of keys. As he regained his balance, Lily pushed open the door and ran into the living room, just as he surged forward towards her. For a few seconds everyone stared at one another, wondering what had happened, before Kumar escorted Vinod out of the room by the ear.

CHAPTER TWENTY

November 2006

I ris emptied the contents of the carrier bag onto her bed. She was annoyed at the way her grandmother had stuffed the letters into it, not bothering to order them. Containing her eagerness to read them, she first arranged them chronologically by postmark, noting that some had been sent from America.

She was astonished by the quantity, counting 62 separate items. Her father had written to her every other day for the first couple of weeks after his departure, then weekly for several months, dropping to fortnightly then monthly. There were exceptions, when he sent postcards or packages of sweets and stickers outside of his regular schedule. His last letter had arrived just before her grandmother's stroke, which meant the next was overdue, perhaps because he would be sending a parcel for her ninth birthday.

Iris still couldn't comprehend why her grandmother had said nothing when they received the postcard that summer, keeping quiet when she had said that it showed her father didn't love them if that was all he could be bothered to send in two years. Her bizarre determination to get to the post first, even when she was poorly, now made sense.

When she was satisfied they were in the right order, Iris picked up the first letter. She was irritated to find it had already been opened. She picked up the next one and turned it over – to her relief it was still sealed. She did not think she could have contained her fury at her grandmother if she had found them all open.

Iris took a deep breath and unfolded the flimsy piece of note paper. It didn't explain why her father had left but was full of love. She wondered why her grandmother thought it would be better for her not to see that her father loved her. The letter also said he would call. On the rare occasions that Iris answered the phone, usually when Flora was in the bathroom, she would always hope that it was him. It never was.

The next few letters were on the same sort of paper, followed by a stint on thick pastel letter writing paper. When he had finished that set, the next few arrived on a mix of postcards and paper ripped from a note book, before resuming on writing paper, this time decorated with Snoopy and Woodstock. Some of the parcels had been sent by recorded delivery, which her grandmother had no doubt signed for.

Iris was overwhelmed by her father's persistence, even when it must have seemed like she was ignoring him. In nearly all the letters he had closed by saying that she must be very busy with school but when she had a moment he'd love to hear from her. She found it hard not to cry each time she read it.

A favourite subject was You the cat. She giggled as her father described how he and her uncle had tried to cure her of hiccups by trying to scare her. Many of the letters featured sketches of You's exploits.

Iris was impressed with the obvious care her father had taken with his handwriting. Soon after he left, before it was turned into her grandmother's bedroom, she would go into his study and look at his things, picking up pens and books and paperweights. She would try and decipher the scribbled notes on his calendar. The writing in her letters was not a scrawl. Though by no means pretty, it was writ carefully and large to ensure she could read it.

She wanted to savour each letter. With the first few she had tried to remember what she had been doing at the time of writing, but she was also keen to get through them quickly so she could be up to speed with her father's movements. She resisted the urge to skip to the most recent ones, wanting to build up a picture of his life and movements chronologically. Once she had done this, she would write to him and, hopefully, meet him. She stopped herself when she caught her mind drifting. She had to be disciplined for progress to be made.

She took a handful of letters down to dinner and read them as she ate. She knew it was probably bad manners, but her mother said nothing. Iris did not join her in the living room to watch TV afterwards, but went back up to her bedroom and continued reading, even after her mother kissed her goodnight and switched off the landing light. In the course of her reading she had discovered a handful of items for her mother. There was one envelope that only had her name on it with no address, which perplexed Iris. She was curious to read it but restrained herself. She would pass them on in the morning.

Among the packages were a paint set, various books - including an illustrated edition of Grimm's Fairytales and a boxed set of The Chronicles of Narnia (all things she had since read), a small telescope, vouchers, stickers, keyrings, pens, soft toys, a gold bracelet and several packets of sweets, some of which were now out of date. What she appreciated most were the occasional photos of her father, nearly all accompanied by the cat. He looked kind, she thought.

Not like a bad father at all.

Her mother had said her grandmother had probably been trying to protect them from getting hurt, but Iris wondered how she could have got it so wrong. Adults were supposed to know exactly what to do, especially those as old as her grandmother. She had picked up bits of information throughout the years about her grandfather. He had abandoned them, and her father's behaviour probably reminded her grandmother of him. But Iris was not yet ready to forgive her. She didn't feel she could let her off the hook so quickly when she had let them suffer for so long.

Iris was startled by a knock on her bedroom door. She glanced at her alarm clock, it was 1.34am. Lily pushed open the door and walked over to the bed.

'Sweetheart, I know you want to get through them all but you need to sleep now.'

'I need to know what they say, so I know what to write to him.'

Her mother sat on the bed.

'If you're too tired tomorrow you won't be in the mood to write anyway. Plus there's the small matter of school.'

'Does grandma hate daddy because of what grandpa did?'

'I don't think she hates him. She just didn't want us to get hurt anymore.'

'But this hurts...Things might have been different, I mean, if we knew he loved us?'

'I don't know.'

'Why did he leave? He doesn't say.'

'Irie, now's not the time. It's past 1.30.'

'Please tell me.'

Lily looked up at the ceiling. 'There was a woman at the university. They had a...relationship. It didn't last long but he felt it would be better for him to leave. So he did.'

At first, Iris did not understand what her mother was saying, but as the words became clear she felt as if her chest had caved in.

She slid down beneath the bedcovers, causing letters to cascade to the floor. Lily kissed the top of her head, which was still visible.

'I'm so sorry, darling... Do you want me to stay with you?'

Iris shook her head. Her mother stroked her hair, then eventually she felt the mattress spring up as she stood. She listened for the sound of the door closing and her mother's bedside lamp being switched off, which didn't happen for some minutes. What her mother said made sense. She had even thought about it as a possibility once or twice, before firmly rejecting it. The man of her letters gave no hint of this betrayal, she thought, as hot tears streamed down her face.

*

Iris took her seat at the front of the class. She had lost her treasured window seat in a recent reshuffle. Now she felt exposed, especially since becoming the preferred target of abuse of the class bully.

Prior to this, Iris had managed to get through her school life unnoticed by most of her peers, even when she was moved up a year, but then she was offered the role of Dorothy in the school's Christmas production of *The Wizard of Oz*. The classmate in question, Sky 'Psycho' Lacey, had been given a non-specific role in the chorus and had asked to swap. When Iris refused, Sky commenced a campaign of petty annoyance.

'Have you got nits?' Sky asked, as she peered at Iris's scalp.

Iris said nothing.

'Something's moving in your hair. You need to get that sorted so we don't catch nothing off you.'

Iris sighed and opened up her reading book.

'I'm trying to help. No need to be rude.' Iris felt pressure on the back of her head, before Sky strode to the back of the classroom to gasps and laughing.

Iris tentatively reached back. Her fingers landed on the still warm chewing gum that Sky had pressed into her hair. Rage and disgust flared up in her chest as she desperately tried to pull out the sticky mess.

'Put your head in the freezer - that's supposed to get it out,' Sky offered from the back of the room.

'What's so hilarious?' Mr Faraday, their teacher, asked wearily as he walked into the classroom.

'A nit's just laid a giant egg on Iris's head!'

'Alright, enough of that. Settle down.'

Iris started to pack away her belongings, confident that her teacher would not notice, even though she was directly in front of him. He had been given the name Mr Faraway for his tendency to stare out of the window even while teaching. After taking the register, he stood and started writing on the whiteboard.

While his back was turned, Iris got up and walked quietly out of the classroom. She would have liked to shove the chewing gum onto Sky's forehead, then throw her out the window, but even Mr Faraway would have noticed that.

Iris wondered how long it would be before anyone said anything. She wasn't sure if any of her classmates had even noticed her departure. She continued down the empty corridor to the reception, remembering the last time she had been summoned out of class, just weeks ago. It thrilled her to be alone in the silent passageway, not contained behind closed doors, like the rest of her peers. She carefully opened the main door, grateful the receptionist was away from her post. Once outside, her pace quickened as she crossed the playground, until she was running. She pushed open the school gate, which should have been electronically locked but had been faulty for weeks. She had always thought misbehaviour required a lot of effort, so couldn't believe how easy this was.

After her grandmother's accident, Iris had been given a house key. For the past fortnight she had been letting herself in, waiting alone until her mother returned from work. Lily had reluctantly agreed to this after a short-lived arrangement with one of the mothers from church. Iris had complained of being 'forced to watch baby programmes' with her younger twins, and being unable to concentrate on her homework because of their 'constant whining'.

Though Iris had got used to being in the house alone, it felt odd in the middle of the day. She poured herself some squash and found a packet of crisps before making her way up to her bedroom. She was keen to change out of her school clothes as they somehow added to the sense of strangeness.

She then tried to extricate the stringy remains of the gum, which were now stubbornly entwined with her hair. Their location at the back of her head made them difficult to locate in the bathroom mirror, added to the infuriating nature of the task. Her arms started to ache with the effort. She walked to her grandmother's room and rummaged around her sewing drawer, not caring about disturbing its orderliness. She returned to the bathroom with a pair of dressmaking scissors that her grandmother would have scolded her for using.

With some effort Iris managed to remove the offending gum, but cut more hair than she intended. It would give Psycho Lacey another reason to mock her. She threw the thick chewing gum-laced lock into the bathroom bin, returned the scissors and went back to her bedroom.

Before she could resume reading, she had to reorder the letters she'd displaced from her bed the night before. She wanted to see if her father gave any hints of what he'd done or explanations for his behaviour.

Half an hour later the phone rang. Iris thought on balance it was better to ignore it, as well as the five subsequent calls. Eventually she heard her mother's key in the door.

'Iris?' Lily's voice was anxious more than angry.

'Yeah,' Iris answered quietly. She heard Lily's footsteps on the stairs, noting that she hadn't paused to remove her shoes. Her bedroom door was pushed open. She braced herself for a tirade.

'Thank God. Why did you do that, Iris? I was so worried.'

Iris shrugged. Lily pulled off her shoes before entering the room, then perched herself on the bed by Iris.

'I know you've been through a lot, but I didn't know-'

'Would you have taken him back, mummy? If you had known about these letters?' Iris interrupted.

'I don't know.'

'Everything would have been so different.'

'There's no point thinking like that. Grandma did what she thought was best. She made a mistake. Things are as they are. That's all.'

Iris wanted her mother to ask her why she had walked out of school. She wanted to pour out everything she had been holding in. Instead, Lily got up and walked towards the door.

'Are you going to send me back to school?'

'No,' her mother said, then picked up her shoes and went back downstairs.

Iris got up and closed the door before continuing to plough through the letters. She was now wary of her father's expressions of love. She was more interested in searching for clues - references to other people in his life. When he made a passing comment about an acquaintance, she would wonder if it was a woman and if this casual mention belied something deeper.

Her mother was quiet at lunchtime. She had seemed distracted for weeks, ever since the fire. Iris had excused her for not noticing her own subdued behaviour, aware that her mother had a lot to deal with, but was now annoyed at her lack of attention.

'I'm going to see grandma this afternoon,' Lily said as she cleared away the plates.

Iris said nothing.

'I feel sorry for her. I don't want her to feel...'

Lily sighed and made no attempt to complete the sentence.

While her mother was away, Iris continued reading through the afternoon, pausing now and then to daydream about a parallel life in which her father hadn't left them and was as attentive as his letters suggested.

By the time her mother returned, the house was dark around her, apart from the reading light. She heard her mother slip off her shoes, then the kettle being filled in the kitchen. She walked down to join her.

'You must be hungry, darling.'

'What did she say?'

'She kept asking about you. She understands you're hurt and hopes you'll forgive her. She was hoping you might visit her tomorrow, but I told her that might be too soon.'

Iris leaned on the counter.

'She loves you, darling.'

'I know.'

It was another sombre mealtime. Iris wanted to ask her mother about her father, but she seemed absorbed in her own thoughts. Neither of them turned on the radio.

After eating, Iris completed the last of her father's letters. She did not have the energy to write to him yet. She would draft something the next day. A sudden lurch of anxiety filled her chest at the thought of returning to school. She traipsed downstairs. Her mother was staring blankly at the television screen. A soap was on that she didn't usually watch.

Iris sat down next to her. She had decided to tell her mother about the problems she was having in class, in the hope that she might consider home schooling her.

Annoyingly, the phone started ringing and her mother rose to answer it. Iris turned down the volume on the television to try and ascertain whether it was worth eavesdropping in on the call. Her mother was quiet, listening to the other person, but when she spoke Iris could tell from her tone that something was wrong. She turned off the television and went into the hallway. Her mother's expression was identical to the one she'd seen in the school reception on the day of the fire.

'Has something happened to grandma?' Iris asked as soon as Lily put down the receiver.

She nodded. 'Get your jacket, we have to go.'

CHAPTER TWENTY-ONE

October 1960

L ily scanned the dining hall for a suitable seat. A stern-browed dinner lady pointed to a spot she had dismissed, surrounded as it was by a group of older boys.

'Well, go on!' the dinner lady insisted when Lily hesitated.

The boys, who had been laughing, stopped and watched her as she reluctantly sat down at the end of the bench.

'What's that smell?' one of them asked and the others sniggered.

Lily kept her eyes down as she opened her lunchbox. Her mother had made fish cutlets, her favourite, but she was in no mood for them. Wanting to finish her meal as quickly as possible she took an uncharacteristically large bite.

She was familiar with this feeling. She had noticed people staring at her and her mother when they travelled by bus and walked down the street. She would try to decipher their mutters, confused by their hostility. What had they done to upset these strangers? Did they really just hate their dark skin?

'What's that?' the boy asked.

'Is it a scotch egg?' another responded.

Lily continued chewing as the boys craned their necks towards her. She wished she could eat faster, but had always been slow.

'What are you eating?' the first boy said condescendingly slowly, bringing his hand to his mouth in an eating gesture. 'English. Do you understand English?' The others cackled.

Lily looked pleadingly in the direction of the surly dinner lady, but her attention was elsewhere. The boy opposite her, the ringleader, used the opportunity to snatch her lunchbox. He grabbed a cutlet and sniffed it. 'Dunno what it is.'

He passed it to another who also smelled it, before another seized it and took a bite. 'Urgh, it's disgusting!'

Lily put her hand up, hoping desperately for the dinner lady to look in her direction, finally calling out 'Miss!'

'Mi-iss!' the boys mimicked her.

One of them took the remaining cutlet from

the lunchbox and threw it in the air. They laughed hysterically as it landed, squashed on the floor.

Lily grabbed the lunchbox and fled, to the sound of their squeals behind her. 'Where's she going? She didn't finish her lunch,' she heard one of them say.

She ran to her classroom, hoping no teacher would be around to shoo her away. Her usual practice was to go to the school library after lunch but she was in no mood to face any-one, not even the other unassuming children who also sought solace in its shelves. She, like them, had been glad to discover the scantily resourced room, which offered respite from the playground despite its limitations. It was unfor-tunately closed during the other breaks, so Lily would take her time putting on her coat and mittens, then take a leisurely stroll to the play-ground, while others raced ahead. She would then hover around the assembly line so she was first in queue at the bell, thus minimising the time spent standing alone in the cold.

Lily had been attending Grayford Primary school for a month and wondered how long she would have to endure its misery before they re-turned to the comfort of Ceylon. She had asked her mother repeatedly, but was yet to receive an adequate answer.

They had moved out of her aunt and uncle's house shortly before she started at the school.

She was not sure exactly why they had left, but her mother had announced they were moving after an argument with her aunt, which Lily had only partially overheard.

A fortnight later they had moved into a terraced house a thirty-minute bus ride away, crammed with fellow Ceylonese. They had a bedroom to themselves with a gas hob and sink, but shared a bathroom with the six other occupants – one young couple, the rest single men. The house was gloomy and cold, worse than the London flat, with creaking floorboards and damp walls. Lily couldn't understand why her mother had brought them to such a place.

As she sat in a corner of her classroom, hugging her knees for warmth and comfort, Lily sobbed at her situation: the stupid boys, the horrid house, her faraway father. To be happy again, to feel safe, seemed an impossible hope.

'Why are you crying?'

Lily looked up. A girl, with the orangest hair she'd ever seen, was watching her with interest. She stopped crying abruptly, embarrassed to have been caught like that.

The girl's accent was different to the other children's. It sounded more like the voices she'd heard in London. She got up from her chair, walked over to Lily and stretched out her right hand. 'I'm Elizabeth Bairstow. I'm new. You can call me Lizzy.'

Lily, unrehearsed in the art of handshaking,

took Lizzy's hand with her left, 'I'm Lily.'

'Nice to meet you, Lily. We're almost name twins.'

*

'Mummy, I made a friend today! She's called Lizzy, which is short for Elizabeth, like the queen and she's from London.'

'Really, darling? That's wonderful. I told you you would.'

Lily could tell her mother was distracted. She was walking briskly and Lily was finding it difficult to keep up. Flora had started a new job that week, providing reception cover at a surgery in the neighbouring town. Before leaving Frieda's, Flora had surreptitiously asked Kumar for contacts who might have work for her. He had wearily given her a list, advising her on those most likely to be fruitful. 'It's only because I know you're stubborn like your sister that I'm giving you this,' he had said.

As they turned the corner to their street, Flora started running. 'Mr Biggindale!'

Lily found it difficult to keep pace with her mother, who had been a keen sprinter in her youth, and stumbled, grazing her knee. Flora stopped and pulled her up by the wrist.

'Mr Biggindale, please, just a minute!'

The man she was pursuing turned and stared at them indifferently.

'I have the rent. I couldn't get back any

sooner.'

The man remained where he was, waiting for them to reach him. Flora took her time as she walked towards him, Lily limping beside her, then handed him an envelope.

'I'm not a charity, Mrs Ratnam,' he said, mispronouncing their surname in a way that made Flora wince. 'The very least I expect is that you pay your rent on time.'

Flora was silent but Lily could feel her fury in her tightening grip. Mr Biggindale looked down at her, then again at Flora, before turning and continuing on his way.

'Stupid little man,' Flora said, not quite under her breath. Once inside the house, she washed Lily's knee in silence, then tied a scarf around it.

As she finished, there was a knock on the bedroom door.

'Who is it?'

'*Acca*, can we borrow some sugar? I'll buy you some tomorrow.'

It was one of the other tenants, Ashwin, a friendly rotund young man. Unlike the others, he spoke to them in English. Flora opened the door without a word, then went to find the sugar. Ashwin timidly stepped inside.

'*Aiyo*, bubba. Why are you so sad?'

Lily smiled. She was always grateful for friendly conversation.

'That's better. What happened to your leg? Did you get into a fight?' Ashwin came and sat next to Lily on the bed that also functioned as a sofa and dining table.

'No!' Lily answered, incredulous that he could make such an assumption.

'Here's the sugar,' Flora said. Her tone made Ashwin stand up immediately.

'Thanks, *acca.*' He retreated backwards out of the room, bumping into their clothes horse on the way out, which made Lily giggle. Ashwin smiled, then closed the door behind him.

'Darling, I don't want you talking to anyone if I'm not around, do you understand?'

'Yes, mummy.'

The prospect of her mother not being around terrified Lily, but she felt it best not to raise this at the present time.

They ate their meal of fried rice and egg, curled up on the bed. It was the place Lily felt safest, though this was only relative to everywhere else which seemed actively dangerous.

Flora had decorated the room as best she could. Kumar had stopped by Reuben's flat on a trip to London and collected the remainder of her belongings. The bedspread was one she had brought over from Ceylon to remind her of home, its oranges and reds bringing some warmth to the dreary surroundings. She had draped a mustard coloured sari on one of the walls, saying that her mother would never have approved of such frivolous use of clothing. Lily's eyes would trace its embroidered patterns as she lay in bed, waiting for sleep.

They had fallen into a sad routine. After collecting Lily from school, Flora would give her milk and a biscuit, then cook a simple meal on the hob, which they would eat while listening to the radio. Afterwards, Flora would sew while Lily read. After prayers, Lily would lie awake, listening to the sound of her mother's pen busily updating her journal or writing letters home. On occasions her mother would let out a deep sigh that ended with almost silent weeping. At such times Lily found it impossible to suppress her own tears, but tried to make them fall as quietly as her mother's.

'We won't be here for very long, darling,' her mother would tell her. 'Just a little while, then things will be well again.'

As it was a Friday evening, Lily was allowed to stay up a little later and they played snap and solitaire. It was her favourite time of the week as it had the longest gap between having to go to school, which was even worse than being in the house, though the arrival of Lizzy was an encouraging development.

What she dreaded most about the house was the bathroom. By day its filth was evident: alarming stains on the bath, sink and toilet seat, which Flora had tried in vain to scrub away, as well as rampant mould creeping up the walls. They had invested in a bucket which they used to wash themselves as they stood in the bath, rubber slippers on, unwilling for their skin to come into contact with any of its surfaces. Lily found it worse at night, despite the grime being less visible. The flickering light bulb would occasionally cut out completely, leaving them in deep, smothering darkness, before coming back on again after several seconds. The landing light had been fused since they arrived, so they used a torch to climb the stairs, which created eerie shadows on the walls, adding to the horror of it all. It reminded Lily of her experience in her aunt and uncle's attic.

Early on, Flora and Lily had learnt to control their fluid intake in the evenings to avoid the need for excursions upstairs in the middle of the night. Lily adopted the same approach during the day, having discovered the school facilities were just as grim.

Flora walked closely behind Lily, one hand on her shoulder, the other holding the torch, as they briskly made their way up for their final bathroom visit of the day. Low murmuring came from one of the rooms, followed by laughter, which Lily found threatening like that of the boys at lunchtime. A rhythmic creaking sound came from the young couple's room.

'Friend, have some consideration for your brothers,' a man called out in Tamil, from the room with the laughing. Lily turned to Flora for an explanation, but she was looking straight ahead, pushing on towards the bathroom.

After they had washed their faces, both Lily and Flora examined their reflections in the speckled mirror. Their eyes were hidden by shadows.

As they shuffled out of the bathroom, they were startled by a figure waiting on the dark landing. They couldn't make out the face, only the cigarette smoke escaping from his mouth and nostrils. As Flora herded Lily down the stairs, they could feel him watching them.

*

Flora never let Lily lie in past eight o'clock at weekends, keen to complete all morning ablutions before the men woke from their drunken stupors. Then, after washing and hanging out their clothes - apart from underwear, which was always dried indoors - they would do the grocery shopping.

Lily found the friendly people were friendlier than those in London, but there were also proportionally more unfriendly ones than those who just ignored them. She had also noticed that her mother's pace had quickened in England. It was only on their weekend excursions into the nearby country lanes that she slowed down and her grip was less tight. Even in church, they would leave immediately after the benediction, scurrying back to the bedsit for a lonely lunch.

As they walked back to the house, having completed their Saturday morning errands, Lily could see someone standing by the front door. It was her aunt Frieda, recognisable by her red coat which stood out against the gloomy backdrop of the house, and in fact everything else around it.

'Flora, come back. You can't live like this,' she said while they were still a few paces away.

'We can't impose on you any longer,' Flora said as she walked past her to unlock the front door. Lily noticed her aunt's worried expression as her mother then struggled to unlock the stiff padlock on their bedroom door.

'It's quite a good size,' Flora said as they entered. 'It's the biggest room in the house.'

'Come back. I didn't mean for you to leave.'

Lily looked at Flora hopefully. After being left in the attic by her cousins she had felt less comfortable in the house, but would rather put up with that than the current arrangement.

'You were right though - I shouldn't get too comfortable and hide. I need to make a decision about what to do. This will help clarify things.'

'You can stay with us until you make that decision,' Frieda said as she sat down on the bed. 'Have you heard from Reuben?'

Flora started filling the kettle. 'Tea?'

'Come home with me and at least spend the weekend with us.'

'Can we, mummy?' Lily asked.

'Think about your daughter, Flo.'

Flora turned sharply.

'Do you think I haven't been thinking about

her? Do you think this is what I want for her? Is it my fault that we're in this mess?'

'Flora, you know that's not what I meant.'

'You keep judging me, Frieda, when it's Reuben who's responsible for this.'

'Why do you have to be so dramatic? I'm trying to help,' Frieda said, standing.

'I'm grateful to you and Kumar for putting up with us for as long as you did. As soon as I'm able to, I will recompense you.'

'Flora!'

'I have to do some things now, so please can you make sure the front door is properly shut when you leave.'

On her way out, Frieda stroked the side of Lily's face. They heard her slam the front door behind her.

'After lunch we'll go for a nice walk. You'll like that won't you, darling?'

Lily let her tears fall silently.

*

By the time Monday morning came round, Lily's excitement at the prospect of seeing her new friend had dissipated. A sense of dread had enveloped her and she feared her misery would never end now that her mother had upset her aunt, and her father had disappeared from their lives. Flora had tried to cheer her with promises of sweets and trips to the seaside, none of which had any impact whatsoever.

'This evening, let's make a rag doll. That will be nice won't it, darling? We can sew some dresses for her,' Flora said as they approached the school gates.

'I don't want a doll, mummy. I want to go home,' Lily said, before walking off without a goodbye kiss.

'You look sad, what's wrong?' Lizzy Bairstow asked her at break time, as they walked to a corner of the playground to stand in the sleeting rain.

'I hate it here,' Lily said. 'I hate everything about it. I want to go home.'

'Do you hate me?'

Lily looked at her. 'No.'

'Well you don't hate everything then, do you?' Lizzy took her by the hand and started running. As they ran around the perimeter of the playground, Lily felt a sense of exhilaration that she had never experienced before.

'We're eagles!' Lizzy cried.

At lunchtime they sat together, sampling each other's food and assigning nicknames to all the dinner ladies and classmates who annoyed them most. Afterwards, they sat in a corner of the library, taking it in turns to read pages from their favourite books, as quietly as possible, in between being shushed by the duty teacher.

When Flora came to collect her, Lily was buzzing with excitement.

'Have you had a good day, darling?' Lily nodded, but before she could say anything, Flora continued. 'I'm glad. See, I told you things would get better. Darling, I have to go back to the surgery to do a few things for Dr Kitchener. I won't be long, I promise, but I need to leave you for a little while.'

'Leave me? On my own?'

'Just for an hour or so. You can snuggle up in bed. Just don't answer the door to anyone and I'll be back before you know it.'

When they reached their room, Lily watched anxiously as Flora warmed the milk for her.

'Do you need the toilet?'

Lily shook her head.

'Don't answer the door to anyone. Don't even say anything. Just wait quietly. Go to sleep if you can and soon I'll be home.'

'Not even Ashwin *ana*?'

'No. He can come back if he needs to. Alright, darling. After I go out, bolt the door. I will say it's me when I come back. Use the chair so you can reach it.'

Flora kissed her on the forehead, then shut the door behind her. 'Bolt it, darling,' she said from the other side.

Lily climbed onto their solitary wooden chair and reached up to bolt the door. Her mother had asked Ashwin to fix an extra bolt to complement the small one, which he had fixed at his eye level – approximately six feet from the ground.

Lily waited for a moment, listening as her mother opened and closed the main door, before alighting the chair and crawling into bed. She switched on the radio for the comfort of the voices, not taking in anything they said as she solemnly munched biscuits.

As she began to drift into comfortable sleep, she was disturbed by two quick knocks at the door. She froze. After a short pause, there were another two impatient knocks.

'Open the door.'

The voice sounded like it belonged to one of the men from upstairs, though she couldn't tell which one, only that it wasn't Ashwin. This one was gruff and angry. The radio volume was already low, but she turned it lower, her heart racing. The door knob turned and she could see the door straining against the bolts. She got up and rushed to the window. She pulled up the handle, remembering that her mother had struggled to open it before. She was relieved when it opened and sat up on the windowsill. She watched the door to see if it would give way, ready to jump out onto the street if it did.

Eventually the door stopped moving. After watching five minutes take a lifetime to pass by on the wall clock, Lily got down from the windowsill. She dragged the chair and placed it back by the door, adding also the clothes horse. She found a paring knife by the hob and returned to bed with it, grasping it firmly in one hand, with the torch in the other. Thus armed, she prayed for her mother's speedy return.

It was a quarter past five when she heard the front door open. Her grip on the knife tightened until she recognised her mother's footsteps.

'Darling? It's me.'

Lily sombrely stood on the chair and unlocked the door.

'Darling, why's the window open?' Flora asked cautiously, before noticing the knife in Lily's hand.

'A man tried to open the door and I was getting ready to escape. I couldn't shut it.'

The next day when Flora had to work late again at the surgery, she took Lily with her.

CHAPTER TWENTY-TWO

July 1951 – February 2005

Frieda dug her toes into the baking sand and closed her eyes. They had found a shady spot on Hendala beach, but she had slid forward so that her feet could be warmed by the sun. It was a sensation she had enjoyed from childhood, though the rest of her body couldn't tolerate it. As she drifted into sleep, she felt a sharp kick from within her belly, followed by another and another.

'Doc, your children are already keeping me awake. I blame you.'

Kumar removed the handkerchief covering his face and turned to Frieda.

'It's my fault is it?'

'Who else?'

Kumar had been the first proposal Frieda received. She was twenty-three at the time and had been called into the sitting room where her mother, father and aunt Rani were waiting, all clearly nervous about raising the matter. She was told that he was a doctor with excellent prospects. Both parents were lay preachers. Her aunt had said excitedly that she may even get to live in England or America, a possibility that had terrified Frieda at the time. She had been furnished with a photograph of a man with thinning hair but a friendly smile, who looked at least a decade older than his thirty years.

She had said nothing, but returned to her room and cried vigorously, wondering how her parents could do such a thing to her. Her mother had come to the door and whispered, 'Just meet him, Frieda. See what he's like. He may be a good man.'

To her surprise, Frieda found her mother was right. She had been disarmed by Kumar's kindness and modesty, and decided that yes she could love him. Her only condition had been that they remained in Ceylon for at least two years, before taking off to any foreign lands. This would give them the opportunity to get used to each other somewhere familiar, before having to cope with other variables. Kumar had readily agreed.

Frieda eased herself up, assisted by Kumar, so that she was sitting. She looked towards the horizon, the gentle waves sparkling as they caught the late afternoon sun. Once the twins were born, they would start preparing for the move to England. She wanted to absorb as much of the landscape as possible before they left.

'Can't we take it with us?'

'Mmm, what?'

'This. The sea, the beach, the breeze.'

'It's an island too, Fred. They have plenty of sea.'

She raised her eyebrows at him.

'It'll be slightly different, of course,' he relented.

Frieda scanned the beach, squinting. There were a few lounging families snacking on mangoes and patties, and skinny youths playing cricket, loudly contesting every ball. The main demographic on this Sunday afternoon, though, were promenading young couples. She fixed her eyes on one such pair walking on the edge of the shoreline. There was something about them that made them stand out.

'Oh look, it's Reuben and Flo,' Kumar said, raising his hand to wave, having also noticed them among the others.

'Leave it, Doc,' Frieda hissed.

Kumar sighed and slid back down onto their blanket to resume snoozing.

Frieda continued to watch them, embarrassed she hadn't recognised them. She was certain it was not their familiarity that had made them more noticeable. There was something about them that made them look different to everyone else. Perhaps it was their height. Their clothing was not particularly distinctive, but the way it hung on their bodies seemed somehow more modern than on the others, more glamorous even. While a few couples were daring to publicly hold hands, Reuben held Flora close to him, his hand resting on her hip. As they got closer, she could see he was laughing. Flora was smiling.

Frieda looked down and placed the handkerchief over Kumar's face again.

'What's going on?'

'Shhhh.'

Once they had walked past, Frieda struggled to her feet.

'Where are you going?'

'I'm going to see what they're up to. Did you see how he was holding her? Like she was a -'

'Careful, Fred.'

'If they're behaving like this in public, what are they getting up to when they're alone?'

'They're getting married, Frieda.'

'I don't trust him, Kumar.'

'*You* don't have to.'

*

March 1957

Frieda watched Reuben as he sat in a corner

of her parents' sitting room, reading a paper and smoking. At the other end of the room, Flora was serving ice cream into steel dessert bowls, while their mother placed them carefully, one by one, into the hands of a waiting crowd of expectant children. Their father was sitting in his armchair, Lily on his lap, reading from a picture book of Bible stories, which she had just received for her third birthday.

'You could make a bit more effort, Reuben. It's your daughter's birthday after all.'

'I'm here, aren't I,' he replied without looking up.

*

December 1959

'Mama, look! She's got no clothes on!'

'What?' Frieda had been trying to ascertain the level of flirtatiousness of a conversation taking place on the other side of the room, between Reuben and a niece of Theva and Elsie. She looked down at the double page spread of Titian's *Venus of Urbino.* 'Where did you get that book?'

'It was on the table.'

'Go and put it back. It's not for little boys.' Frieda looked up again. Reuben and the niece were nowhere to be seen.

'Doc, did you see where they went?'

'Who went?'

'Reuben and the girl.'

'What girl?'

Frieda sighed and made her way across the packed room of Ceylonese ex-pats towards the door. Theva and Elsie had been inviting them to their Christmas parties since they first arrived in England seven years earlier. They had been unwilling to make the journey down to London from Lancashire when the children were small, but had decided they would make the effort this year. They had also gone to a pantomime, *Cinderella,* which she had thought somewhat vulgar, then seen the lights on Regent Street and Oxford Street. That the trip offered Frieda an opportunity to check on Reuben was merely a coincidence. As she reached the hallway, she could see the front door was open. She headed towards it and stepped outside.

'Frieda, always a delight to have your company,' Reuben said as he lit a cigarette.

'Where's your friend?'

'Who?'

'The young girl with whom you were getting rather friendly.'

'Was I? Will you be reporting that to Flora?'

'I know what you're like.'

'I will in future refrain from talking to, or associating with, any women. Is that what you want? Or is it alright if they're ugly, because that would allow me to continue being harangued by you?'

Frieda sighed and went back inside.

'Sorry, Fred, that was un-gentlemanly,' Reuben called after her. 'You're a handsome woman. I'll happily stop talking to you.'

*

August 1960

Flora paced up and down the living room.

'How can a man show such a complete lack of self control?'

Frieda felt like she'd had the same conversation with Flora a thousand times, but knew she had to let her unburden.

'Flo, that's Reuben. That's what he's always been like, the only difference is that now he's been caught out.'

'And we're caught in the chaos.'

'You need to decide what you're going to do, Flo. The school term starts soon - what are you going to do with Lily?'

Flora sat down and shrugged.

'I know this is hard for you, but you need to make some decisions.'

'Reuben keeps talking about going to France. Says he'll meet us there.'

'You're not seriously contemplating that?'

'No...'

'You already know what I think you should do.'

'You want me to return to Colombo to face

the humiliation of my husband's adultery yet again?'

'You don't have to tell anyone! Anyway, what's the alternative? You can't stay here forever in limbo.'

'I realise that, Frieda. I'm grateful to you and Kumar for putting up with us.'

'I didn't mean that. I mean-'

'I realise we've relied on your hospitality for far too long.'

'You know I didn't mean that, Flora! You're welcome to stay here. I mean you can't just hide here forever, hoping your problems will go away. You need to make a decision at some point.'

'You're right. And I will. We'll be out of your hair as soon as possible.'

*

July 1985

Frieda looked over at Flora weeping, Lily's arms around her, trying to soothe her while her own tears fell. Between her and them, on the bed, was her father's body. She remembered him being so tall, filling rooms with his presence. He had diminished after being forced to take early retirement. By the time he joined them in England, he seemed to be half the size of the man she remembered. Grief, following the death of their mother, had consumed huge portions of him.

297

Now his shell looked so frail, so grey under the bed sheets. Not like her father at all.

*

February 2005

'Drink this, Fred. Come, open.'

'No, Flo. Can't.'

'Stop being so stubborn. This is good for you. How will you get better if you don't eat?'

'I miss him, Flo.'

Flora put down the bowl of *rasam* on Frieda's bedside table.

'Vinnie? Do you want me to call him? Ask him to come?'

'No, he and Shirley have just bought a house. They can't afford the airfare right now,' Frieda said, though it was not her son who had been uppermost in her thoughts. 'I'm sorry things didn't work out for Lily. I shouldn't have interfered.'

'Don't be silly. I asked for your help. You weren't to know what would happen.'

'I had such a happy marriage, Flo. Doc was such a good man. He put up with me.' Frieda stopped, worried she might break down, as she so often did lately, even though Kumar had passed away ten years earlier. 'I often wonder why you and Lily didn't...didn't get the happiness you deserved.'

'None of us deserve anything, Fred. And anyway, we did get it. It was just a different kind of happiness.'

CHAPTER
TWENTY-THREE

November 2006

The album lay open on Flora's lap. She had taken out a photograph to examine it more closely – one of herself and Reuben standing in front of his motorcycle, laughing. They had asked a passer-by to take it and the sea breeze had caught their hair the moment the shutter clicked. She brought the photo closer to her eyes, looking for traces of uncertainty in her expression.

She remembered that day, from the early weeks of their engagement. It was her first time riding a motorbike. Her mother had looked anxious as she watched them from the gate. Flora too had felt an underlying sense of guilt throughout the day, wondering if it was quite decent for a young woman to straddle such a vehicle. She had often felt a sense of unease with Reuben in those early days, aware that he was a man of the world, who knew and had experienced things that the other young men of her acquaintance had not. She would worry that she had allowed him to get too close, given too much of herself. But her misgivings were always overruled by longing.

Frieda had always been the more romantic of the two of them. Flora had thought of herself as sensible and had been cynical of the romances her sister loved to read. She would often wonder how she had allowed herself to become so strongly drawn to Reuben. She was not willing to accept that it was just his looks and charm. He had made her feel significant. She'd later seen him do this to others too, men and women. When he eventually discarded them for someone or something else, rather than be offended, they sought his attention again. She had read about research that claimed attractive people generally did better at life, were more likely to succeed, more likely to convince juries of their supposed innocence. She hated to think she had been so superficial.

Flora returned the photograph to the album, carefully placing it behind its cellophane veil, frustrated by her shaking hands. She quickly flicked through the following pages, peppered with people from a period she wanted to forget.

Though she had decided to forgive them, she did not want reminders of that time. She stopped when she reached a photograph of Reuben holding Lily as a baby. There were very few of just the two of them. Lily had been plump then, and Reuben was nuzzling her cheek as she smiled toothlessly. Flora removed the image and held it in front of her.

A knock at the door interrupted her thoughts.

'Hello, Flora. Is everything OK?' It was Jude, who she found to be less like her husband by the day.

Flora nodded, eager to return to her reminiscing.

'It's Kay's birthday. Her daughter's brought cake. Would you like me to bring you some?'

Flora shook her head.

'Are you sure?'

'Yes, I'm fine. Thank you,' Flora said, her voice gruff from lack of use. Jude nodded then closed the door behind him.

She continued through the album, pausing at a solemn group shot, taken at her father's sixtieth birthday party. Her family and neighbours stood around a table, at the centre of which was a large square cake. The only person smiling was Lily, four at the time. Flora's parents had defiantly insisted on going ahead with the celebration, even though the country was in the middle of the '58 riots. Reuben had sped through the dark streets on his motorcycle, with the lights off. She had held Lily tightly between them, uncertain of the wisdom of their venture, but Reuben had insisted.

That evening had been the first time she had seen him cry. He had received devastating news about a childhood playmate, Raj, the only son of his family's maid. Raj had been returning home from work when a mob had confronted him and demanded that he read from a Sinhala newspaper. When he was unable to, they had beaten him to death. His eight-year-old son had come out to look for him, concerned by the delay in his return. He had found an old man, a local shopkeeper, trying to pull out his father's body from an open drain at the side of the road.

Flora had told Reuben they need not go to the party, but he was adamant they should, as a gesture that they would not be cowed by what was being allowed to happen by the government.

The birthday party had been more like a wake than a celebration. Others spoke of atrocities they had witnessed or heard about, but they had found some comfort in sharing their grief and anger.

Flora kept flicking through, occasionally taking out photos to examine them more closely. She cried when she came to the last one she had of her mother, taken at the prayer meeting they had held the night before she left for England. At the time she had not noticed how thin her mother had become, too caught up in her own worries.

The UK photos were in a new album. She was surprised at how happy Lily looked in the early ones taken at Frieda's house. In most of them she was holding the dog that she had become so fond of. There was nothing from their time in the bedsit, though she remembered vividly the day they left. It had been a perversely bright December day. She had turned and stared at the house for some time, wanting to remember it, wanting to wallow for a moment in the horror that she would be free from.

A letter from her father had been their ticket out. She knew Frieda must have written to him, as she had never shared in her letters all the details of their circumstances. He had announced that he had sold the house and also their land in the north. He was planning to leave Ceylon for good and was due to arrive in England just before Christmas. His role now, he had said, was to look after them. His only regret was that he would be leaving his beloved wife alone, in the soil of a country he had come to hate.

Theva and Elsie had invited them to stay a few nights before going to meet her father's ship in Southampton. As they had journeyed by train through the crisp countryside, she had begun to feel the hope of the season. As children, she and Frieda had dreamt of Christmases in Europe, believing that log fires, snow-covered fields and winter coats were essential parts of the celebration, even though the original events had taken place in the Middle East.

Her only anxiety had been about seeing Reuben. In the end it had been a brief and awkward encounter, as she left Lily with him at the flat. The other woman, Amanda, had been there with the baby, confirming the end of their marriage. Even though she was aware of the situation by then, seeing it had still crushed her. As she descended the checkered steps, Reuben had accompanied her and whispered that he would sort it out, that the arrangement was temporary. If she didn't like the idea of France, perhaps they could go to America. She had walked away without turning back, ashamed at herself for wanting to believe him.

They had spent Christmas at Frieda's. It had been tense at first, until her father scolded them into reconciliation, for which she was grateful. Then in the new year, a house was found in a quiet road a few miles away. It was to be her home for the next thirty years.

Flora rifled through the album in search of one photo in particular. It was of Reuben and Lily, standing in front of a motorbike, just like the earlier picture from her courtship, except that while Reuben was smiling, Lily looked serious, scared. It was the last one she had of Reuben and it filled her with an acute pain that made her breathless.

He had come to visit them in the new house,

riding from London in the early morning on a colleague's bike. She had been unnerved when he phoned to announce his arrival, fearing he would bring chaos into their comfortable, ordered lives, just as he had done before. Yet she had looked forward to seeing him. Her father had not come out to greet him and had said that while she couldn't deny him access to Lily, she should have nothing more to do with him.

Reuben had insisted on the photograph, asking that she send him a copy, as he had none of Lily. It was the first time Lily had ridden alone with him. She had looked nervous, and when they returned from their trip to the frozen seaside, she was pale and ran to Flora crying. Despite that, she had been unwilling to let go of Reuben when he turned to leave and pleaded with him to return soon.

Flora too had been reluctant to see him leave, worried for his safety riding in the dark rain, which was getting heavier. She had wanted to ask him to call to confirm he'd arrived safely but had said nothing. A terrible fear had overcome her that evening and, unable to sleep, she had called the flat. The phone had kept ringing, unanswered even by the woman, so she had called Elsie and Theva, begging them to find out what had happened. They agreed to go in the morning, leaving Flora to a fitful night's sleep.

The next day they called her with the news of Reuben's accident.

Lily had not displayed much of a likeness to her father, but in this photo, despite the difference in their expressions, Flora could see a similarity. Both had sallow cheeks and sunken eyes. Reuben always had a sadness in his, she remembered, even when he was smiling.

Flora thought of his darkened eyelids as he lay in the hospital bed. Without hesitation she had rushed down to London with Lily, with her father's tacit agreement.

As she sat by his bedside with Lily, the other woman had stood in a corner of the room quietly weeping. Flora had pitied her but resented her presence, especially when she wanted to tell Reuben he was forgiven, that she knew he was sorry.

When Theva and Elsie invited the woman, Amanda, to join them as they prayed, she had stepped forward, but then retreated when they started singing from the Methodist hymnal of Flora's childhood. She had held Reuben's hand throughout, feeling every twinge. She was certain his grip had tightened when Theva read from 1 John, '*If we confess our sins, he is faithful and just to forgive us our sins, and to cleanse us from all unrighteousness.*' And then, in the middle of *Blessed Assurance*, she felt his hand loosen, suddenly heavy in hers, and he was gone.

She had sobbed uncontrollably in a way she only did when full of grief. She had cried for her parents and sister in the same way: unrestrained, wild. The only times in her life that she had let go of all inhibition. She had never thought it would end like that, in a foreign hospital on a dark February afternoon.

They did not see Amanda or the baby after the funeral. She made no claims on Reuben's estate, for which Flora was grateful, even though the sums concerned were modest. As a child Lily would occasionally ask about the boy, having been told by a tactless relative at the wake that he was her brother, but made no requests to see him. Flora would occasionally think of them, even imagining that she had passed them on the few trips she made to London. She wondered if Reuben's son looked like him.

That morning, in the early hours, Flora had dreamt of Reuben, and of Frieda and her parents. She knew of people who had reported dreaming of passed loved ones, before themselves passing on within a few days. There was not much time to put things right. She had to reconcile with Lily and Iris without delay.

She rose early and wrote to Carl, then called Lily, describing the dream and begging her to visit that day. Lily told her to forget about the dream but nevertheless agreed to come. Flora wondered if she recognised its significance.

*

Even though it was a cloudy day, because they were flickering, the fluorescent lights in the dining room had been switched off, so it was particularly gloomy.

Flora surveyed the room. Her fellow inmates were either deep in concentration as they attempted to feed themselves or stared blankly ahead as someone else fed them. She had no appetite, but felt thirsty. She tried to pour more water for herself, but the jug was too heavy for her. She looked up towards Jude, but he was busy talking to a pretty new care assistant. Flora sighed and worked her way through the bland lunch, as ever, uncertain of what it was. She wondered if her daughter would be willing to take her home. She couldn't bear to end her days here.

After lunch she was surprised to find Lily waiting by her bedroom door. She tried to stand, but immediately fell back into the wheelchair.

'I didn't expect you so soon. It's so good to see you, darling.'

'I left work early,' Lily said as she took over from the assistant in pushing Flora into her room.

'Darling, I don't have much time left. I need to put things right,' Flora said as Lily closed the door.

'Have they said you can leave?'

'No. I mean not much time left...in general.'

'Don't talk like that, mummy. You've been getting better.'

'I told you I dreamt of your father last night, and Frieda, and *uppa* and *umma*. The Lord is preparing me.'

'Iris walked out of school today.'

Flora gasped. 'It's my fault. I need to see her.'

'Give her time.'

'I don't have time!'

Lily turned to look out of the window. The wind was whipping up the fallen leaves.

'I wrote to Reuben. Told him what I did.'

'Reuben?'

'Did I say Reuben? I mean Carl.'

Lily was silent.

'I'm sorry, Lily. I've made so many mistakes.' Flora closed her eyes and held her hand to her mouth.

Lily walked over and bent down to embrace her. 'We all make mistakes, mummy.'

'Not as many as me. But the Lord has been kind to me. He gave me you and Iris.'

'Don't talk like this, mummy.'

'I'm sorry for what I put you through, darling. In that house, with your father...'

'Why are you bringing all this up now?'

Lily sat down on the bed next to her mother's chair and held Flora's hands in both of hers.

'That day, when daddy came to see you in the house. On the motorbike. Sometimes I think I should have told him not to come. Not until he'd sorted himself out, at least. It was foolishness getting you on the motorbike and...maybe he'd still be-'

'There's no point thinking like that, mummy.

What happened, happened. It wasn't your fault. I know you always meant the best for me.'

'Did I? If I did, we would have gone back to Frieda's, or maybe even back to Colombo. I would have listened to Frieda when she suggested proposals for you. My pride has always got in the way.'

'Your speech is much better now.'

'I don't know why I hid the letters. I suppose I wanted to punish him. And then, as time went on, I didn't know how to undo it.'

Lily stroked her mother's hands.

'Will Irie forgive me? Is she alright?'

'Of course she will.'

They sat in silence for a while.

'Why don't I put a cassette on?'

Lily got up and chose one from Flora's modest collection. They listened to Johnny Cash sing hymns until the sky darkened and Flora fell asleep. When she woke, Lily had put on her coat and was drawing the curtains.

'Are you going already?'

'It's nearly teatime for you. And for Iris.'

'You'll tell her that I love her so very much and that I'm so sorry?'

'Of course.' Lily planted a kiss on the top of Flora's head, while Flora gripped both her elbows.

'Can you visit tomorrow? With Iris? There's not much time left.'

'Stop saying that, mummy. I'll ask her, but I

don't know if she's ready. Shall I take you to the dining room?'

'Not yet. Just leave me by the door. Please ask Iris. Tell her I'm begging.'

Flora watched Lily walk down the bright corridor to the exit and continued looking even after she had gone. The carers' station was opposite her bedroom. She could hear them chatting. She could recognise Jude's voice, his Goan accent standing out, but couldn't make out what any of them were saying. There were occasional bouts of laughter. She wondered what they had to laugh about when they were surrounded by so much sadness and death.

She tried rolling her chair forward, to gain a better position to hear what they were saying, but was too weak to handle her own weight. She tried again and rolled forward a couple of feet, bringing her nearer to the door. She recognised Blink's voice, loud and clear above the others.

'...behaves like the Queen of Sheba but wets herself like the rest of 'em. Seriously - if she don't take the pads and then goes and has another accident, I'll kill 'er!'

Flora desperately tried to turn the wheelchair so she could return to her room. As she struggled, she was aware that someone was now standing in the doorway. She leaned heavily to the right, trying to manoeuvre. As she did so, she tipped the chair and herself to the ground.

CHAPTER
TWENTY-FOUR

December 1960 – No-vember 2006

The room was illuminated only by the glow of fairy lights on the sparsely decorated Christmas tree. Lily sat on the edge of the sofa, watching her father's friend Amanda feed Matthew, the new baby. Her father sat in an armchair, also watching, frowning in concentration. She was not used to spending time with him without her mother also present.

'Does she have to keep staring?' Amanda asked. Lily looked down.

'Sweetheart, do you want to play cards?'

Lily nodded. Reuben joined her on the settee and shook the cards out of their packet. 'Snap?'

She nodded again. Though the light was dim,

she could still make out the dark circles around her father's eyes.

'Don't play too loudly. He's just nodding off,' Amanda said.

No one had explained to Lily who Amanda was or why she was now living with her father, with her baby. She had been described only as his 'friend.' There were so many things Lily wanted to ask about the situation but didn't know how to.

Reuben dealt the cards and they started playing, quietly at first but their voices grew louder as they got more involved, until Amanda shushed them. They obliged for a while but were unable to control their volume, so she moodily took the baby into the bedroom.

'How's your mum? Is she happy?' Reuben asked, after Amanda had gone.

Lily shrugged.

'Does she talk about me?'

'Not really. Not to me.'

Reuben nodded. 'No, of course.'

Lily was unable to contain the question any longer, 'Aren't you going to live with us anymore?'

It took Reuben by surprise. 'Oh, tiger lily, yes of course. Things are difficult now. I have to...Amanda doesn't have anyone to help her with the baby, so I have to look after them.'

'But what about us?'

Reuben brushed the side of Lily's face with his

thumb. 'I'll sort something out, I promise.'

Amanda walked out of the bedroom. 'He's asleep.'

They ate a fish and chip supper in the kitchen, the radio filling the long gaps in conversation. Lily and Amanda regarded each other suspiciously, while Reuben occasionally attempted to throw in cheery comments. Lily scanned the kitchen for a clock, hoping desperately that it was nearly seven. She felt sad about leaving her father, but was not enjoying the visit. She wished the woman would go away.

'Lily, would you like to hold Matthew?' Reuben asked as he cleared away the newspaper wrappings. Lily glanced at Amanda, who was looking at her father in annoyance, then turned back to him and nodded.

She followed her father out of the kitchen, into the dimly lit bedroom. Though she had slept in it just a few months earlier, it lacked any sense of familiarity. They peered into Matthew's cot. He was a hefty baby, with low hanging cheeks and dark spiky hair. His eyes were closed. Reuben picked him up and passed him to Lily. His warmth reminded her of Hampshire the puppy.

'He likes the Christmas lights. Shall we take him out there?'

Lily walked slowly to the lounge. She found Matthew heavy but didn't like to say. As she made her way towards the settee, her foot slid under the edge of the rug. She tripped as she took the next step. Stumbling forward she landed on the floor, Matthew beneath her.

'Lily!'

Reuben pulled her up roughly by the arm and retrieved Matthew, who was now awake and crying.

Amanda rushed into the room. 'What happened?'

'Nothing. It was just an accident,' Reuben said, as he pacified the baby.

'Did she do something?'

Lily retreated to the furthest corner of the settee, rubbing her arm.

'Lily tripped on the rug. It's fine. Matthew's OK.'

'Why did you let her hold him?' Amanda grabbed the baby from Reuben.

'I'm sorry,' Lily said, sobbing.

Amanda looked at her disdainfully then went into the bedroom.

'I think I better take you back to your mum,' Reuben said.

'I didn't mean to drop him, daddy.'

'I know, sweetheart.'

As they walked back through the quiet streets, Reuben pointed out Christmas trees in front windows. Lily looked up obligingly, but felt miserable. As they reached Theva and Elsie's house, he crouched down so he was at her level. 'Lily, I know I've not been a very good father to you. But even if I can't see you very often, it doesn't mean I don't love you. Will you remember that?'

*

February 1961

Lily was unsure of her father's idea to go all the way to the seaside by motorbike. She had never ridden with him without her mother there to hold her. Back in Colombo she had felt secure on the bike, snug between them, protected from the dangers that surrounded. But that was a long time ago; now she would be exposed. She could tell from her mother's expression, as she waved goodbye, that she was worried too.

Her grandfather did not come out of the house, but had prayed for her before her father arrived, his hand on her head.

Though she felt a little shy to begin with, Lily held on to her father tightly, holding her breath as he weaved through traffic. She tried closing her eyes but found it made her feel nauseous, so instead buried her head in his back, feeling his warmth through the worn leather jacket.

It drizzled throughout the journey and though her mother had made Lily wear an anorak on top of her woollen coat, neither protected her legs, so her trousers were soaked by the time they arrived at the seaside. She was grateful to take her father's warm hand as they walked along the promenade.

'Not quite Bentota is it, sweetheart?'

The rain got heavier as they walked, but Lily was grateful to no longer be on the bike.

'Let's get some lunch. And how about some ice cream?' Reuben tried to sound enthusiastic.

They found a deserted cafe along the seafront. The owner, grateful for their patronage, gave Lily an extra scoop of ice cream, which she passed to Reuben, having not fully got rid of the cold in her from the journey. Her father had asked her about school and told her about Matthew the baby, but now they were silent, staring at the turbulent sea.

'I'm sorry, Lily,' Reuben said suddenly.

'It's alright, daddy. It's not your fault it's raining.'

'No, I meant…It's OK.'

Reuben looked up. A middle-aged couple had appeared by their table.

'If you're finished, can you vacate these seats,' the man said.

Lily looked around the cafe and counted seven empty tables.

'We're not finished,' Reuben said.

'It looks like you are.'

'Well, we're not.'

The couple tutted and noisily sat down at the table next to theirs.

'I hope they wash their cutlery and dishes

thoroughly after that lot have used them,' the man muttered to the woman.

'It's not right, is it?' she responded tartly.

Reuben started to say something, but stopped himself. He caught his breath and instead asked, 'Is there anything else you'd like, sweetheart?'

Lily shook her head.

'Let's go then, the air's turned sour anyway.'

The rain was torrential when they stepped outside, so they ran into a nearby games arcade.

'Oh, tiger lily, this wasn't such a good plan was it?' Reuben said, as they stood dripping in the entrance way. 'We better dry off, otherwise we might get electrocuted on these machines.'

Lily did not understand what her father was saying, but was happy to be with him, in spite of the circumstances.

'Daddy, please come back and stay with us,' she said as he shook out her anorak.

'Oh, baby girl, I wish I could.'

Lily spent the afternoon watching her father play the flashing machines, assisting him in feeding pennies into the slots and pressing the glowing buttons. She was soon bored as she didn't understand the aim, but said nothing, wanting to delay the ride home for as long as possible. A couple of times a woman, in a short skirt that her mother wouldn't have approved of, came to watch her father play. He didn't speak to her but Lily noticed him looking at her when she walked away.

'We better get going,' Reuben said eventually. 'It'll be dark soon and your mum might worry that I've kidnapped you. And your grandpa will come after me.'

As they started the journey home, Lily studied the scratches on the back of her father's familiar leather jacket and wondered how long it would be before she saw him again. She was grateful the rain had eased off, at least.

*

November 2006

The television was on, but Lily's mind was elsewhere. She was thinking about what her mother had said that afternoon, about her father. That maybe she should have told him not to come that day. But her mother wasn't to know what would happen. Things could have turned out differently, if not for the bad weather that night.

Lily had always struggled to remember good things about her father. Every recollection seemed soaked in sadness, so she avoided thinking about him. She couldn't recall at what point she discovered that he'd had an affair, but was certainly aware of his womanising by her late teens as her mother spoke openly of it by then, warning her about men. She would occasionally think about her half-brother somewhere out in the world.

She had flicked through the photo albums while her mother slept. Looking at images that she hadn't seen in decades. The period before her grandfather's arrival in the UK seemed almost mythical to her.

She had studied the photographs of her father and tried to bring to mind happy thoughts. In the few photos of them together it looked like he loved her. He was so young, she thought. So was her mother, of course. By the time she reached the age that her mother was widowed, Lily had not yet been on a date. She was struck by how beautiful her parents were and wondered if that had been a curse for them.

Lily was glad to have Iris come and sit beside her. She was getting so tall. Carl would be amazed at how much she'd grown. She was annoyed when the phone started ringing.

*

Lily sat in silence in the back of the cab, her throat and temples aching. Iris sat beside her, quietly weeping. They clasped each other's hands. She was using all her strength to retain her composure, certain that if she gave an inch to her emotions, they would submerge her.

After taking the call from the rehabilitation centre, her hands had started shaking and her legs had felt as if they would give way, so she had called for a taxi rather than risk driving. She wondered how she had managed just a few months earlier when she'd received the call about her mother's accident.

She had seen this pattern before, in her church. Elderly people with previously strong constitutions would have a fall or catch a cold and then decline rapidly, and within a few months she would be attending a funeral. She had not expected it of her own mother. Had not been willing to entertain the idea. Was still not willing to entertain it. Her mother had made a strong recovery when she put her mind to it. She could do it again.

She thought about what her mother had said about the dreams she'd had that night. Lily too had heard of people dreaming of passed loved ones soon before their own death, but tried to explain it away in her mother's case, thinking it was just a psychological reaction. She had been looking through old photographs, it was natural that she would start dreaming of those people.

The cab driver was mercifully taciturn, but his tendency to break sharply was bringing up Lily's lifelong motion sickness. She rolled down the window even though it was a brisk evening. The cab driver looked at her through his rear view mirror and shrugged.

When they arrived at the hospital, Lily and Iris rushed through the doors of A and E, which seemed horribly familiar. After informing a weary receptionist of their arrival, they sat near the front desk under the fluorescent lights, which despite their brightness gave the waiting room a dull lustre. Iris held on to Lily tightly. The rehabilitation centre had told Lily that Flora had fallen from her wheelchair and sustained some injuries, including a knock to the head. When she had asked them how serious the injuries were, she had been told, after a pause and a sigh, that it was hard to say. She found it impossible not to read the worst in that sigh.

Lily watched a nurse approach the waiting room, which was almost empty.

'Flora Ratnam?'

Lily and Iris stood.

'Hello, are you Mrs Ratnam's family?' the nurse asked.

'Yes. How is she?' Lily was barely able to speak.

'She's stable, so that's good,' the nurse said, clearly preparing them for the less palatable news. 'She's broken her right arm and leg, so we've put them in plaster. She did take a bit of a knock to the head so she was unconscious on arrival. We've kept her sedated, so she's not in any pain. You can go and see her if you like, but be aware she's looking a bit bruised.'

'Will she recover? Has it affected her brain?'

The nurse sighed. 'She may well do. We need to do some more tests. Why don't you follow me?'

As they walked to Flora's cubicle Lily braced herself for her mother's appearance, but sobbed anyway when the curtain was pulled back.

'Oh, mummy!'

Flora's eyes were closed. Her right arm and leg were in casts, her head bandaged and various wires connected her to machinery.

'Mummy, we're here now. You're not on your own,' Lily breathed deeply. 'We love you very much, you know that.'

'Grandma, I'm sorry,' Iris cried out. She put her face near Flora's and kissed her cheek gently. She stayed close, speaking into Flora's ear. 'I'm sorry for being cross with you...I know you were trying to protect us because you love us...I know what daddy did...Please forgive me. You have to get better, it's my birthday soon and it will be sad if you're not there.'

Iris put her arm across Flora's chest. Flora rasped, but her eyes stayed shut. Iris put her head on the pillow next to Flora's as she stood by the bed. 'We won't leave you alone again, grandma.'

Lily pulled a plastic chair closer to the bed. She held Flora's left hand in both of hers. It felt small and frail.

Iris was whispering into Flora's ear, but Lily couldn't make out the words. It sounded like she might be praying. The room was so hot. Lily felt pressure increasing on her head and feared she might faint. She rested her forehead on the mattress, grateful for it to take the weight. She could hear the heart monitor keeping its regular rhythm. It went on and on, becoming part of strange dreams as she fell into half sleep. Then, after some time, the tone merged into one continuous sound.

Lily jolted up and caught a glimpse of Iris's horrified face, before hospital staff rushed in. She watched helplessly as they tried to shock her mother back to consciousness, dismayed at how events seemed to have spiralled so horribly and rapidly out of control.

Eventually the doctor turned to Lily and shook her head. 'I'm very sorry, she's gone.'

Iris ran to her, barging past medics. Lily felt every one of her sobs as she distantly heard the time of death being recorded as 23:42. She knew she should speak, say something comforting, but she was unable to. She felt completely empty. Just a hollow vessel, incapable of anything.

CHAPTER
TWENTY-FIVE

December 2006

C arl stared at his mobile phone as it bleated at him insistently. Only a select few had his number so he rarely received calls. As he had never saved any contacts, it was impossible to know whether this was worth answering. He tentatively picked it up.

'Hello?'

'Who are these idiots in my house?'

'Edwin.'

'They're saying they live here and that they're going to call the police. *They're* going to call the police - can you believe that!'

'They *do* live there now. You were absent, presumed incarcerated, so I put it up for rent.' Carl smiled apologetically at the people with whom he was sharing a table on the train.

'Oh, so you've been living off the profits, have you?'

Carl lowered his voice. 'It was you who disappeared without a trace, remember? Your debts didn't disappear with you.'

There was a pause as if this reminder had chastened Edwin. 'Hmm, well, sorry about that.'

'I'll meet you later. I've been out of town. I'm on my way back.'

'Where will I go until then? I'm off the booze.'

'I don't know. It's quite mild, go to the park.' Carl lowered his voice even further, to a whisper. 'You could at least have let me know you were alive, Ed. It's been two years.'

'Yes, sorry, I've been busy. Look, I better go, before the cops turn up.'

With that, he hung up. Carl put down the phone on the table. He was frustrated at his brother's insistent unreliability, but he was pleased he was back. And alive. He looked up to find his travel companions staring at him. Both immediately turned their gaze downward, but he continued regarding them. The older man was probably Carl's age, with a grey crew cut and close beard. The younger one was clean shaven and had a wistful look. Both had narrow, blue eyes. A father and son, presumably.

They had boarded the train at Oxon Road, a station from Carl's previous life. He occasionally had to pass through it for work. A couple of times he had disembarked and taken a bus to the family home. He had found a tree on the *cul-de-sac* that afforded a good view of the house, while its width allowed him to hide from his mother-in-law's surveillance. He had lingered by it, looking for movement by the windows, in between pretending to look at his diary. He never stayed too long, remembering the efficient Neighbourhood Watch, of which Flora was a keen member.

Once, he had gone to Iris's school. He had watched her being collected by his mother-in-law. Iris had grown and her face was thinner. He had almost called out.

He had cried on the bus back to the station. He had heard a woman whisper to her companion that he was probably drunk. On returning to his room he had poured himself a large whisky, downed it, then drafted a letter to Iris.

He wrote that he'd seen her and that his heart had almost burst with love and sadness and would she spare just five minutes to write to him. He had sealed and stamped the letter straightaway. The next morning, he tore it up.

Carl had remained at Edwin's house for another month after his absconding, in the mistaken belief that his brother would return. He had also harboured hopes of Lily turning up, in response to his letter. When neither occurred, he put the house up for rent, setting up a separate account for the income in the event of

Edwin's eventual return, siphoning off a little to cover his costs.

He took a room he had seen advertised in a newsagent's window. He had chosen it for the rent which had seemed mistakenly low for the part of town it was in. He had asked for clarification of the amount two or three times during the viewing. Each time it was confirmed by the landlady, a Miss Patricia Ripley, who had also been willing to welcome the cat, You, into her home at no extra cost.

Patsy was about twenty years senior to Carl, but her robust figure - maintained by regular consumption of pork pies and profiteroles - and mischievous cheeriness, belied her years.

Carl had enjoyed this period of homely indulgence, even gaining weight. He got used to the abundance of pastel pink satin and lace which seemed to cosset everything in the house (including Patsy, and occasionally You). He had not discouraged the light flirting that occurred when she took an extra glass of sherry at the weekend, relishing the feeling of being the younger object of desire. At around the same time he had been offered a full-time job at the university, which he accepted though the pay was considerably lower than his previous post.

Then one day he returned from work to find an ambulance outside the house. Patsy had suffered a fatal heart attack while on the phone to the electricity supplier. Carl had believed her to be somehow invincible to the ailments of normal people. Even encouraging her to enjoy life and to continue eating and drinking as she pleased. It was only as he helped clear out her belongings that he found her stock of medication. He was bereft, and disappointed at the scant turnout for her funeral.

Shortly after, he accepted an offer from the university in Boston in which he had completed his sabbatical. Though lucrative, he had initially been hesitant to accept, not wanting to be away in case Iris or Lily tried to contact him. In the end he thought the break might do him good. He reluctantly left You with a kind but absent-minded colleague.

Carl found that he slipped into this new phase of life surprisingly easily. He enjoyed getting reacquainted with old colleagues and being invited for dinners, and the smell of his comfortable room with its green leather Chesterton and formidable walnut desk. He agreed to the extension of his contract from three months to six, but when they asked him to stay for the following academic year, he declined.

Loneliness had taken hold and he couldn't shake it off. Though he hadn't seen his family for two years, he felt that proximity would somehow help. To be walking on the same land rather than separated by an ocean. Plus, he unexpectedly missed You. On his return, he found himself a one bed apartment within walking distance of the university, who were grateful for his return. The flat was not unlike the one Nadia used to have.

Carl gazed out of the train window. They were twenty minutes away from their final destination. The carriage seemed quieter than usual, which normally he would have appreciated, but for some reason he now found annoying. It also made him more self-conscious about his earlier conversation with Edwin.

He turned towards the father and son. The boy was reading a thick book, while the older man held a tabloid, which he folded and put down on the table. He turned towards his son as if to say something, but then changed his mind. A moment later he tried again.

'Nearly there, son.'

The younger man nodded and closed his book, which struck Carl as odd.

'You're not nervous, are you? You've got nothing to be nervous about,' the older man said.

Carl turned back to the rapidly passing countryside.

'A bit.'

'There's no need. You'll knock 'em dead.'

The man grabbed the back of his son's neck affectionately, then quickly retrieved it.

Carl caught the older man's eye and smiled. The man smiled back sheepishly.

'Off to university?' Carl asked the younger one.

'It's just an interview.'

Carl wondered if he should volunteer the information that he worked at the university. He decided against it.

'Well I wish you all the best,' Carl said, then started rifling through his briefcase in search of some papers to pretend to look at. He was unsure why he had initiated the conversation but was now in no mood to continue it.

'I am proud of you, son,' Carl heard the man say quietly. 'I want you to know that, whatever happens.'

As countryside gave way to industrial units, Carl stood up and retrieved his coat. With a last smile at his companions he walked towards the exit. He was in the middle of the carriage so had the choice of either. He was relieved to find the father and son choose the opposite one.

Carl planned to go to the house, apologise to the student tenants and then find Edwin. He had not yet decided what to do with him. He was reluctant to let him stay at his flat. He wondered if he should give the tenants notice, but it would be unfair in the middle of the academic year. He started to become anxious about what to do.

He was relieved to find that Edwin was not at the house. He knocked on the door and waited. He knocked again and rang the doorbell knowing full well it didn't work. After what seemed like a reasonable period, he opened the door with his key. The stench of cigarettes and stale carpet hit him.

There were footsteps on the landing floor-boards before someone called, 'Boz, is that you?'

'No. It's the landlord.'

'Oh. Some bloke was here before.' A young woman in pyjamas appeared at the top of the stairs.

Carl looked at his watch, it was nearly 1pm. 'Yes, sorry about that.' He retrieved a pile of mail that had been stuffed behind the radiator, alarmed to see that the first thing was addressed to him.

'Um, is this my mail?' Carl asked the dishevelled figure walking down the stairs.

'Dunno, sorry.'

Carl followed her into the kitchen, which he was amazed to find in a more squalid state than when he and his brother were resident.

'I thought I asked for stuff to be forwarded. There shouldn't be much coming here now.'

'Did you? OK, well leave an address then.'

Carl sighed.

'Well, see you then,' he said, and left.

Once outside, he flicked through the envelopes. He found one with a handwritten address. He turned it over. It was from his mother-in-law. He ripped it open.

'Dear Carl,

I am about to die and would like to make amends before it's too late. I want to apologise for my behav-

iour towards you. What you did was inexcusable, but I too am guilty of a gross error of judgement and I hope you will forgive me for it.

Until yesterday afternoon I had not passed on any of your correspondence to Iris or Lily. I mistakenly believed this would protect them from further hurt.'

Carl became short of breath. He lowered himself so that he was sitting on the doorstep, then continued reading.

'Your letters are now with their intended recipients. Needless to say, they are deeply hurt by my behaviour, but that is something I will have to deal with. I am writing to say that I will no longer be a barrier to you. If you feel you would like to contact them, then do so. I leave it to your judgement and only ask that you are mindful of what they have been through. I believe they would like to see you, Iris in particular. You are blessed with a wonderful daughter. Please do not hurt her again.

With my sincere apologies again,
Flora Ratnam'

Carl's hands were shaking. He felt giddy with the possibilities. Should he return to the train station and see them straightaway? He felt he should be more angry with his mother-in-law. He was annoyed that she had caused Iris to believe that he had forgotten her, but he was also filled with an ecstatic hope.

He tried to steady his hands to go through the

remaining letters. Flora's was dated from early November, over a month ago, and he wanted to see if any others had arrived. She would be wondering why he hadn't responded. He went through the rest of the pile, discarding the catalogues and charity requests until he came to a padded envelope. The writing on it was neat but childlike.

'Oh, darling Iris,' he said out loud, causing a passerby to turn and look at him. Carl carefully opened the package. In it was a book of poetry and a pale yellow envelope. He opened it, his eyes full of tears which he desperately tried to clear so he could read the card inside.

'Dearest Daddy

You are probably quite surprised to hear from me. In case you're wondering, this is Iris.

Well, I don't really know where to start. I don't know if you know, but grandma passed away two weeks ago. It has been very sad for us. I miss her a lot and can't believe she has gone. I keep thinking she will walk into my room. The house is so empty without her.

I know that you have written lots of letters to me daddy. I only just found out. Grandma kept them from me. It's hard to understand but I think she thought it was the best thing to do so please don't be angry with her – there's no point now anyway. I have been reading them. Now I know about You and Miss Patsy's puddings and big American portions.

There's a lot I can say about me. Well not a lot really as I've just been at school mainly, but I've been in a few plays and won a few competitions. The school moved me up a year so I am the youngest in my class. It would be nice if I could tell you more in person.'

Carl had been smiling as he read, now he had to catch his breath.

'What do you think? Our number is the same as before so maybe you can call us. In case you've forgotten I've put it at the top of this letter, with our address. We don't have your number. Mummy tried ringing the one that you wrote on her card and some other people answered. Do you have an email address? I've put mummy's at the top (we bought a computer two years ago).

Mummy is alright. Obviously very sad about grandma. She knows that I am writing to you.

I hope you like the Christmas present I sent you. It is a book of poetry. You once mentioned that you visited John Keats house in London in one of your letters. This book has some of his poems. My favourite is the one about Autumn.

Anyway, I think that's all for now. I hope you can write soon and we can meet each other soon. It will be something to look forward to.

Lots of love.
God bless you.
Iris
xxxxxxxx

P.S. Mummy told me why you left. I forgive you.'

Carl had to catch his breath again. He looked up to find a pigeon staring at him from the front wall.

'I'm so happy,' he told it.

CHAPTER
TWENTY-SIX

January 2007

T he winter had so far been relatively mild, but unrelentingly grey. To Lily, the greyness seemed to have a weight to it, which burdened her shoulders and caused headaches.

She had been back at work for two days. They had spent Christmas with her cousin Veena. Her children were much older than Iris, but had been kind to her. Then Liz, who had flown in from the States with her new young American husband, had taken them to a rented cottage in the Highlands. They had been good company, making a special effort to entertain Iris so that she wasn't bored with only adults around her.

When the holidays were over and they returned, the house seemed quieter than ever.

Lily had dreaded going back to work, having been absent for almost two months, but felt if she delayed any further she might never manage it. She found the effort of appearing resilient and continuing as normal exhausting.

Added to grief was disappointment. She had hoped the reappearance of Carl in their lives might temper their sadness, but it had been weeks since Iris wrote to him and they had heard nothing. Not even for Iris's birthday or Christmas. Lily had given him an allowance of excuses: there had been a postal strike; perhaps he hadn't received either Iris's letter, or her mother's. Perhaps he had and it was his letter that had gone astray.

She no longer had the strength to continue hoping. Perhaps her mother had been right all along. Better that they kept him out of their lives and had no expectations. But, he had never failed to make a payment into her account. And that card he had written to her, in between all the letters to Iris...

As she walked to the train station, she passed discarded Christmas trees on the pavement, waiting to be collected. Bereft of their Christmas decorations, the houses looked mournful, their windows like dark sad eyes.

*

'Nine times four, Iris.'

Iris stared at her exercise book. 'Forty-two?'

'Come on, Iris. That's not like you. Fourth finger down: thirty-six.'

Iris shrugged and watched Mr Faraday write on the whiteboard. She had once overheard him say to another teacher, while on playground duty, that he didn't even like kids. She used to have such faith in adults, but now doubted their trustworthiness. She turned to gaze out of the window and willed the lesson to end.

*

Lily checked emails as she ate her lunch. It was past three o'clock. She had worked through her lunch break to meet an unexpected deadline thrust upon her that morning. Her new manager, Carol, had failed to mask her annoyance at Lily taking extended time off over Christmas, when she'd already had compassionate leave a few weeks earlier.

'Thanks for this.' Carol perched herself on Lily's desk, crushing some papers.

Lily looked up at her wearily, fearful of being thrown another deadline. She had wondered if she should have told her earlier that she was being unreasonable. And whether agreeing to the deadline meant she would continue to be taken advantage of. But - like for so many other things - she found she didn't have the energy or temperament for a confrontation.

'There were a few typos though,' Carol continued.

340

'OK, I'll correct them.'

'You should really go through your work before you hand it to me. I don't have time to be checking for this kind of thing.'

Lily said nothing and wondered if Carol was speaking slightly louder than usual.

'I've marked them on here. I mean it's basic stuff, Lily: 'their' with an 'I' instead of 'there' 'R.E.'. It'll be embarrassing for the department if we send stuff out like this.'

Lily snatched the document from her. 'OK, I'll correct it.'

She was aware of her colleagues' raised eyebrows. She was used to containing her fury, but that didn't make it any easier.

*

Iris tried to ignore her teacher as she packed away her books. He was standing directly in front of her desk.

'I was just wondering if you're OK, Iris?' he asked uncertainly, as she heaved her rucksack over her shoulder.

Iris pondered for a moment. She had no desire to share her feelings with Mr Faraday, but was tired of pretending everything was alright.

'Not really, sir,' she said and walked out of the classroom.

Her best friend, Amma, had gymnastics practice that afternoon, so Iris had no one to walk home from school with. The temperature had dropped so she pulled on her mittens, knitted for her by her grandmother the previous winter. Iris had chosen a golden yellow wool, hoping it would brighten up the winter gloom, but now regretted that decision, thinking they looked babyish.

She had cried profusely for the two weeks following her grandmother's death, then after the funeral, the tears ceased, leaving only deep sadness that she felt would never go away.

Although she had briefly returned to school in early December, she had asked her mother to tell them that she wouldn't be able to take part in the Christmas production. She had watched jealously as classmates were called out of lessons to rehearse, but knew she didn't have the heart for it, not even for the chorus role she was offered in compensation.

Christmas had been a welcome distraction, but she had keenly felt her grandmother's absence. They had not made love cake that year, which was normally the first thing they did to herald in the season. Her grandmother would chop the cashew nuts by hand, stubbornly eschewing modern technology, while she and her mother sliced the pumpkin preserve and glacé cherries - family additions to the recipe. The aroma of the cake baking, made large enough so that it could feed all the neighbours and church Women's Fellowship, was for Iris the smell of Christmas.

They had not decorated the house either, and she had gone shopping for her mother's Christmas present alone. All things she would normally have done with her grandmother, that had been part of the excitement of the season.

When she and her mother returned home after New Year, the house had looked so bare, and seemed too big for the two of them. It even smelt empty.

Iris had written to her father the day after the funeral, in the hope that he could bring some happiness into her life. It had taken half a day to draft the letter, which she posted with his Christmas present the day before she turned nine, a full month before Christmas as she had heard something about postal strikes. Several weeks had passed since then and she had heard nothing from him.

She had hoped that he might deliver her birthday present in person. Her mother had baked her a chocolate fudge cake and they had gone to the cinema with a couple of friends. In the evening, their pastor and his family had come over and they'd played Monopoly and had Chinese takeaway. It had been mildly enjoyable but she had been angry with her father, sulking when the takeaway was delivered, having hoped it was him at the door. He hadn't even sent her a card.

To make up for all that had happened, her mother had said that she could have two birthdays, like the queen: the official one and another in the new year when they would take the long-promised trip to Disneyland Paris. Iris wondered if she would be in the mood for it, or whether her misery would follow her to France.

Nothing had arrived from her father for Christmas either. She couldn't bring herself to cry over him anymore. She was angry that his words to her were lies - he didn't really care about her at all.

As she trudged home, she became aware of someone who had fallen in line with her step. Iris continued walking without looking up.

'Hi, Iris.'

Iris gave a quick sideways glance. It was Simone McKenzie, a Sky Lacey hanger on. A long time ago they'd been in Sunday school together.

'What do you want?' Iris asked wearily.

'I heard about your grandma. You know my granny knew her from church?'

Iris resumed pavement-gazing.

'I don't know what I'd do if my granny died. I'd be in pieces.'

Iris looked up at Simone again. She was staring at her shoes, contemplating the horror. She turned to Iris. 'I just wanted to say I'm sorry. You must be so sad. And, and I think you would have been better than Katie in the school play. Sky was really annoyed they didn't choose her to be Dorothy but she wouldn't have been any good either... Anyway, I better let you get on.' Simone slowed her pace to allow Iris to continue alone.

Iris stopped. 'You can walk with me if you like. What did your granny say about my grandma?'

*

Mrs Barker had replaced Aiden's usual History teacher, who was on maternity leave. She had insisted on them using her surname and had taken an unprovoked dislike to him. He had wondered what it was about him that she had taken such offence to, as he was one of the more unassuming students. A friend had suggested that perhaps he reminded her of someone.

At the end of the lesson he quickly packed up his things, not wanting to stop for small talk with anyone. He was annoyed to be further away from the door than usual because Will Gardener had taken his seat next to Angie Ludlow, on whom he had an unrequited crush.

He walked at speed to the station. He was one of the few to commute to college by train. There was definitely a chill in the air that had not been there earlier. He pulled up his collar. The train was warm when he boarded. He closed his eyes.

*

Nadia emptied the contents of the box onto the dining room table. She planned to unpack and deal with all the remaining items still boxed up from their move, before the birth of her son in four weeks.

This particular carton was full of smaller items: souvenirs from holidays she'd taken in her youth, an appointments diary from 1998 that she had kept for some reason, tennis balls, trinkets that had been gifted to her that she had initially discarded but now had a liking for. She gently prised open a small blue velvet box and dropped its contents onto her palm - a pair of antique silver earrings.

Carl Jansen had given them to her as a birthday present during their brief affair. She had thought about him occasionally in the intervening years, sincerely hoping he had reconciled with his wife. She would take the earrings, along with some other items, to the charity shop in the morning.

She walked upstairs and into the nursery, where Dylan was meticulously painting the skirting boards.

'I think he likes it, I just felt a kick,' Nadia said.

'You shouldn't be in here, the fumes aren't good for you.'

Nadia remained where she was. 'Look, Dylan. It's snowing.'

*

Lily stood in the hallway as Iris ran upstairs. She took the glove out of her pocket. The other was now with the young man on the train.

'Darling, I'm so sorry. I'm so careless, I know,'

she called up.

She walked to the kitchen and stared at the tiles. She wanted to cry, thinking it might be cathartic, but no tears would come.

She laid the glove on the counter and put the kettle on the hob.

*

Gordon sat in his chair. He knew he should be getting tea ready but he was in no mood to be dealing with frozen pizza. He had over-reacted. It was just a stupid glove. But what did it mean? Maybe nothing. He gulped down his tea, which was now tepid. A letter had arrived that day from Aiden's preferred university. He had restrained himself from opening it. He noticed the postmark was from three weeks earlier. Stupid postal strike.

He grabbed his walking stick and stood. He hobbled out of the room and up the stairs. He hated the way each step creaked under foot, as if they were mocking his infirmities. When he reached his son's bedroom door, he stood for a moment. Then, after rehearsing what he would say, gently knocked.

*

Iris launched herself onto the bed. She held her pillow tightly as she wept. Her mother had become more careless lately, forgetting names and words. She had been so careful and ordered before. Iris reached forward and grabbed Mrs Chicken, her toy rabbit, from the end of the bed. She held it against her face, finding comfort in its softness and smell.

She took it with her into her grandmother's room. The bed was made, though Flora had not slept in it since the fire. At the foot of the bed was a folded crochet blanket that Iris had watched her grandmother make. She picked it up and took it to her room. It smelt of her grandmother's talcum powder. She had been sleeping with it every night, returning it each morning.

Iris wrapped herself and Mrs Chicken in it as she sat on the bed. On the bedside table was a selection of her father's letters that she sometimes read, though she hadn't for a couple of weeks. She wondered if she should try and forget about him. Accept that he had gone and would never come back.

She pulled back the net curtain of her window. It was snowing. Already the garden was coated with a thin layer of white, like the powdery icing sugar on the top of her mother's Victoria sponge cakes. Iris opened a window and stretched out her hand to catch some flakes. She brought them close to her eyes to examine the delicate patterns before they melted and disappeared forever.

She remembered her grandmother telling her about the first time she saw snow. How excited she and Lily had been. They had wrapped themselves up and gone out and danced in it, even though it was late at night. She had shown her the photographs her great grandfather had taken, capturing their joy.

*

Carl sat on the sofa, a glass of whisky in his hand. On his lap was a battered parcel. It was his birthday present to Iris. The Post Office had decided that the return address, which he had put on the back, was in fact the recipient's address, despite him writing 'to' and 'from' in the appropriate places. Because of the postal strike there had been a delay in it being 'delivered' to him.

He was distraught that Iris would think he had forgotten her. He had not posted her Christmas present, having planned to deliver it in person. Now it looked as though he had twice-snubbed her. And after her beautiful letter.

Carl had tried calling them the day after receiving Iris's parcel. He hadn't called straight away, wanting to prepare himself for it so that he didn't mess up his words. When he did call, no one had answered. He had called every day after that, sometimes once or twice an hour, before accepting that they must be away for Christmas. Despite this, on Christmas Day he tried ringing several times on the off chance they had returned, then again on Boxing Day, and every day until New Year's Day. He had not yet tried the email address. It was not a form of communication he was fond of and he hadn't wanted it to be the method he used for his first contact with them, which now seemed stupid.

He had spent Christmas, rather improbably, at his aunt's. His brother had also been present but then left to an undisclosed location, promising to be in touch in a couple of weeks.

It had been over a week since he last tried calling. He had almost lost his nerve, fearing it was not meant to be and they would be better off without him back in their lives. The returned parcel had given him new resolve: there was now an urgency to explain. If he was unsuccessful again, he would go to them, camping out in his car if necessary, until they returned. He had set aside the next day, Saturday, for this venture. As a last resort he would email. He took a sip of his drink and picked up the phone. He beckoned the cat to join him on the sofa for moral support. He was pleased that she obliged.

*

Lily gazed through the kitchen window at the snow swirling around the garden. She held her hand to the glass, feeling the chill through the pane. She heard footsteps behind her and turned to find Iris dressed in her winter coat and boots.

'Shall we go outside, mummy?'

Lily smiled and wrapped her arms around her daughter.

She unlocked the back door, bringing in the

roaring winter night. Iris raced out and started dancing jubilantly, her palms up trying to catch snowflakes.

'Come outside, mummy!'

'Let me get my coat, sweetheart.'

Lily rushed to pull on her coat and shoes, then hurried outside to join Iris, a rare feeling of exhilaration flaring up in her chest. Iris grabbed both her hands and they started spinning around, faster and faster, hearts racing.

'Mummy, if we go fast enough maybe we can fly!'

Inside, in the comfortable warmth of the kitchen, the phone started ringing.

Outside, Lily and Iris were still spinning, laughing, giddy with excitement, ready to take off into the brilliant night sky.

THE END

ABOUT THE AUTHOR

A.N.P. Emmanuel is a pen name of Anushka Rasiah. Anushka was born and raised in London, England; her heritage is Sri Lankan Tamil. This is her first novel.

You can read more of her work, including poems and short stories, at cloud-cocoa.com.

NOTE FROM THE AUTHOR

Thank you for taking the time to read my novel. I am genuinely grateful and hope you enjoyed it. It has been a long journey to publication. It started one snowy January evening as a short story, which got longer. And longer. There have been delays, detours and near derailments, but here we are at last. And I think there are more journeys to come...

47628731R00209

Printed in Poland
by Amazon Fulfillment
Poland Sp. z o.o., Wrocław